The Beginning

The Richard Jackson Saga, Volume 1

Ed Nelson

Published by Eastern Shore Publishing, 2024.

Table of Contents

Other books by Ed Nelson

The Richard Jackson Saga
Book 1: The Beginning
Book 2: Schooldays
Book 3: Hollywood
Book 4: In the Movies
Book 5: Star to Deckhand
Book 6: Surfing Dude
Book 7: Third Time is a Charm
Book 8: Oxford University
Book 9: Cold War
Book 10: Taking Care of Business
Book 11: Interesting Times
Book 12: Escape from Siberia
Book 13: Regicide
Book 14: What's Under, Down Under?
Book 15: The Lunar Kingdom
Book 16: First Steps
In the Richard Jackson World
Mary, Mary
Stand Alone Stories
Ever and Always
The Cast in Time series
Book 1: Baron
Book 2: Baron of the Middle Counties
Book 3: Count
Book 4: Earl
Book 5: Earl of the Marches

Dedication

This book is dedicated to my wife, Carol, for her support and help as my first reader and editor.

This fictional journey started with the Bellefontaine Ohio School class of 1962

Professionally edited by Janet E. Rupert

.

Quotation

That's the way it happened, give or take a lie or two.

James Garner as Wyatt Earp, describing the gunfight at the OK Corral in the movie *Sunset*.

Copyright © 2019

Chapter 1

"Your homework for your first day of English class, due tomorrow, is one on your summer vacation," said Miss Bales.

This should be interesting. Do I tell the truth or make up the usual crap? We went to the beach on Lake Erie or to Columbus to the zoo.

I should explain why I am even thinking of making something up. I have proof of what happened, but I don't know if I want all the nonsense that will go with it when it comes out. It will become public anyway after that last bit in Philadelphia, so I might as well go for it.

It all started in late May of last year. I had just finished 8th grade, and my dad Jack Jackson and I discussed what I would do for the summer.

Dad was a child during the Great Depression and had been in the Civilian Conservation Corps as a youth out in Idaho, killing coyotes. During World War II, he was in the Army, where he met my English mother. I think I was why they got married. I could do arithmetic.

My name is Richard Edward Jackson, known as Rick or Ricky to friends and family; I am large for my age at five-foot-ten inches and one hundred seventy pounds. Judging by my father's, cousins', and uncles' sizes, I still had a lot of growth left. I am fourteen years old, turning fifteen in October.

Anyway, Dad said, "By the time I was your age, I had been all around the country. Hell, when I was twelve, I ran away with the carnival, but your grandmother had the sheriff chase me down. Later, she swore she should have just let me go."

"You wouldn't mind if I traveled around a bit?"

"Not at all, but your mother might care."

"If I mention it to her, would you say it is okay?"

"That would be better than running your paper route and sitting around reading."

Dad was happy that I had been working since fifth grade. He didn't mind that I read all the time, which was easy because the library was a stop on my paper route. What he minded was me sitting on the porch swing for hours at a time, reading and getting a little pudgy.

Taking my life in my hands, I broached the subject at dinner that night. My two younger brothers and sister had not acted up, and Dad hadn't gone on a toot (what he called a drinking spree) for a while, so there wasn't any tension at the table. Additionally, money must have been okay because Dad had moved up from the extra board as a switchman on the railroad to become a conductor.

This job wasn't like a conductor on a passenger train. His job as a supervisor was putting together a freight train by having the cars placed in the correct order. The switchmen and brakemen had to take their direction from him. This promotion irked two of my uncles, who did those jobs.

I asked, "Mum, would you care if I saw a little of the country on this vacation?"

"What do you mean?"

"Well, I only go up to Indian Lake, about ten miles, with you and Dad. Would you care if I rode my bike or hitchhiked up there?"

In those days, hitchhiking was quite common and not considered bad.

"I might even get to Cincinnati to see a ball game!"

"That sounds ambitious; I doubt you would have the nerve for that. It is one hundred miles there."

"I won't know if I don't try."

Mum looked at Dad and asked, "What do you think?"

"Well, I sort of put it in his mind, so I am okay with it."

Mum then gave me a look and said, "You can do it. Now tell me what you actually have in mind?"

I should have known I wouldn't get anything past her.

"I would like to hitchhike out West and see as much of the country as possible during the summer."

"I thought it was something like that. I don't see anything wrong with it. You have the size and seem to have common sense. I certainly did more adventuresome things when I was your age."

"Like what?" I asked.

"Well, you know we lived in Grays, a small town on the Thames River near London. We used to make rafts to cross the river. You don't know fear until an Ocean Liner blows its horn for you to get out of the way while you are on a homemade raft. So, I do understand. Just be careful of who you take rides with."

And so, my summer vacation started. I had saved forty dollars from my paper route, which I no longer had. These savings were almost a grown man's week's wages in those days.

I had a thin sleeping bag, ground cloth, shaving kit, and an old army rucksack to carry several changes of clothes. Plus, the Barlow pocketknife, which was required of all boys my age, and a comb.

What I did have that was unusual was my American passport. Since Dad was a GI and Mum British, I had dual citizenship. My parents thought we could afford a trip to England several years ago, which didn't work out, but I did end up with an American passport. It was very handy for impressing the girls.

It was the only ID I had besides my library card. Mum gave me five dollars to be used in an emergency and told me I had to send a postcard every few days, so they knew where I was.

I had already learned that what parents approved one day might change the next. So, I was up early on May 31. The school calendar was easy to follow during those years. School ended the day before Memorial Day and took up again the day after Labor Day. The dinner conversation was on Thursday night, May 30, and school was over for the year. I passed eighth grade going on to the ninth.

I was up at daybreak and packed. Mum had breakfast waiting. It was my favorite bowl of cereal. Quaker Oats puffed rice. While I ate, she made me two baloney sandwiches for lunch. Dad had left an Army surplus canteen for me. He was at work, but both figured I wouldn't waste time once I had permission.

After a hug from Mum, I walked the five blocks to Main Street, which is also US 68 in Bellefontaine, Ohio. From there, I started walking south. It didn't take long before Ernie Nevers slowed down. He was an older paperboy who could drive. Ernie offered me a lift. He thought I was heading out to the fairgrounds south of town.

When I told him I was heading toward Springfield, he questioned me. I explained my summer mission, seeing the West.

He scoffed, "You will be home tomorrow, but I will take you that far since I'm heading to Urbana."

We spent the half-hour drive talking about going west. The truth was neither of us knew much. If I went to Springfield and followed US 40 to the ocean, then turned left, I would get to LA. In those days, the interstate system was just being built, and US 40 went all the way to San Francisco.

Anyway, Ernie dropped me off in the center of Urbana at the roundabout, and I started walking south. It took me about half an hour to get to the edge of town and stick my thumb out. Of course, the first person to stop was a county sheriff's deputy.

He was polite and wanted to know who I was, where I was going, and the usual things a cop might ask, like had I run away from home. I politely told my story.

He laughed and said, "Few people do that anymore. I tried it just before the war. I got clear to Indianapolis before I got homesick. Good luck, and have fun."

Things were different in those days.

An old farm truck slowed down, and the deputy flagged him over.

"Hey, Bill, we got a young man on his way west. He needs to get to Springfield to pick up 40."

"Well, hop in, youngster! I remember those days; I used to ride the rail when I was your age. We would jump a boxcar to Dayton, then go south to Cincinnati to watch a ball game at Crosley Field. We were thirteen and would drink Hudepohl beer. The kid who sold it to us was probably ten. It was a dime a bottle."

The old farmer regaled me with the fun stuff he did as a kid. He let me out at his turnoff and wished me luck.

My next ride took forty minutes, and it was an insurance man going to his office in Springfield. He wanted to know where I was from and did my parents need insurance. I couldn't answer him, so it was a quiet ride. He let me off in downtown Springfield on the main drag, Route 40.

Chapter 2

It being Memorial Day, a parade was lined up on 40 getting ready to head west. One float, the Future Farmers of America, had boys and girls my age.

One of the girls, a cute brunette, said, "Hi," as her float was slowly going by.

Of course, being nobody's fool, I said, "Hi" back.

She laughed. "Oh, I am sorry. I thought you were someone else."

Her words created an opportunity to ask, "Who did you mistake me for?"

She named some guy I had never heard of while I continued to walk along the float.

A more general conversation ensued, with me telling her and the other kids on the float about my big trip. This led to an invitation to ride the float to the edge of town. All the kids thought it was neat that my parents would let me do that. We weren't cool in those days, just neat.

I felt like I was the King of the World on that ride. Then reality caught up with me as we reached the cemetery at the edge of town. I went my way, and they went theirs.

According to my glow-in-the-dark Timex watch, I stood by the road with my thumb out for half an hour. I became bored standing, so I started walking, putting my thumb out whenever a car came by.

It took me the rest of the day to reach Dayton. It was getting dark, so I left the road and camped in a small, wooded area. My food long gone, I was tired, hungry, lonely, and scared of being out alone. I jumped at every little sound.

I managed to get through the night. If there were tears, you would never know. Daylight comes like it usually does, so I did my morning duty and headed out. But for some reason, no one wanted to pick me up.

Later at a small gas station, I caught a glimpse of my reflection. I wouldn't have picked myself up. I cleaned up as best as I could. I bought a couple of candy bars and a Coke to hold me until I got to real food. The station also sold other goods, and I found a small metal mirror. I could use my comb and avoid looking like some deranged killer from now on.

Not too far down the road was a small diner. I paid seventy-five cents for two eggs, bacon, hash browns, and my first-ever cup of coffee. Everything but the coffee was good. I had to kill the taste with so much sugar and cream that the waitress laughed.

I made fifty miles that day. At that rate, it would take me two months to get to California. I kept trudging along.

I learned that the Burma Shave signs were further apart than I had thought, and the Mail Pouch Tobacco advertisements painted on the side of barns weren't really put on that well. The fancy work from a distance was sloppy hand painting when viewed up close.

I realized I was far from home when I had to reset my watch after passing through Indianapolis. I dialed my watch one hour from Eastern Standard Time to Central Standard Time.

A week later, I left Indiana for Illinois. I saw a farm truck with a flat tire and an elderly lady—at least forty—sitting inside.

I asked if she needed help. She told me she couldn't handle the spare. I changed the tire, and she gave me a lift down the road to her farm. She invited me in for lunch. Her husband came out of the field to eat with us. And she asked me why I was hitchhiking.

Her husband laughed at my story and said, "I bet you would like nothing better than a bath right now."

"Yes."

"I thought that would be the case, I was all over Europe with Patton, and a bath was the goal of every soldier. Home and girls were the dreams, but a good soak was the goal."

While I cleaned up, Mrs. Whaley washed my clothes. They had some old clothes I could wear while mine were on the clothesline.

It was getting late, and they invited me for dinner and the night. I wasn't shy. It felt so good to be under a roof.

During dinner, Mr. Whaley asked if I would mind staying for a couple of days to help with some chores. He had some fencing to replace, and it was a two-man job. He would pay me five dollars for the two days plus meals and a bed. I immediately took him up on it.

The next day they asked if I had let my parents know how I was doing. Of course, I was in the middle of my second week and had not done so. Mrs. Whaley gave me a postcard and one of the new four-cent stamps.

Postage had gone up since my trip had started. On June 1, it went from three cents to four cents. The way prices were rising, we would all starve, at least according to Mrs. Whaley.

I wrote several lines saying I had just got into Illinois and that I was fine. I put it in the mailbox and raised the flag for the mailman.

After two days of fencing, I was ready to move on. Mr. Whaley paid me my five dollars, we shook hands, and I was off again. Mrs. Whaley had packed me a little something for the road. If I was careful, it might last for three days.

By this time, I was getting my road legs. I chose to walk with my thumb out rather than stand and wait. Walking became easier, and that pudginess was going away. Losing weight got me feeling all virtuous, so I decided to do pushups and sit-ups every morning. I thought it would only last a few days as I had tried this before, but it took, and it became part of my morning ritual.

I hated St. Louis. It took me an entire day to walk across town. It was all sidewalk, so my feet were killing me when I hit the western city limits. And now I was halfway through my money and my shoes were wearing out.

I put cardboard in the shoe's bottom, but the sole hole was getting too large. I had to stop at a farm store and buy a stout pair of Mason work shoes. They were hard to break in. By the time I had hitched and walked to the Kansas border, I had blisters.

Ready to stop for a while, I bought a loaf of bread, baloney, mustard, and band-aids at a local IGA. I then found a secluded dell and took the next two days off.

I woke up feeling like a new person on the third morning, so I hit the road again after performing my new morning ritual.

After many different rides, Mr. Serling dropped me off just over the Kansas state line in Colorado.

He had to say, "Toto, we aren't in Kansas anymore."

I laughed and wished him well in his writing. His delivery of that line was sort of spooky.

I got lucky and caught a ride with a long-distance hauler who took me to Craig, Colorado. In those days, Craig was a small town that was little more than a crossroads.

When Chet let me off, he joked that I should be careful and not get lost in town. With a grin and a wave, he took off like all the other recent people in my life.

Chapter 3

My first goal was to exchange my last and only money in the form of a twenty-dollar bill for smaller bills and change.

Seeing The First Bank of Colorado, I walked in. I was fifth in line, and the tellers were friendly. They were so neighborly that I had only moved up two spaces in fifteen minutes. No one else had come in, so I was still the last in line. I turned to look when the door behind me opened.

Two men walked in with guns in their hands!

"Stick 'em up. It's a robbery," one yelled.

He pushed his way to the front of the line, handed the teller a pillowcase, and said, "Fill it up!"

The other came up beside me and thrust his handgun close to me, and said, "We are taking it all. Give me your money."

Without thinking I grabbed his hand and turned the barrel away from me. I almost ripped his finger off as I turned the gun.

He let go, and I had it. I pointed it at his chest and pulled the trigger. Bang. H went down.

The other guy turned towards me, but I was facing him with the gun already aimed in his direction. Bang.

The robbery attempt was over. I had just killed two men. And it all happened so fast that the other people in line had no time to move.

I stood there gun hanging down, trying to process what had happened. All heck broke loose as a teller set off the burglar alarm. The bank guard came out of the back room and immediately grabbed me.

The tellers got him straightened out as the police came charging in heading for me.

Again, the tellers got it all sorted out. I surrendered the handgun to the police, which I would later learn was an M1911A .45 caliber semi-automatic. The cops found the getaway car around the corner with the engine running.

They closed the bank and set me in a conference room. A male teller brought me a glass of water and closed the door behind him. I promptly got the shakes.

I was pretty well settled down when the FBI showed up two hours later. The agents were nice to me, and I appreciated that they didn't pull their guns on me as everyone else had. It was more like a conversation than the grilling I expected.

My version of events confirmed what others had told them. They then proceeded to tell me that the two guys, brothers by the name of John and Ernest Johnson, were wanted for bank robbery and murder in three states.

They had robbed nine banks and killed six people, wounding four others. These were bad men. I was eligible for the reward because it was dead or alive, and there was no doubt about the dead part.

The rewards totaled twenty-five thousand dollars! The agents helped me fill out the paperwork and attested to the facts. The bank was kind enough to let me use their phone to call home.

Boy, was Mum surprised and relieved to hear from me. I assured her all was okay. She was mad that I had only sent one postcard.

I told her about the robbery. She got all shook up and even madder when she learned that I was almost killed. When I told her of the reward, she got quiet. I asked for Dad's checking account numbers so the money could be deposited there.

"Mum, when you get the money, pay off all our debts, buy a new house and a new car."

"It is your money!"

"I know, but what do I need all that for? Let's do some good for our family. And I only mean our family, don't let Uncle Wally get his hands on it and drink it away. Maybe you can let Dad go on one big toot, but that is all."

"Jack doesn't need to go on a toot; he will be too busy house hunting and buying new furniture."

"Your call, Mum. I want to help the family."

"It is appreciated. Now, don't wait so long until you let us know how you are doing."

"I won't, Mum, talk to you later."

When I got off the phone, Mr. Weber the bank president was waiting to talk to me. "Ricky, our board of directors has authorized five hundred dollars on top of the reward you have earned. Do you want it sent with the other money?"

"Could I have it in cash?"

"Do you think that will be safe?" he coughed. "I remember what happened to the last person who tried to take your money. Of course, you can have the cash. I will be right back."

He returned with the money "The FBI has asked that you stay in town for several days in case something else comes up."

"I guess I have no choice. Is there anywhere I can stay?"

"I checked, and there aren't any hotel rooms available. I did make a phone call, and a member of the local school board, Clint Easterly, is willing to put you up. He's here in town and will be stopping by in a few minutes."

Chapter 4

It was a short few minutes because Mr. Easterly walked into the room just then.

"I hear there is a young man who needs a place to stay."

Mr. Weber introduced us. I told him I would be pleased to have a room as I got tired of sleeping outside. I was willing to pay for it, but he would have none of that. In short order, he had me in his pickup and headed out to his ranch.

I met his wife, Sally, who treated me like a long-lost son. I had a bath before dinner and put on my only pair of clean clothes. At dinner, I mentioned that I had to find a laundromat in town. She laughed and asked if I had looked in a mirror recently.

Of course, I hadn't. It appeared that I was now six feet and one-half inches tall. My pants and shirt sleeves were both too short. I needed all new clothes! Fortunately, I now had the money.

The next day Mr. and Mrs. Easterly took me into town. Our first stop was the local newspaper. They wanted my description of what happened during the robbery.

The newspaperman, Jimmy Olsen, chuckled when he first introduced himself, telling me he wasn't a photographer.

I laughed and said, "You must be asked about Superman a lot."

"You have no idea, but I have learned to live with it."

The laugh we shared got us off to a good start, but I still felt overwhelmed by the sheer number of his questions.

He asked me so many questions that I felt more intimidated by him than the FBI.

Mr. Easterly let me fend for myself during the interview but later told me I did okay. Not much praise, but I thought that an "Okay" from him was a lot. He also promised to mail a copy of the article to my parents.

The next stop was at a newly opened Sheplers. They specialized in Western gear, so I ended up with cowboy boots, several pairs of jeans, cowboy-style shirts, a belt with a large brass buckle, and a straw cowboy hat.

Ignoring that I had only ever ridden on a fairground pony when I was young, I was a rough-riding cowboy.

I mentioned that to Clint, and he told me he had the cure. I thought he was going to put me on a horse, not one of the Brahma bulls he raised and provided to the rodeo.

He gave me the basics and lifted me on the back of one. I'm sure he thought I would go flying. I was as surprised as he was when I stayed on.

It seems I had the natural reflexes and balance required. Mr. Easterly gave me some pointers on showing off on the ride by waving my arms and hat during the eight-second ride. All of which I did without any problem.

After riding two more bulls that morning, he said he had never seen such a natural.

He taught me how to saddle, ride, and care for a horse. It all came easy and was fun. Except for the half dozen times the bulls and horses threw me off.

Three days later word came from the FBI that I wasn't needed anymore and could move on.

Clint asked if I wanted to join him as a helper on the rodeo circuit. I would also be a wrangler on several other projects. I learned that wrangler was just the fancy word for helper and dung shoveler. Those bulls needed a lot of wrangling!

Since he was headed towards California, it made sense. He was giving me a ride and paying me. The pay was for spit, but since he helped me, I would have done it for free. Our first stop was outside Denver to provide the riding bulls for a rodeo. The rodeo was a lot bigger than I thought it would be.

I assumed it would be like our local Logan County Fair. It was more like the Ohio State Fair. He had talked me into joining the American National Bull Riding Association Junior Division so I could enter the events.

I thought it would be neat to tell my friends in school about entering. It was more than neat when I won the Junior Division at the rodeo.

The prize was one hundred dollars, and they gave me the neatest big silver buckle for my belt, a trophy, and a blue ribbon with the rodeo name and date on it.

We boxed the trophy and ribbons up and shipped them to my parents. They would be surprised!

We then headed up to a rodeo in Cheyenne, Wyoming. And wouldn't you know it, I won first place and another one hundred dollars.

I packed the trophy, mailed it, then headed down to Fort Collins, Colorado for the third rodeo. It was almost anti-climactic when I won that one, but their first prize was two hundred dollars.

I now had more money than I had ever dreamed of. I started talking about becoming a professional rodeo rider. Clint told me not to get too big for my britches.

I had enough points in the Junior Circuit to enter the Grand National Junior in Dallas at the end of August. Again, he helped me with the forms but let me know that I would now be going against the real riders and had to step up my game.

Heck, I was happy to hang on. How could I step that up?

We went out to a dude ranch in Nevada near Reno. They were filming *Adventures of Spin and Marty*, a show which was part of the *Mickey Mouse Club*. There was to be a segment about rodeos, and we were providing the bulls.

When the child actor who was supposed to be the bull rider refused to get on one, Clint pointed out that I rode and even won some rodeo contests. They had me join the Screen Actors Guild and made me an extra.

It turned out to be a little more because the writers heard Annette say I was cute. That gave them the idea to have me in several episodes.

I won the rodeo in the first episode, and Annette swooned over me, much to Spin and Marty's dismay. I made headway with her the next one, and they got more frustrated.

In the third one, the writers had me overstepping my bounds and trying to kiss Annette (Gasp!). Spin and Marty catch me in the act and toss me in a horse trough. And that was the end of my Disney career.

I didn't get a chance to know any of the actors. As soon as a scene was finished, they would disappear into their trailers with their chaperons, ending my boyhood fantasy.

The scenes were shot out of sequence, so my work was done in two days. They wouldn't let me keep the black hat they had put on me.

Chapter 5

After Reno, we headed south to Yuma, Arizona. Clint was providing the bulls for a movie down there starring John Wayne, Elvis Presley, and Tab Hunter with a working title of *It Never Happened*. My job was to clean up after the bulls and feed and water them.

I was taking care of the bulls on our second day when John Wayne came out all hot and bothered.

"Where the hell is everybody, we got a scene to shoot," he bellowed as only John Wayne could.

He saw me and yelled at me, "Get your butt over to costuming now. You are not being paid to stand around."

I was being paid to stand around with the bulls, but when you're fourteen, and John Wayne yells at you, you move!

It was just around the corner of the set, and since my dress met the requirements, they strapped a prop gunfighters rig on me, mounted me on a horse, and gave me my direction. Now, if I could ride, it would have ended up differently.

My job was to be in the back of the pack of bad guys, and when I hit the mark in the sand, I would slide off my horse away from the camera.

Everything was good until I tried to slide off the horse. My boot got caught in the stirrup and the horse tried to shake me off.

My weight was enough that the horse tried to walk away from me. Dragging me right in front of the camera. He went about a hundred feet down the road and stopped. I worked myself free.

When I stood up, Wayne and the director were followed by the rest of the cast and crew. Wayne wanted to know if I was okay. The director wanted to know if I could do a retake if they didn't get the shot.

I guess my mouth hung open because they all started laughing at me. Elvis accused me of being a scene-stealer. He was laughing, so it was okay.

Clint showed up around then, and it came out that I wasn't even an extra but a bull wrangler. When I confessed that Wayne's yelling got me in the scene, they all thought it was a hoot.

Since I had a Screen Actors Guild card on the Mickey Mouse set, they decided to use the shot as it was too dramatic to pass up. Most stunts were live in those days.

The next few days, I bummed around with Elvis, and we both learned Western gun handling with real Colt .45s and how to quick draw. We even got to go out in the desert and plink at tin cans. Elvis was a little upset that I could hit them repeatedly and make them "walk". He couldn't do either.

The shooting ended for the week. Elvis and Tab Hunter asked me to go to Tijuana with them. Since Clint was heading home, I told them yes. Clint reminded me that I was entered in the National Junior Bull Riding Championship and not to forget to go to Dallas. I promised him I would go. We parted company on a good note.

We arrived in Tijuana early on a Saturday night. We walked around eating food from the street vendors. I stayed with corn on the cob as it was the least likely to give me stomach problems. It worked, but then neither of the other two had problems, at least of that sort.

What I remember of Tijuana was the stop signs, and the shoeshine boy, and the buses. I had never seen so many people on a bus.

They were old school buses, which ran up and down the main road. Those who couldn't afford or were too cheap to pay would hang from the frames of the open windows outside the bus. Some would climb and sit on the roof. It lent a new meaning to being full.

The stop signs were something else. They said, "Alto", Spanish for "Stop", But the bottom of the sign said, "Drink Seven Up". Apparently, the Seven-Up bottler sponsored the stop signs!

We were followed by street urchins the whole trip. Finally, through persistence, one got to shine my boots. They gleamed when he was done. I gave him a US Dollar, a gross overpayment. I regretted it two days later when all the stitches on my boots dissolved.

I had to walk over a mile to buy a new pair while the soles flapped with every step. I have no idea what was in that polish, but it was potent. However, that would be several days in the future; we were in Tijuana tonight to have fun.

I found Elvis and Tab's idea of fun was to go to a cantina, drink too much and flirt with the pretty girls. They were all pretty to them after drinking. I didn't care to drink, and I didn't think the girls were that pretty.

This led to them getting in a fight with their boyfriends. It was one heck of a brawl with the three of us against about eight of them.

We were holding our own until we heard the police whistles. Everyone raced for the backdoor. I was the only one of our three that made it out. The others got jammed up in the doorway and hauled away by the police.

When I got out of the backdoor, I followed the guys I had been fighting. They jumped up on the roof of a low-standing shed. We all hunkered down. It is a wonder the cops did not hear the giggling above them.

The boy next to me said, "That was a good fight *gringo*."

"Yeah. It was fun."

"It is a shame we can't bail our friends out. They will have to spend the night in jail."

"If you show me where the police station is, I will bail everyone out."

I was led to the police station. They had everyone stuffed in the drunk tank. It cost me fifty dollars for Elvis, Tab, and three Mexican boys.

The police took group pictures of Elvis, Tab, and me in various poses.

They recognized Elvis when they saw his ID. Tab was put out that he had to tell them who he was.

I was nobody, but they included me in the pictures anyway. Everyone shook hands and declared it a wonderful night when it was done. I loaded my friends in an international cab and headed back to the US.

Fortunately, we had all managed to hang onto our IDs, so we made it across the border okay.

We checked into a suite at the Coronado Del Rey, a fancy hotel in San Diego. The next day was a bad one for Tab and Elvis. I worked on my tan. They both swore eternal friendship to me for bailing them out of trouble.

They avoided a night in jail, but the cops sold the pictures to *Variety* magazine, the trade journal for the movie industry. Wayne mailed a copy to my home and signed it to me with a note saying, "Wish I was there."

Chapter 6

These events were all in the future. Early Monday, Tab and Elvis headed to their next destinations. As for me, I stuck my thumb out and headed north on Highway 101.

It was an easy trip, and I found myself out by Long Beach in the midafternoon. One of my rides told me he knew the oil rigs were always looking for roughnecks if I was looking for work.

Being a roughneck was a high-paying, hard dirty job that required a strong back and a fairly weak mind. I met those qualifications. All the walking and daily exercising I had been doing had me in better shape.

I got a hotel room for the night. Sleeping on the ground in Long Beach was out of the question and I could not resist the name Hotel California. When the song came out years later, I wished I had sent some of their postcards.

After breakfast, I checked out and left the Hotel California. Then I was off to the Union hiring hall.

My SAG card and ten dollars got me into the International Oil Rig and Drillers Union. I asked the guy who took my money if he thought I would have difficulty getting on. He just pointed to all the derelict drunks sleeping on benches in the hall.

One oil rig hired roughnecks at sixty dollars a week for a two-week stint. They had some extra stuff going on and thought they would need the help.

So, I was hired. I had to buy a hard hat, safety glasses, and steel-toed work shoes. I was taken by water taxi to the rig not far from shore. I spent the next week dirty, tired, sore, and certain that I would never want to do this regularly.

They had so many men on board that we had to hot bunk. One guy would get up and another would take his place in the bed. Drilling for oil was around the clock; talk about a stinking mess of unwashed, farting men. The food was a horrid greasy mess, and the showers were salt water. This life was not what this Ohio boy was ready for.

I toughed it out but knew I would never come back. All but one set of my clothes were ruined in the first two days. I saved one set after realizing I would have to buy new ones when the job was done. They gave us coveralls, but they didn't help.

The guys working the rig were a hard lot, but they didn't seem to resent me and would give me pointers on how to do things. I quickly became known as Kid. "Hey, Kid, do this," "Hey, Kid, wake up," "Hey, Kid, get your head out of your butt." All this was yelled, but never in a mean way.

I mentioned that to one of the supervisor types one day. He told me, "Kid, these are really hard cases; they have learned to be polite to each other and the world in general. They have nothing to prove, and if a fight broke out here, there would be dead men. You don't want to see a dead man."

I didn't tell him that I had already killed two men at my young age. No one on the rig had asked my age, and I didn't volunteer.

Events took a sudden turn on the second week when I heard a big voice yell, "Hey, Pilgrim. What are you doing here?"

I turned, and there was John Wayne. It seemed he was doing some location shots for a movie called *Hell Fighters*, a take on Red Adair, the oil rig firefighter. That was why the extra crew had been added on.

Since I already had a SAG card, I was hired to be an extra in the movie. I was being paid again to do the job the second time, so they could take pictures of me. When the finished movie came out, you had to look quickly to see my face.

My stock certainly went up with the other roughnecks when Wayne told a group at lunch one day how I had got in a fight down in Mexico and had to bail my buddies Elvis Presley and Tab Hunter out of jail. That's when I found out there were pictures in *Variety* magazine.

After my second week, the job and the movie deal were done, so I hitched a ride back to shore with John Wayne. He had his boat, which we took directly to his house on the water in Newport Beach. His wife made me clean up at once and throw all my old clothes away. I had no problem with either.

After dinner that night, we went to the recently built Del Webb Hotel and listened to a new group the Waynes knew, The Beach Boys.

During one of their breaks, John let Brian Wilson know that I was a bull rider. Brian asked, "Rick can you sing?"

"My singing scares the cattle, but not bad enough to start a stampede."

"Seriously, we are hunting for a cowboy type to sing a song. It doesn't meet the image we are establishing, but it is too fun not to do. We would be the backup band, and our studio would handle all the distribution."

In a moment of weakness, I agreed to an audition the next day. The first thing I did was replace my destroyed wardrobe. I learned all the fancy terms like wardrobe from hanging around the movie sets.

The wardrobe on the oil rig was funny. Instead of the rig's grey coveralls, we wore red ones. That was the extent of the difference; I even used my own hard hat.

I bought several sets of jeans, Western shirts, a pair of boots, and a new belt for my largest buckle; and splurged on a real black cowboy hat, made by Resistol. The brand wasn't as famous as Stetson, but I thought it was a better hat. It cost sixty dollars but looked sharp. I had wanted one ever since the Disney show.

Everyone knew the bad guys wore black hats, which was the look I was going for. Hey, I was fourteen!

I had grown again. I was now six feet two inches and weighed one hundred and eighty pounds. I was tall, thin, and hard from all the work and exercise I was doing. No longer the pudgy kid who left Bellefontaine!

My audition went well enough that we did the record. After several false starts on my part, we did a complete cut, and "Rock and Roll Cowboy" was born.

The band carried me since my voice wasn't that strong or even pleasant sounding. Brian gave me his business card and a copy of my contract.

He asked me to call him in a couple of weeks to see how things were progressing. I promised I would. That also reminded me to send a postcard home. I was doing better at mailing postcards and meeting my weekly goal.

They only said I was doing fine, everything was good, etc., but they let my parents know I was alive and where to start the search party if I went missing.

I hitched up to San Francisco and finally got to see the end of US 40. I ended up on the Berkeley campus while exploring the area and merged with a group heading into a hall.

I wasn't thinking, just going with the flow. Next thing I knew, I was being welcomed to freshman orientation. I was too embarrassed to get up and leave, so I listened to the talk, and I am glad I did. I heard something that would get my education headed in the right direction.

"If you want to do well here, then read the book and work all the problems at the end of the chapter *before* you come to class. This way, you will understand what is being said, and you will know what you don't know so you can ask the right questions.

If you are really lucky, any homework will be problems you have already done. If not, you will have a firm understanding of the material. Treat going to school like a job. Plan to spend the time to do it right."

For some reason, that rang true to me. I had straight A's up to the eighth grade, but I never had to study. My eighth-grade grades dropped to Bs and Cs. Maybe I would have to do some work!

Chapter 7

Sheer curiosity and the fantasy that I would find my fortune led me out to the gold fields. I stopped at a working gold mine where they let tourists pan for gold.

They gave an interesting lecture and movie on gold mining, but it didn't take me long to figure out that they were mining the tourists for their gold. I had rented a pan and was taught how to use it. After an hour of swirling sand, I had one small flake or what the miners called a "color".

I took it up to the young attendant, who said it looked like a nickel's worth. He took my pan with its single speck in the remaining water and held a strange-looking gun with a two-inch barrel.

When he flipped a switch on it, it blew extremely hot air on the water, drying it quickly.

I asked about it. The guy replied, "It's an industrial heater. It has a heating element inside and a small fan blowing hot air. "This machine is much better than having an open flame around the tourists."

He then offered to sell me a glass vial to keep my gold in for a dime, but I declined and let him keep the flake.

I decided I would rather spend my time hiking in a nearby National Forest. It was really neat, and I enjoyed my outing immensely. Those big old trees made it feel like being in church, though my family weren't churchgoers.

One of the things we had been shown in the gold mining movie was to look for quartz. It was associated with gold. If we found a big enough outcrop, it might even have a pocket of gold in it. It would be in nugget form still, as erosion hadn't broken the gold down into fines.

At the head of the hiking trail, there was a sign that said, "Do Not Feed the Bears". I didn't have any food with me, so that wouldn't be a problem. I did have the nasty thought that a bear might consider me food!

That put a different, much stronger connotation on not feeding the bears. A sheet pinned on the sign gave information about the local black bears. Strange enough, the black bears were mostly any shade of brown but not black.

The important information to me was that bears have the right of way. In other words, if you see one, get out of their way. Don't turn and run. Just slowly back up until you are out of sight. Then turn and run.

It sounded like a good plan to me. The chances of me running into a bear were slim and none, but now I knew what to do.

The hike was very pleasant. The giant trees gave a hush to the area that felt peaceful.

That peaceful feeling continued until I heard a grunting sound. Two half-grown black bear cubs walked out onto the trail right in front of me. The brochure was right. They were more brown than black.

I don't know who was more surprised, them or me!

I stopped dead and slowly started to back up. The bears just watched me. I felt like I might get away when a roar came from the trail. Momma had shown up.

I kept backing up, but Momma started towards me. Now the instruction said to calmly back up until you were out of sight before turning and running. But of course, I immediately turned and took off.

I could hear growls and yowls behind me. I wasn't about to turn and look. I wasn't a fast runner, but I set a personal best that day.

I was still on the trail with bears on my heels when I came to a turn. I had just traversed this part, so I knew what to expect. The turn was at the top of a rise, not a big one. If I followed the trail, it would steadily take me down to a creek.

Instead, I went straight, half running and half plunging down the hill to the creek. Gravity is a wonderful thing. I picked up speed. At the bottom, the creek wasn't wide or deep, so I high-stepped it across, splashing as I went.

I risked a look back when I got to the other side. Momma and the kids were still at the top of the trail. The bears had stopped and were sniffing around. It appeared that I had gotten far enough away they couldn't see me anymore. The question was, did they care enough to track me? I continued downstream, and thankfully, they turned and started back up the trail.

Now my only problem was that I had left the trail and had to get back to it. I knew it wouldn't be that far down the creek, but my goal was to find it and get out of there.

As I made my way downstream, I saw the small footbridge ahead which marked the trail.

On my way to it I saw a flash in the corner of my eye. The sun reflected on something. It was an outcrop of quartz that appeared to be newly uncovered by a small mudslide. It had rained heavily in the last few days. Being no dummy, I used a large rock from the creek bed to break up the quartz.

They were correct; there was a pocket of gold nuggets. Later at home, it weighed out at a little over one hundred and twenty pounds. I now had the problem of being two miles deep in a National Forest, and I had taken a bus to get to the area. How to get the gold home?

I first carried the gold nuggets to the nearby stream and collapsed part of the bank to bury them. I hiked back to the tourist gold mine and caught the next bus back to town.

From there, I rented a hotel room for several days. In those days, they were a lot easier about renting rooms. The fact I had a passport for identification and paid cash upfront was all it took.

I bought a heavy-duty three-wheel bicycle with a basket in the back the next morning. I also picked up a shovel, some feed sacks, and shipping cartons. I took the cartons to the hotel.

I pedaled the six miles back to the forest, dug the gold out of the stream, and then loaded it into the feed sacks. Then it was back to the hotel to package the gold in the shipping cartons.

I took the cartons down to the railroad station and paid extra to have a wooden crate built to contain the boxes of gold.

Then I shipped the crate via Railway Express back to my parents in Bellefontaine with a note to not open it till I was home. At the gold mine, they had explained that gold was legally priced at thirty-five dollars an ounce, but they talked about taking the price controls off. If they did, that gold might go up to four hundred dollars an ounce.

I sold the gold in 1979 for eight hundred dollars an ounce, or one million four hundred thousand dollars.

Chapter 8

It was time for me to head to Dallas for the Rodeo Championships. I hitched most of the way there. I had finally learned to stick my thumb out near restaurants where long-distance trucks were stopped.

There were even some places out West that had combination restaurants and gas pumps. They called these Truck Stops. I could get longer rides much quicker.

My ride luck had worn out in the middle of nowhere Texas. I was on a deserted road with nothing in sight, and it was getting dark. Rather than fight it, I walked over a small rise beside the road and unrolled my sleeping bag. I dropped right off but was awakened around three in the morning by the sound of cattle.

I peeked over the hill and saw two cattle trucks and a pickup towing a horse trailer. One of the trucks had already been loaded. I crept close enough to hear them talking about the easiest heist and most profitable job yet. These were cattle rustlers!

There were five of them. Three of them rode out and collected the cattle, and two stayed with the trucks. I checked the loads on the two Colt .45s Mr. Wayne had given me for target practice.

On the movie set, we used special pistols that would only fire blanks. People had been killed on sets where they used live weapons.

When the three galoots left to rustle more cattle, I snuck up on the two who stayed behind. They talked and didn't have any weapons in sight, so I just stepped out with weapons cocked and told them to reach for the sky.

I knew the lingo; I had been watching Westerns for years. They were surprised and put their hands up.

I was like the dog that chased the car and caught it; now what was I going to do with them? I had them drop their jeans down to their ankles. Both wore boots and were now effectively hobbled like a horse.

I checked around the truck and trailers and found a rope. I had them lay on their stomachs near where I had been sleeping and tied their hands behind their backs. They looked like they were related and were of different ages. I asked the younger one if the older guy was his dad. He said, "Yes."

I let that go. I checked the three trucks' cabs out and found several empty lunch sacks from the Fort Worth Cattle Auction House. I wandered back over to the kid (early twenties) who I had kept apart from his dad. I asked the kid his name.

"Eric,"

"What's your dad's name?"

"John, John Bear."

"After you drop off the cattle at the Fort Worth Auction House where were you heading?"

"Home, I guess. Mom doesn't like us to be gone too long."

"Okay. Just be quiet, and this will be over soon."

Over soon, I thought. Your mom will be mad when you and Dad don't get home for another five to ten years.

I waited patiently for the other three to return and load the next truck. When the others got back, one of them yelled for the other two. They went over to the smaller truck with the horse trailer when the others didn't appear.

They dismounted to talk, and I braced them in the same manner. Jeans to ankles, down on their stomachs, and hands tied behind their backs. I also ran a rope between their legs and up and over their jeans. The hogtie locked them together.

I had found a full five-gallon gas can and several bales of hay in the trucks. I had a nice fire going in the center of the road, and about fifteen minutes, two Texas Rangers pulled up.

It didn't take long for them to figure out I was the good guy and had captured five rustlers in the act.

One Ranger stated that I had done it as if John Wayne had taught me. I let it go.

I showed them the lunch sacks and shared what the youngest rustler had told me. They talked to him separately like I had, and he reconfirmed that they were meeting someone he didn't know. He would recognize him but didn't know his name.

The Rangers told me that this gang had hit the area pretty hard, so they were on patrol. They questioned the other guys, but they wouldn't say anything.

The Rangers weren't surprised as this had happened before. The low-level people, when caught, kept quiet and had all sorts of high-level legal talent on their side. They would get truly short or suspended sentences.

I asked, "Why don't we deliver the cattle? The boy seems dumb enough to help us."

They went and struck a deal right there. If the boy and his dad took us to the leader in Fort Worth, we might lose them in the heat of the moment. If two low-level rustlers got away, no one would spend a lot of time and effort chasing them. They agreed to the deal.

We loaded everything, including the other crooks, and headed to Fort Worth. Our numbers added up. There were five, just like the gang. We pulled into the Fort Worth Cattle Auction House. There was a guy with a briefcase waiting for the trucks to pull in.

Later, I learned that the dad in the other truck pointed out the guy and said he was their contact. I was with the son in the truck with the horse trailer. The Rangers had deputized me so I could legally hold a gun on the young guy if needed. I kept it handy, but he made no moves.

Dad got out of the truck, and the guy with the briefcase came right up to him and handed him the case. The Rangers were right behind the guy and collared him. They had him in cuffs immediately.

The guy blustered and asked if they knew who he was.

"Yes, you are the guy with a briefcase full of money buying two loads of stolen cattle."

"I'll have you know that I am the biggest donor to the governor."

That probably was the wrong thing to say because that governor had been trying to cut the Rangers' budget and powers for years. Texas did get a new administration in the next election.

I noticed that Dad and son had disappeared. I hoped they got home before mom got mad.

The Rangers explained that this was a big deal, and it would make the national news. I told the head Ranger, Mr. Walker, they could have all the credit and leave me out of it.

He told me that wasn't possible. He would like the credit, but they couldn't lie about this. It would bite them in the butt if they did. The Rangers would look good from this, but so would I.

The reward for the information leading to the capture and conviction of the largest cattle rustling operation in the twentieth century was eighty-five thousand dollars. I wouldn't get that until after the trial and conviction, which wouldn't be until sometime next year.

In the meantime, they gave me a real Texas Ranger badge and swore me in as a permanent deputy.

I was told this was an honorary position, and I wasn't to wear my guns and arrest people. There was even an ID card and a leather case to hold it and the badge. I bet when I was old enough to drive, this would get me out of speeding tickets!

Chapter 9

The Rangers delivered me to the rodeo headquarters and got me checked in. Being escorted raised some questions about a young rider being in the custody of the Rangers. They told the people at the check-in desk that they were making certain I got to where I needed to be as an unaccompanied minor.

After checking me into the rodeo, the Rangers took me to an address Clint Easterly had provided. When helping me register for the championship, he contacted some Dallas people he knew to have a place to stay with a local family, the Ewings.

They had a ranch and a lot of oil wells but were nice to me and became my supporters at the event.

They did seem uptight about the Rangers showing up with me but soon relaxed when they were told what had happened. The older brother was quite pleased to hear the sitting governor would have some questions to answer. Seems the Ewings were a power in Texas.

My skills as a rider held up, but that wouldn't have been enough to win the Championship. I got lucky; the last bull dislodged me and tossed me to the right. I hung on and the bull tossed me back to the left and then swung me right back onto its back.

Watching the movie reel, it looked like I planned the move. When asked later how I had perfected it, I said it was a once-in-a-lifetime gamble and did not recommend anyone else try it.

I received a check for one thousand dollars and the largest silver belt buckle and trophy I had ever seen. As promised, I found a payphone and called Brian Wilson to see how our new song was doing.

Brian was really glad I called. He had been contacted by the TV show, *American Bandstand* and they wanted us to appear as soon as possible while the song was still hot.

I only had one week left before I had to be home, so we agreed to do it the following week. I was to fly to Philadelphia on Eastern Airlines, and he would have my flight met by a car and driver.

I also called Clint Easterly and thanked him profusely for introducing me to bull riding and that I was now the American Grand National Junior Champion. I had to describe the ride and my winning move.

He mumbled something about being born with a horseshoe up my butt, but I probably misheard him. We promised to stay in touch and ended the call.

I took a taxi to a local Sheplers and bought more new clothes and suitcases to carry them in. There was one carry-on bag for suits that had compartments for boots! The outline of the boots showed on the outside. It was really neat.

The salesman convinced me that I needed a suit and the carry-on, and I should probably have new boots while I was at it.

The grey suit with gold edging had that Western look; it went well with my black Resistol hat. I had a hard time choosing between the Ostrich skin and Alligator boots. The helpful salesman pointed out that I could buy both, keeping one pair in the carry-on while wearing the others. I left my old rucksack and sleeping bag with them as they were plumb worn out.

I was buying my ticket at the airport when I was asked if it would be first-class or coach. I found that it would only cost seventy-five dollars for first class. I peeled the money off my money clip and paid the lady. Having this much money sure was a change from the beginning of the summer!

The flight on the brand-new jet plane was smooth, and I looked out the window most of the flight. The view was neat, and I decided I would learn to fly one day.

The meal was a nice fillet mignon and they brought me Cokes the entire flight. I needed to pee when the flight landed. I learned later they had toilets on the plane.

I thought about swiping the silverware as a souvenir but decided it didn't fit my new status as a Texas Ranger. I was learning about pictures on paper.

A man with a sign met me at the airport, and after a quick trip to the restroom, we went out to the car. It was a long stretched-out car he called a limo. He took me to a big old hotel downtown. At the front desk, they were expecting me and told me my suite was ready.

A man in a funny uniform took me and my bags upstairs and showed me all around my room. He seemed reluctant to leave. He stood there with his hand in his pocket, jingling some change. I didn't know what to do, so I looked back at him. He turned and left but didn't seem happy.

Brian Wilson called my room and asked me if everything was okay. I told him it was but that the bellhop seemed unhappy. He asked how much I had tipped him. Uh oh! A small-town kid strikes again. Brian and I agreed to meet in the lobby to go out for dinner.

I got cleaned up, put my fancy new suit on, and went down early. I explained my error to the bellhop at the front desk and asked what a proper amount to tip. They told me a dollar a bag was normal, but five dollars would go a long way to making the guy happy if I could afford it.

I was lucky, and my bellhop was still on duty. I gave him five bucks and explained I was green as grass. He told me he figured that was the case and thanked me.

Brian and I had a really good dinner at a Bookbinder's restaurant or something like that. The other guys in the band were going elsewhere. I got the idea it might involve drinking and women. Recently things like that sounded attractive, especially the women part.

The next morning, we had breakfast in my hotel suite and went to the studio where they recorded *American Bandstand*. The host Dick Clark was nice to Brian and me and introduced us to another singer a little older than me, Paul Anka.

We waited in a room called, for some reason, the Green Room, which was painted grey, and had a really good talk about my possible career as a singer.

Paul had listened to my song. Both Paul and Brian agreed I didn't have the voice for a career. The song was a novelty hit, but that was it. I didn't disagree with this harsh estimate of my talent.

Paul, who turned out to be an astute businessman, said, "You might consider donating all the profits from this song to a charity. From what little I know of your story from Brian, you will be hit with some hefty taxes."

Brian agreed that made sense, so I decided to right then and there.

When we were introduced, I told the audience that this was a fun song and that I wouldn't have a career singing, so I decided to donate all my profits to the Leukemia Society. Later I was told that was a little overboard. I had just blown fifty thousand dollars.

Before I got off the air, I had a phone call from the Leukemia Society wanting to get it in writing. It turned out to be a good move, according to Dad's tax accountant.

The show went well, but I later learned that TV did it in spades if newspaper stories got around. I had worn my Texas Ranger badge on my suit. The cameras focused on it several times.

Having the badge caused questions of the Texas Rangers, who told the whole story of my help with capturing the cattle rustlers. My story made national news. Since it wasn't breaking news, it didn't come out till the weekend, when I was safely home.

It was a week until school started, so it was time to head home. The next morning, I flew to Dayton, Ohio, hiring a taxi to drive me to Bellefontaine and home. I had too much stuff to hitchhike now. There was only one problem when I got home. There was no one there.

The house was empty! A neighbor Twyla came out and told me where we had moved to. It was in the nicest area of town, Indian Heights. The driver took me there, and I had a wonderful welcome this time.

That was my summer vacation in 1958 and exactly how it happened, give or take a lie or two.

Chapter 10

The cab dropped me off at my new home a week before school started. My parents had moved while I was on my summer trip, but they left word where we had moved. I knew right away that it was the correct house. My two younger brothers were shooting hoops on the basket attached to the two-car garage.

Denny, the oldest, yelled, "Mum, he's home!"

My younger brother Eddie took the opportunity to steal the ball from Denny. This set off one of their typical yelling matches. Yep, I was home.

To say my arrival home was tumultuous would be putting it mildly. I had been gone all summer and had enough adventures for a lifetime. On top of that, I raised our family's standard of living by providing a new paid-for home, a new car, and money in the bank.

Mum came running out the door and swept me into a hug. Dad was right behind me and started to shake my hand but instead swept me into his hug. Mary wrapped herself around my leg. At first, it was a continuous babble about the new house, new car, me being home, and the adventures I had. No order for any one of us. The words just flowed. I was home!

Things finally settled down, and Mum gave me a tour of our new house. I was shown my new bedroom. Each of us had our own bedroom in the five-bedroom home. There was an eat-in kitchen, dining room, living room with fireplace, family room, and a mudroom between the kitchen and garage. The master bedroom suite was downstairs. The upstairs had a junior suite with a small bathroom which was mine.

The other kids shared a bathroom. I suspected that my four-year-old sister Mary and I would be switching rooms one day.

There was also a full basement with a recreation room. The rec room had a regulation-size pool table, with a table tennis top set on top of it. There was also a fireplace and a wet bar. The laundry room was big and airy, and there was a laundry chute on each floor so you could drop dirty clothes into the laundry room!

The lot was about one acre, which meant I would have much mowing to do. Fortunately, the neighborhood was new enough that the trees were not full-grown, so I wouldn't have to rake any leaves. I would miss burning them, though. There was a brick fireplace out back for grilling, and I could still burn the trash in it, so my inner firebug would be satisfied.

The house had a gas furnace which meant I wouldn't have to shovel coal and clean out ashes like the last house. I wouldn't miss working with the coal furnace at all. There was nothing worse than getting out of bed on a cold morning with the coal fire banked, going to the basement to get it going, and then waiting for the house to warm up. There would be five of us standing on the main warm air register on cold days.

I didn't know if we would have a garden here as we did at the old place. There weren't any in our new neighborhood. There wasn't a clothesline strung, but there was one of those whirly things that always seemed to need restringing.

After I toured our new house, the family settled into the family room. Things had quieted enough we could have a real conversation. They had a hundred questions about my trip.

My rodeo and ribbons were brought out, and I showed off the belt buckles I had won. After showing off my Colt .45s, Mum insisted that I keep them locked up in the gun cabinet in the basement.

My brother Denny pontifically stated, "You told us you camped in a dell. Dell is a proper name, like Mum's sister Aunt Dell."

"Denny, Dell can be a proper name like Aunt Dell, but when it is not capitalized, it refers to a small, secluded valley, similar to a dale.

However, while a dale is a small valley, it is not necessarily secluded," I told our budding young grammar Nazi.

"A Mr. Michael Dell even gave me a ride out in Texas, so Dell can be a first and last name."

My now pouting brother was told to quit interrupting or go to his room by Mum. I started to talk about the bank robbery, but Dad broke in, "We will talk about that later."

John Wayne had sent the autographed copy of *Variety* that talked about how Elvis Presley, Tab Hunter, and I had got in a fight in Mexico, and I had to bail them out of jail. The Mexican Police had sold pictures of us with the police, so that I couldn't deny it. Mum and Dad were okay about it.

Mr. Wayne's writing, "Wish I was there," helped.

They wanted to hear all about the movies I was in; even Denny and Eddie were impressed that they would see me on an upcoming *Mickey Mouse Club* TV show.

They both thought it a shame that I hadn't had a chance to get to know Annette. Denny even wanted to know if I kissed her. As if I could get past those chaperones!

Mum and Dad wanted to know all about John Wayne. They also let me know that Elvis had been drafted and was now in the Army! They also liked how I had worked my way across the country and not just hitchhiked.

The story about the Texas Rangers and the rustlers had everyone in their seats. Mum made a point that I was lucky not to get killed. She seemed to forget I was the one with the guns.

My singing career was amazing to the whole family because we weren't noted for our ability to keep a tune other than in a bushel basket. None of the family had seen my appearance on *American Bandstand*. But they were all interested in how I was treated in Philadelphia.

When I told them about my promise to the Leukemia Society, Dad about had a cow. His words were unprintable when I told him about Paul Anka's and Brian Wilson's comments on taxes.

He hates taxes. He blames all of those on President Eisenhower. When he calmed down, he concluded we would have to talk to an accountant.

Luckily, I had kept all the paperwork from my trip. These papers included the record contract, reward notices, rodeo winnings, movie and TV pay, plus my roughneck pay. Mr. Easterly had paid me out of pocket, and it was only twenty dollars a week for three weeks.

My brothers and sister left us alone after establishing that I had not brought them any presents. I wish I had thought of that, especially for Mum and Dad.

I told them I was sorry about not bringing them gifts.

Mum laughed at me. "Ricky, you just gave this family a wonderful new house, and you haven't even seen the 1958 Buick Roadmaster we have in the garage!"

This news led us to a financial discussion. I had sent home twenty-five thousand dollars from the bank reward. There would probably be another eighty-five-thousand-dollar reward within six months, but we wouldn't count that till it happened.

I also had nine hundred dollars left over from my trip, but I intended to keep that separate for my use.

The house cost sixteen thousand dollars and the car twenty-four hundred. We had over six thousand dollars left after the new furniture, electric washer, and dryer. My parents asked me what I wanted to do with that. I turned the question around to them.

"You know more of what the family needs than I do. What do you think?"

Mum and Dad exchanged looks, and Dad started.

"Rick, work hasn't been good. You know I'm only on the extra board on the railroad. I only get called for work after all the regular full-time employees have been scheduled for their forty-hour work weeks. Many weeks there aren't forty hours of work available to me."

"I thought you had been working there since you returned from the war. Don't you have seniority?"

All railroad kids knew about seniority. Dad's time book kept track of his hours and even had a list of employees and their starting years. When he started in 1946, the most senior person had been there since 1898.

"I have, but the railroad has been declining faster than my seniority has been building. Trucks, buses, and the new jet planes are taking over the freight and passenger business. I am afraid the railroad days are numbered for me. We own some stock in New York Central, and it keeps going down. I don't think the government will let it shut down, but it will be much smaller and consolidated with fewer employees."

"What are you going to do?"

Chapter 11

"Mum and I have an idea; we have been talking about this since you sent the reward money. We still own the house on North Detroit Street. We would like to fix it up and rent it out. If that works, we would like to buy others and do the same thing."

"How will the finances work?"

"The Detroit Street house is worth eleven thousand dollars. We put twenty percent down and started with an eighty-eight-hundred-dollar mortgage. At two percent interest, for thirty years, that works out as thirty-two dollars for the monthly house payment.

"We have checked with two local realtors, and they both suggested we ask for seventy-five dollars a month for the house. We would put away twenty dollars a month for repairs, insurance, and when it is sitting empty.

"That would give us twenty-three dollars a month for the family budget. Our thinking is to get that house into shape, rent it out, and then buy others.

"Duplexes seem to be the best bet as the cost wouldn't be that much more, and you could rent each side out for sixty dollars a month. That would be one hundred and twenty dollars a month income with a set aside of forty dollars or eighty dollars to the family for every duplex we own."

Mum stepped in, "If we owned five units like that, we would be making four hundred dollars a month which would more than replace Jack's railroad income in a good year. Seven units would allow for units sitting empty. Ten, and we would be rich."

"Let's go for rich," I replied.

"Dad, I am big enough. I now can help with home repairs and keeping lawns mowed and things like that. We have enough leftover that we could buy two units right now with twenty percent down."

"Rick, we can do better than that. The North Detroit house has seven thousand dollars in equity," said Dad.

"What's equity?"

The difference between what the house is worth and the amount we owe on it. We can take out a new loan for up to eighty percent of our equity. We can start with five duplexes if we are careful about what we buy and how much we need for repairs."

"What do we have to do to start?"

"We have identified three units we would like to buy if the price and building conditions are right."

"I am all for it!"

"Okay, son. Your mother and I feel that ownership should be set up so that the houses go to you if anything happens to us. We will talk to a lawyer about how to make that happen."

And that was the beginning of Jackson Housing.

My parents had one last question, "What is in the shipping box marked 'Do Not Open'?"

I told them about finding the gold and what the gold miners told me about deregulated gold. Dad remembered everyone having to turn in their gold during the Great Depression. He remembered because it was a bitter joke in his house; they had no gold to turn in.

They agreed to consider that possibility because it could be a small fortune. In the meantime, Dad would look into a safe deposit box to store it.

They also had some information for me.

Dad said, "George Weaver of the *Bellefontaine Examiner* will be contacting you. He was called for information on you by James Olsen out in Colorado after the bank robbery. George did not know much other than you weren't known as a juvenile delinquent and had been a paperboy."

While not a loner, I didn't have any close friends in my junior high years. Those friends from my grade school days had moved away. I knew most of the kids from my grade school but didn't get invited to their birthday parties.

That was how you knew your social status in those days. I hadn't any social status. I wasn't an outcast. I just wasn't in any of the groups.

The next day, the first thing I did was go to J.C. Penney and buy new school clothes. All that I had that would fit me were my cowboy outfits. Those would do for the rodeo circuit and my singing appearances but would get me teased to death in Bellefontaine.

Even if I must say so myself, I looked good with my Ivy League pants (a buckle in the back) and a cardigan. I also splurged on a pair of dirty bucks, a brown suede shoe. I thought about blue suede shoes, but Elvis hadn't worn them when we went out together, so I figured they must be from the song.

I had mixed feelings about the start of the school year. I couldn't wait to try the idea of reading ahead and working on the problems in advance of the class.

But I hated going back to school because I was fourteen years old, and all fourteen-year-olds disliked going back to school. I think it was a rule or something. I liked the idea of being in high school instead of junior high. A new school meant I would be meeting new people (girls).

I didn't know how I would be treated once word came out about my summer vacation. I wanted to tell everyone my story, but I didn't want to be a braggart.

Getting the story out was taken care of before school started. George Weaver of the *Bellefontaine Examiner* rang the doorbell of our new home and asked for me.

He knew I was due home about now and wanted to talk to me before they printed anything. When Mum and Dad told me about the interview, we agreed that I should tell him about the whole summer and share all the evidence that it was true.

Dad was downtown talking to a lawyer about setting up a business, so Mum sat in on the interview. Mr. Weaver asked me to tell my story.

I prepared him with, "The story is more than you know, and I hope you have some time."

I then launched into my summer trip.

The run up to the bank robbery I covered quickly. I shared the news article written in Colorado and the reward posters for John and Ernest Johnson. I also had a carbon copy of the FBI report and a deposit slip for the rewards.

I then moved on to bull riding and winning rodeos right up to the National Championship. I had trophies, ribbons, silver belt buckles, and prize money receipts.

I showed him my Screen Actors Guild card and the deposit receipts for my *Mickey Mouse Club* appearances. They also gave me the viewing dates, which were still a month away. At this point, Mr. Weaver looked like he was having a fit. He was bouncing around in his chair.

He couldn't sit anymore when I got to the John Wayne and Elvis parts. He kept notes while walking around the room. I showed him my salary receipts for *It Never Happened* and *Hell Fighters* and my John Wayne autographed *Variety* copy.

I showed him my Oil Workers Union card and paycheck stub for being a roughneck.

I thought he would have a heart attack when he learned about the rustling episode and my Texas Ranger badge.

We had to stop the interview for a while in fear for Mr. Weaver's health. This news was the biggest story he had ever had. Mum offered him tea, but he declined by saying he had an ulcer. She then brought him a glass of milk, for which he was grateful.

The last news I had to tell him was about "Rock and Roll Cowboy" and being on *Bandstand*. I think he was numb because he just kept taking notes. When I finally finished, he asked if he could use the phone.

He called his office and had them send a photographer out. He then spent the next three hours going over my story for the fine details. He was professional, and I didn't feel pressured.

After the pictures of trophies, ribbons, badges, etc., he told us that the story was long enough to spread out several days next week or even the week after. He wanted to get this one right as he thought it might go national.

Chapter 12

The first school week was short as Labor Day fell on a Monday. So, on Tuesday, September 2, 1958, I started my high school career. The previous Friday, I went to the school office, picked up my class schedule, and paid my school fees.

These were for a biology workbook and some poor frog. I would have to cut up the frog. There were two locks for my coat and gym lockers.

I also took the time to check out where my classrooms and homeroom were. Since my junior high was attached to the high school, I knew the building fairly well.

Afterward, I walked downtown to G.C. Murphy Five and Dime and bought a three-ring binder for my homework, pencils, paper, and a fountain pen. I splurged on the paper; they now had a green tint with narrow lines instead of the boring white paper with wide lines. I soon regretted purchasing that the first time my assignment was, "Write one full page on...."

The first day was taking attendance and getting seating assignments straight. Some teachers didn't care where you sat. Others wanted you in alphabetical order. Books were handed out, and we wrote our names on the pasted-in book slip on the inside cover. I also got the soon-to-be-famous "What did you do on your summer vacation" English assignment.

I ran into several kids I knew at lunchtime, and it was amazing how much some of them had grown over the summer. The boys up, and the girls out. Many of the girls were taller, but that isn't what I noticed. I was surprised when my growth got the most comments.

Not only by growing taller but by being in shape. My friend Tom Pew wanted to know what I had been doing. I went all mysterious to him and told him he would have to read about it in the newspaper like everyone else.

He laughed and moved on with a "See you later, alligator."

I brilliantly rejoined with, "After a while, crocodile."

He came back with, "Don't get wise, beady eyes."

Then I gave the conversation topper, "Understand, rubber band." We were such wits.

My growth was brought home to me in gym class. Coach Crowley gave us the rules of the road. We were told what type of shorts, shirts, and shoes we had to buy. It was made clear we had to shower after class and bring a clean towel from home. We might even want to buy a gym bag!

He then went around and talked to some of the freshmen. I knew this was to talk to the kids going out for sports. I was surprised when he came up to me and asked if I would try out for football.

The regular varsity team had been practicing for two weeks, but they had freshman tryouts after the school year had started. They did this because of teenagers' growth spurts between the eighth and ninth grades.

"I never thought about it."

"Did you grow a lot this summer?"

"I did, Coach."

"I thought so, or I would've noticed you before. You are of a size; you could be a running back or even a quarterback if you have the arm."

"When are tryouts?"

"After school this Thursday; come on out to the football field if you are interested. We could use some new players this year. We lost most of our first-string varsity to graduation last year."

"I will give it serious thought. I never thought I would be big enough to play, so I haven't given it any thought."

Coach laughed. "You know I teach one of the English classes. You might want to think about how often you used 'thought' in that sentence."

"After I said it, I thought it might be a problem."

Coach gave me a light hit on the arm and moved on.

I got home that afternoon at about 3:45, and my first duty was to wrap all my schoolbooks in book covers. I used the ones sold by the band club.

They were expensive at fifteen cents each, but they were in the red and black school colors and had BHS with a bell on the front.

I then proceeded to get ahead. I read the first chapter in the English book. It was the start of diagraming sentences. It took about half an hour to read the lesson and diagram the practice sentences at the end of the chapter.

I found that the correct answers were at the back of the book, and I had them all right. I could see this would work out well. I was going to English class tomorrow and would understand what Miss Bales was talking about.

She was a tough grader, and I needed every break to make an A in her class.

Algebra was easy after getting it through my head that subtracting a negative number turns that number into a positive. Does that mean two wrongs make a right? It only took about twenty minutes to get the problems worked out. The correct answers being in the back of the book sure helped.

Latin was easy but tedious; I wrote out each vocabulary word ten times while saying its meaning aloud. Then I had to translate the simple sentences in the back of the chapter. Again, the back of the book helped a lot.

Biology took a while because I had to read the first chapter, then do the first chapter in the workbook. The workbook questions were fill-in-the-blank, so I did them as I went. I had no correct answers for those, so I would have to wait and see.

World history was not so easy. After reading the chapter, the questions required writing a paragraph about each event covered in the book. It also referred to other references that I didn't have.

We did have an Encyclopedia Americana, so I used that as my basic reference. It took about ten minutes to write about each question. I wrote each out on a separate sheet of paper to turn in what was requested.

I got everything done in time to watch the *Mickey Mouse Club* with my two brothers. After that, I helped Mum by setting the table for dinner. After dinner, I told her I would wash the dishes.

She wanted to know who I was and what I had done with her son! This surprise didn't stop her from letting me do the dishes. When I was done, Dad asked to speak with me.

We went down to the basement, and he closed the door behind us after telling Mum to keep the children upstairs.

I was beginning to wonder what was going on! It came out quickly.

"Rick, let's talk about that bank robbery. You killed two men. How do you feel about that?"

"Dad, I don't know how I feel. It all happened so fast that it didn't feel like I did anything. All of a sudden, they were dead."

"How did you react after the shooting was finished?"

I proceeded to tell him how I just stood there almost in shock and felt numb for several hours.

"Have you had dreams or intense memories of what has happened?"

"How intense are the memories you are talking about because I think about it at times."

"Do you suddenly feel like you are there again, happening again?"

"No."

"Good, let me tell you why I am asking. I saw some fighting during the war but not like some people. You know Bill Samson, who always sat on the wall down by the courthouse?"

"Yes, he would be there every day if he wasn't on his front porch drinking a beer."

"Well, Bill and I got drunk one night, and he told me about his war. He was on the second wave of landings that hit Omaha Beach on D-Day. Bill was with the 29th Division, a group from Virginia. He told me how he could hear the bullets rattle off the front of their landing craft and knew that most of them would die when the front was lowered to let them out.

"He was lucky; he was one of the last off. He had to climb over his dead friends to get out. They had landed in the wrong spot because of the wind and tide. They had to scale a cliff with little cover rather than the smooth beach they were supposed to be at. All-day long, his friends were killed, and he had to keep going.

"Today, almost fifteen years later, he still can't sleep a complete night. He wakes up screaming, not wanting that landing door to open. That is why he never was able to hold a job."

"Was? What happened?"

"He committed suicide last month. He stuck his pistol in his mouth and pulled the trigger. He left a note saying he was leaving to visit some old friends.

"Anytime death is involved, it can affect people, especially if it is by violence. Your mother and I were concerned about how you were handling this."

"Dad, I haven't felt anything like you are describing."

"I am so glad to hear that. It was so fast that it didn't register with you. Please let us know if you start to have flashbacks about the shootings."

"I will."

Dad then changed the subject. "I talked with Eugene Burke, an attorney. He suggested that we form a corporation. It will be expensive, two hundred dollars, but it will protect the family from general lawsuits from the business and split everything between your mother, you, and me.

"That sounds like it sets us up as you talked about. Do I have to do anything?"

"No, as a minor, we sign for you. The corporation will be split three ways with a third for each of us."

"Sounds like a plan."

That night in bed, I thought about Bill Samson. We kids had joked about the town drunk for years. If only we had known. Another thought that kept running around my mind was that I thought I was a tough guy after the bank shootings.

Sitting in that boat waiting for the door to drop and let in all those bullets was frightening beyond belief. I wasn't a tough guy.

Chapter 13

The next morning after going through my exercise routine, I had pretty well shaken off the dark thoughts of the night before and was looking forward to the school day. It only took about ten minutes to walk to school from our new home.

Several kids were going toward school when I came out of the front door, so it was natural to join them. We kept picking up kids until about ten or twelve of us arrived at school.

We had a casual conversation on the way to school. But I couldn't tell you about anything we discussed.

School on Wednesday proved interesting in several ways. First of all, I had never felt so on top of things in my classwork. I quickly learned that I only had to pay half attention to the lecture as they were going over material that I had studied the night before and felt comfortable with. I started reading the next chapter ahead. That worked very well.

At the end of Algebra class, I realized something I didn't understand in the next chapter. Mr. Buckley, our teacher, gave out that night's assignment in the last fifteen minutes of our forty-five-minute class session and told us to get to work.

If we had any questions, we were to raise our hands. Since every other problem was at the back of the chapter, I had those done correctly.

I raised my hand, and Mr. Buckley came to my desk. I showed him what I didn't understand. He started to get a little huffy about working on the problems at the end of today's chapter.

I quickly showed him that I had worked on *all* the problems. He smiled big, invited me to his desk, and showed me what I missed on tomorrow's homework.

I couldn't finish all of tomorrow's Algebra problems, but it wouldn't take that long at home or in study hall. I had two study halls on Monday, Wednesday, and Friday. Tuesdays and Thursdays only had one because of gym class.

World History was a revelation. Mr. McMillian told us we could pick any question at the back of the chapter to write an essay on. All the references quoted in the book were either in the school library or the study hall library.

Since I was excited about schoolwork, I decided to do every question at the end of the chapter. Fortunately, we did one chapter a week, so I only had to do one essay a day.

Mr. McMillian then really made my day by saying we would get extra credit for every essay we turned in over and above the one required.

One interesting thing other than schoolwork was girls. They noticed me! It was nothing exciting (other than to me) or sexual. Just that the girls that sat next to me in every class would say, "Hello," and make inquiries about my summer or the fact that I had grown so much. I gave nothing away about my summer and made polite conversation for one or two minutes before the teacher began.

Thursday is when it all started. The beginning was when I got my English paper back.

It had the comment, "Well written, but I did not ask for a work of fiction."

The grade was an F. I was crushed, and I didn't know what to do, so I did nothing. I guess I flushed very red because Miss Bales glared at me like she waited for me to open my mouth. She was well known for assigning detention. I kept my mouth shut.

After thinking very evil thoughts, I realized that the *Bellefontaine Examiner* article would clarify that I was telling the truth. I would approach her with a copy of the paper and ask her to revise my grade.

The rest of the day went by quickly. I had to hustle to keep ahead in my reading and answer all the questions. I was doing about twice as much as most students.

I say most students because I realized that other kids worked diligently in study hall in the libraries every day. Until I stumbled into that orientation session at Berkeley, I had never known that this level of schooling existed.

I hadn't planned any goals in life, but it did not take much to figure out this would keep many options open.

After school, it was time for football tryouts. I want to report that I was a natural, and the coaches wanted me to play on the varsity team for Friday's first game.

The reality was that I was strong. I could catch the ball; I could pass the ball fairly well but couldn't run worth a darn. I didn't have the stamina needed and was too slow to boot.

My discouragement must have shown because Coach Crowley took me aside and explained that stamina could be earned. I just had to run every day.

I had to run long distances to build my wind and sprint to work on speed. As he pointed out, I had grown a lot recently, and my body hadn't had a chance to catch up.

"What time do you get up in the morning, Rick," he asked.

"Seven o'clock to be at school at 8:30."

"Try getting up at six o'clock and see how far you can run. Don't push it, just get a comfortable speed, and keep at it as long as possible. At first, you will be able to go for five minutes before walking for a while.

"Keep that up for several weeks, and I guarantee that you will be able to run for the whole hour. Not real fast, but your stamina will have increased that much.

"In the meantime, we will carry you on the squad and let you practice. We aren't limited on how many we can carry for the first month."

I decided that I would get up early and run. I'm not certain what was driving me, but I controlled my life and made good things happen.

When I got home that night, Mr. Weaver had dropped off a copy of the story that would run in the paper for three days starting Monday. It was all correct, but it made me look like some super kid.

All the high points were there, but none of the low points like camping in the desert because of no ride, that first lonely night on the road, or how falling off a horse got me in a John Wayne movie. I wondered if this was how most hero stories went.

On Friday, I set the alarm for 6 a.m. and crawled out of bed. I did wonder how anyone could jump out of bed. I ran and walked till 7.

Okay, I walked more than I ran.

When I came into the house, Mum said, "PU, up to the bath with you, boy."

The bath in my room also had a shower with it. I tried it for my first shower ever. I don't think I have taken a bath since.

My hair was still wet when I left for school. I wished I had one of those industrial dryers I saw at the gold mine.

Before I went to my homeroom at school, I stopped in Miss Bale's room and asked her if she had a minute. She did.

I handed her a copy of Mr. Weaver's story and explained that it would be published in the *Examiner*. She took the papers absently and laid them on her desk. I didn't get any reaction from her.

When I went to English class late in the day, I did get that reaction. She started with a statement.

"There is a student to whom I owe an apology. Mr. Jackson turned in his paper on his summer vacation, and I gave him an F. I asked for a factual report on your summer. He turned in a well-written piece of fiction, or so I thought. His grade has been changed to an A, and I urge you to read the Bellefontaine newspaper Monday evening.

This statement, of course, had the school speculating for the rest of the day on what would be in the paper. More kids came up to me and asked what was going on. More than I usually talked to in a month.

I told everyone, "Just read the paper. It is too long to tell here."

Chapter 14

Friday night was quiet. I went to the youth center, but I couldn't get into the conversation or antics of the other kids for some reason. The only cute girls there were traveling in packs, and I couldn't get close to them, so I went home early. Being in at ten o'clock when I had an eleven o'clock curfew about floored my parents.

They wanted to know what was going on. I told my parents it just was boring.

Dad laughed and remarked, "After your summer, the rest of your life might seem boring."

That was frightening. Had my life peaked at fourteen?

Mum said dryly, "I suspect he will get up to something to relieve the boredom."

I went to my room and listened to records on my portable stereo record player while reading the latest from Robert Heinlein. I made a mental note to get some more of the plastic inserts for my 45 rpm records. The insert went into the large center hole of the 45s so they would adapt to the spindle, which was made small for 33s.

On Saturday, I was up early and did my exercises, including my new one-hour run-walk. My stamina felt better. I could see how someday I could run the whole distance without getting winded. I would get a stitch in my side the first couple of tries, but coach had told me to run through that. It worked. I guess that was the second wind.

The bad part was that I couldn't seem to run any faster, no matter how much I practiced sprinting. After running, I mowed the lawn. Once I got cleaned up, the rest of the day should be mine.

After taking my shower, I went downstairs to look for some breakfast. Mum was there and came out with a typical Mum statement.

"Your hair is still wet. You will catch your death."

Since it was a beautiful fall day, I didn't think it would be a problem now, but I would have to rethink it when it got cold out. I remembered that handheld industrial dryer I saw at the gold mine. I should check up on that. It would be neat to be able to dry my hair quickly.

I had a Boy Scout meeting at the Lutheran Church, so I rode my bike down the hill, coasting most of the way. The whole town of Bellefontaine was on the side of Campbell's Hill. It is the highest point in the state of Ohio. But at fifteen hundred feet above sea level, it wasn't that tall.

At least it didn't seem that tall going from east to west in town. Going from west to east, you realized that it was long and steep! I could pedal going home, but it was a strain.

The scout meeting was to plan for an upcoming camporee. There would be contests such as knot tying, chopping logs, fire building, swimming, and orienteering. I was a patrol leader and had to decide who would compete in which contests in my patrol. The trick was to pick the best at each event and not leave anyone out. If my patrol didn't have someone good or wanted to perform, I had to do it.

My Scoutmaster cornered me. He asked, "Rick, when will you complete your Citizenship in the Nation Merit Badge? You have twenty-nine badges, so you have more than the twenty-one required for Eagle. You don't have the last required badge, or would you rather switch to the Brotherhood in the World one?

"Last year, you were the Senior Patrol Leader and still are a Patrol Leader, so you have met the leadership requirements. That spring cleaning we did at the church took care of service, so you only need the one badge for Eagle."

"I will complete the Citizenship in the Nation badge within two weeks," I promised. "But why the push to do it now? I have till I am eighteen."

"Simple Rick, it is well established once a boy discovers girls and cars, all thoughts of Eagle Scout go out of their head."

I couldn't disagree with that. As the Scoutmaster talked, a couple of girls walked by the window, distracting me.

"What is holding you up, Rick?"

"The tours of two federal facilities requirement. I have to do that yet."

Mr. Geist, my Scoutmaster, shook his head. "Rick, remember that tour of the radar base on top of Campbell's Hill we took last year?"

"Yes."

"What about the tour of the post office? If I remember right, you organized that when you were Senior Patrol Leader."

"Yes, I had to call the postmaster, Mr. Williams, to make arrangements."

"Who owns the airbase and the post office?"

"Oh, I have been dumber than dumb."

"Who is your merit badge counselor for this?"

"Mr. Wolfe, my eighth-grade history teacher."

He rummaged around in his ever-present briefcase and a blue merit badge card. He then signed off on the federal facility tours.

"Take this to your teacher, and if he has signed off on everything else, you are good to go. By the way, who did you write to, a congressman or a senator?"

"I wrote to Senator Taft about the Russians getting to space before we did with Sputnik. We need to get serious, or they will get to the moon before we do. He replied that he was supporting a bill to do just that. I was able to use the letter and his reply for extra credit in my class."

"That is how we want you to think, how to get the most for your efforts. I expect to see the signed-off card next week now that I know you are so close."

"Yes, sir."

Sunday was a nothing day. We didn't attend church as a family. I got in a pickup football game early in the afternoon. My parents told me I was babysitting while they went to my Uncle Ross's house to play cards.

I was able to get Denny and Eddie to play with tinker toys while I played house with Mary. While it was still light, we all went outside and tried out the new toy Dad had picked up. It was called a hula hoop.

Before long, half the kids in the neighborhood were there, trying to make the hoop go around. Eleanor Price looked good as she twisted around. She was sixteen and had filled out.

We then started a Hide and Seek game, but it wasn't that fun since Mary was with me. Hiding with your four-year-old sister isn't the same as hiding with Eleanor! Of course, Eleanor had never paid any attention to me, as she considered me one of the little kids.

Monday morning opened the school week. I didn't worry about my classes as I read ahead and solved all the problems. I didn't even have any questions for my teachers.

I walked to school with Tom Morton and Bill Cairns. They lived further from the school than I did, so I just blended in with them as they walked by. They were sophomores but were friendly enough.

Tom started with, "Knock, Knock."

I played straight man and came back with, "Who's there?"

"Butter"

"Butter, who?"

"I butter not tell you. It's a secret!"

At our ages, we were great wits.

They had heard that a story about me would be in the *Examiner* tonight. Both of them tried to get me to tell all. I was able to hold them off until Eleanor Price's house. She came out in front of us kids and swayed down the walk. We were so mesmerized that there were no further questions.

Before going to my homeroom, I went to the junior high side, where Mr. Wolfe taught. He was already in, so I explained about the federal facilities I had visited. I gave him the blue Merit Badge card that my Scoutmaster had signed off. He stapled that to his copy which had everything else signed off.

He asked me if I had ever been in a bank, our local National Guard Armory, or out to a Civil Air Patrol show. Of course, I had been to all of them.

"Ricky, all of them, under special circumstances, are part of the federal infrastructure and can be called on at the time of need. Even the New York Central Railroad was nationalized at one point."

I felt dumb again because I knew of all this but never thought of it that way.

"I remember Dad was mad when President Truman seized the railroads to avoid a strike in 1950."

Dad must have been really mad, because I was only six.

I told Mr. Wolfe I had everything to turn in for my Eagle Scout Badge. He shook my hand and congratulated me.

He remarked, "I am looking forward to today's newspaper."

Mr. Wolfe's statement concerned me. It seemed everyone had heard that something was going on. The rest of the day was like that. I did ask for a pass to get out of study hall. My reason was to talk to the shop teacher. Since I didn't take the shop, Mr. Hurley, the study hall monitor, wanted to know why I wanted to see him.

Chapter 15

I told him about the industrial dryer I wanted to find but didn't know where to start, so I hoped he could point me in the right direction.

"Ricky, ask Mr. Donaldson to see the *Thomas Register*."

"What is that?"

"A listing by product, and what companies make them."

"Great, that is what I need."

Mr. Donaldson had a complete set of the 15-volume books in his office. It was dated last year, but he told me that the school would only buy a new set for the shop every three years.

He helped me look up Industrial Dryers. The most promising company was Conair in Franklin, PA. I wrote their address down and thanked him. When I returned to the study hall, I immediately wrote a letter asking for information on their Industrial Dryers.

After study hall, I could buy a stamp at the school office, drop the letter in the mailbox, and still make class on time.

The school day took forever. I was waiting for the newspaper to come out like many others. I wanted the day to end. My schoolwork plan was proving stronger than I thought it would. We had several snap quizzes in Latin, Algebra, and English. I was getting A's without any strain.

Finally, the last bell rang, and I went to football practice. The coach had us run many laps and do pushups and sit-ups. We also had to run through a long row of old tires, lifting our feet. My wind had improved, and I could do almost everything Coach asked. I just couldn't do it as fast as others. I began to realize that I may not have a football career.

After practice, I approached Coach Crowley. "Coach, I have my wind and stamina built up, but I can't seem to go any faster."

"Ricky, I don't have an answer. Your body isn't built for the running speed you would need. You are tall and thin, so you don't have the weight to play the line. I don't want to tell you no today, but you probably won't make the cut."

"I'm disappointed, but only a little. I didn't have my heart set on playing football. You're the one who asked me to try it out. It has been good for me anyway. My ability to run has improved, and that can't hurt. Maybe I can go out for the cross country in the track event."

"That would be an option, but don't get your hopes up. Some boys on the track team have your stamina and can run much faster."

"Darn, there goes my professional sports career."

"Have you thought of something like golf?"

"No, I don't even know how to play."

"You have the body type. Why don't you talk to Coach Stone? I will mention to him that you might be interested?"

"I would appreciate that, Coach. I want to play some sport, but not if I can't do it well."

"So, are you officially dropping from the team?"

"Yes. This has helped me, and I intend to keep running, but I don't want to waste our time."

"Good luck, Rick. I will be watching you win the USA PGA amateur!"

"Yeah, that'll be the day."

"Now we are done with that. What is going to be in the paper tonight?"

I laughed, "You will have to wait till you get home."

I took a shower after my exercise. A couple of kids, led by the ex-Mayor's son Tom Humphreys, started riding me about quitting football.

"Look at the pansy; he is afraid to get hit," came from Tom.

They kept this up for a while, but it went nowhere since I didn't respond.

I walked home and finished up what little work I had to do in tomorrow's lessons. When the newspaper arrived, Kate Smith had just sung "God Bless America". I skipped the *Mickey Mouse Club* on TV to read the story. It was the same as Mr. Weaver's copy, so I had no complaints.

About five minutes later, the phone started ringing. It rang all evening. All my relatives wanted to talk to my parents to see if the story was true. The story starts with stopping the bank robbery by killing two men.

It then continued with my rodeo career. Mr. Weaver took things out of sequence as he went from my third rodeo win to the National Championships.

My Mum and Dad would take turns answering the phone. About seven o'clock, the front door opened, and in staggered my Uncle Wally. He was drunk as usual when he was home.

His job as a union organizer would have him all over the country. He would get a job inside a factory and get the workers all riled up so they would vote for the union. I didn't care for him.

Wally wanted to borrow money as he figured that my parents had control of the reward money. He had a scheme to buy stock in an oil well that would make us all rich. Mum asked him to leave. He kept talking and talking. She finally picked up a broom and chased him out of the house. Mum wields a mean broom!

Dad was lucky. He was on the phone the whole time, so he didn't get dragged into it. We kids watched out the window as Mum chased him to the car, hitting him every other swing.

By this time, Wally had quit talking except to say, "No Peg. Please Peg. Quit it, Peg."

Wally was able to get in his car and drive away. Mum waved her broom in a victory dance as the neighbors looked on. I bet they wondered about us.

The next morning, I met Tom Morton and Bill Cairns in what had become our routine walk to school.

Tom asked me, "Did you kill two men?"

"I did."

"That must have been terrible."

"It was."

Bill wanted to know about the reward money, and did I have it?

"Bill, go down to see our old house on North Detroit Street and look at this. You will see where the money went."

"That doesn't seem fair."

"Well, it wasn't all the money. I was allowed to keep some to spend this year."

I wasn't about to tell them I had nine hundred dollars. Seeing my Uncle Wally in action taught me how people try to get your money. I wondered if Mum would let me borrow her broom.

When Eleanor came out, she didn't take her usual place in front of us. She joined us and started asking questions about the story. This grouping became our pattern for the day. Every guy I talked to wanted to know about the bank robbery, killing people, and the reward.

Girls focused on the rodeo for some reason. The conversation would start with bull riding but quickly go to Western fashions.

What did the girls wear out West? Was it like they saw on TV and in the movies? I was able to tell them the fancy Western dress was for special occasions, that most of the time, the girls wore the same clothes as they did.

I had no idea what they wore when, but I saw they wanted some answer and wouldn't give up till I came up with one.

These questions went on between every class all day long. I walked down to Wilcox's grocery to avoid the cafeteria at lunch but still ran into many questions.

The only question that got my attention was Mr. Hurley's. He took me aside in the study hall and asked, "Ricky, are you having any flashbacks to the robbery?"

"No, sir. My dad went over this with me, and I appear okay. The events seem to be further away and more remote every day. I just remember it in general terms now. Not every second, and I haven't had any dreams about it."

"That's right. Your dad was in the army. He would know. I just wanted to make certain you were all right."

"Thank you for your interest. It is appreciated."

I wondered how Mr. Hurley knew about flashbacks. I thought of the front door dropping open on a landing craft for a moment. I gave a small shudder.

Mr. Hurley noticed and asked again, "Are you certain you haven't any issues."

"No, sir. I recently heard about Bill Samson and what he went through during the war. Knowing what he went through makes what I did seem like nothing."

Mr. Hurley smiled as he said, "You've learned one of life's lessons. No matter how hard, how bad, someone else has had it worse. He was wearing a short-sleeved shirt and glanced down at his bare arm as he said this. He had some numbers tattooed there. I hadn't any idea what they meant.

Chapter 16

I went straight home after school since I didn't have football practice. After shooting hoops with Denny and Eddie and helping Mary with the hula hoop, we marched inside to watch the *Mickey Mouse Club*. Spin and Marty were on, but I wasn't in it yet.

Shortly after the show, the paper arrived with part two of my story. Again, it was the same as Mr. Weaver's advance copy. It was weird when I read about being in the Mickey Mouse segments, two different films with John Wayne, plus bailing Elvis out of jail.

Mum and Dad got home shortly after. They had been grocery shopping, picking up hot dogs, hamburgers, and all the buns plus soft drinks. They told me to answer the phone and just invite whoever called over for a cookout. We would answer questions then. They didn't want to go through as many calls as last night.

They no sooner said this than the phone started ringing. I grabbed my school notebook, kept track of everyone who called, and asked how many they would bring. Altogether there would be forty-three people at the cookout. It was five-thirty. I was to tell them to be here at six o'clock.

Uncle Wally called, and I told him he could come over, but Mum still had her broom. He called me some names I'm not supposed to use. He showed up and behaved himself.

All my cousins and friends wanted to know if I had kissed Annette. I told them it would be on the show next week, and they would get to see how close I got to kissing her.

The guys thought it was cool that I met John Wayne. We snuck down to the basement, and I showed them the Colt .45s he let me have. I was careful to lock them back up before we left.

Then we went to my bedroom to show off my black Resistol cowboy hat. I wore the hat for the rest of the evening. No one gave me any grief.

The girls all had questions about Elvis. They were disappointed that I didn't have anything autographed. All the kids wanted to know about the fight in the Mexican Cantina. The guys assured me they would have whipped the Mexicans. I didn't contradict them. However, I remember the eight guys would've had our crowd for lunch.

The adults all wanted to know how much I had been paid. I explained that I received the SAG daily rate for bit players of sixty dollars.

A neighbor exclaimed, "That little!"

Of all people, my Uncle Wally quietly asked him, "He made that in a day. How much did you earn last week?"

That cut that conversation off.

We all had a good time. My little sister Mary kept answering the phone. She would say, "Jacksons, come on over," and hang up. Listening to and watching the serious look on her face was fun. We were surprised when Mr. Weaver showed up. He said, "Mary told me to come on over. I wanted to follow up and see how the story was being received.

He was invited to have something to eat. He promptly dug in and asked almost everyone what they thought of the stories of the last two days. They all agreed the bank robbery was scary. The rodeo wins puzzled them because I wasn't a known athlete. The movies were all "wow, that lucky stiff!"

Again, I was surprised when my Uncle Wally said, "Just think, Ricky wouldn't have had these adventures if Jack and Peg weren't willing to let him take a chance."

Wally puzzles me. When I have him pegged as a bum, he acts like he has tonight.

The evening ended at nine o'clock as it was a school night. Mum and Dad told everyone they were doing it again tomorrow. It worked much better than being on the telephone till eleven at night. As he left, Mr. Weaver asked if he could come the next day.

Of course, he could. He was becoming a member of the family.

Mary looked at him and said, "You don't even have to call first."

He thanked her profusely. He also said, "I will behave myself; I hear your Mum can hit hard with her broom."

My mum said, "Yes, I can, George, and if that is in the paper, you will find out how hard." Mum always said what she was thinking.

Wednesday it was raining on our walk to school, so we all rushed to the schoolhouse. There weren't many questions on the way. The day was like a replay of yesterday, with questions in the hall between classes and in the cafeteria. The questions were all variations on those asked at the cookout last night.

During study hall, there were so many whispered questions Mr. Hurley asked if I would mind standing up in front and answering them, so we could put it behind us and get on with our work.

I couldn't say no to him, especially since I had read about tattoos of numbers on arms in the encyclopedia last night. When I thought of the landing craft doors coming down, I would also think of the pictures of the German concentration camps. What a world I had been sheltered from!

One very noticeable thing was that girls my age were going out of their way to talk to me. All wasn't bad!

The rain had let up by the evening, so we had another cookout. The story was about the cattle rustlers, capturing them and being made a Deputy Texas Ranger. The guys wanted to know every detail.

The girls listened but then started with the questions about Brian Wilson, The Beach Boys, and my appearance on *American Bandstand*.

The girls grilled me for half an hour about what the girls on *Bandstand* wore and if Paul Anka was as nice as he was cute. I felt like the police had me under their spotlights.

A couple of people there had seen the show, and everyone loved "Rock and Roll Cowboy". But not one of them had associated Rick Jackson, the singer, with me. I didn't know whether to be insulted or not.

Uncle Wally cornered me and asked if I wanted to make a lot of money. I told him to talk to my parents. He got a little nasty and left. Now I know that he was just trying to get in good with me last night. What a bum!

Thursday at school was a replay of the past two days. Mr. Hurley must have shared what he did with Mr. Gordon, our principal. So, I was called to the office during homeroom.

He asked me if I would take questions from the whole school if they held a special assembly. I agreed to that, and he announced over the school PA system that second period would be an assembly and that teachers were to collect questions from their classes for me to answer.

I had been answering questions for days now and had some answers thought through. When asked what it felt like to be a hero, I replied, "I am not a hero. The bank robbery went so fast that I had no time to think. It just happened. The rustlers didn't have guns. I did. I see nothing heroic in those actions.

"If you want to know about real heroes, read up on what our troops faced when landing on enemy beaches. Imagine hearing the machine gun bullets hitting the door, knowing that the door was about to open and letting them in.

"Think about people who survived the concentration camps and being prisoners of war. Now those were heroes. They all knew what they were facing and kept going. I just reacted."

That quieted the auditorium down. No one had expected this response.

I continued, "I didn't mean to come across so grim, but I learned a few things this past summer. I learned many good people are out there willing to help a stranger. I learned others will take advantage of you, even family members.

"But most of all, I had a lot of fun. Do you think the rides at Indian Lake Amusement Park are fun? Try getting on the back of an eighteen-hundred-pound Brahma bull and going for a ride. Be a roughneck on an oil rig if you want to know about work. Every boy ought to do it for a week. It will show you what hard work is.

"Being an actor is not what you think it is. They work hard to make everything appear easy. They have more patience than I ever will. I saw Mr. John Wayne repeat the same lines twenty-seven times, and he had the same strength and conviction every time. By the way, Elvis can't memorize a script worth a darn." This statement brought the house down with laughter.

I then told my fellow students how my singing career was already over. Paul Anka, Brian Wilson, and I agreed that my voice wasn't strong enough to sing most songs. "Rock and Roll Cowboy" would be a one-time event.

Since Brian Wilson and the Beach Boys had been my backup, I would have to start a new band. This new band would take time and money and wasn't worth the effort.

I then concluded, "However, any cute girl who wants to date a rock star see me after school."

I intended this as humor, and I saw all the boys laughing and nudging each other. The girls were strangely quiet.

Now the time was up, Mr. Gordon thanked me and asked the whole student body and teachers if we could get back to work now.

As I was leaving, I saw Mr. Weaver at the back of the room taking notes. He waved to me to stop as I was leaving.

"Rick, that was a pretty strong speech you made about not being a hero. I had the impression that you were talking about specific people."

I thought for a moment. "Investigate Bill Samson's war record. Since he can't speak for himself anymore, maybe you can. The other story isn't mine to tell."

From behind me, I heard, "George, it's my story, and maybe it is time for me to tell it," Mr. Hurley said softly. I looked at both of them and left.

Chapter 17

As the day went on, I found out I had friends I never knew. I was polite to everyone but remembered something a slightly drunk Elvis had told me at the Coronado Del Rey.

"Kid, they are all sincere. They all want just a little piece of you. You give enough little pieces away, there won't be any of you left."

So, I was polite to everyone but kept them at arm's length. We would see if my classmates still wanted to be friends in a few weeks.

Coach Stone stopped me in the hall.

"Rick, I hear you could be interested in playing golf."

"Coach, I have never played, but I am looking for a sport. My body type doesn't fit for football, but Coach Crowley thought I might be a golfer."

"Well, tall and lean makes you a human lever. Do you have any plans for this Saturday?"

"No, I don't."

"I'm playing a round with the country club pro out at the Bellefontaine Country Club on Saturday. Why don't you meet me here at school by the front door at 8 a.m.? We will loan you the equipment and see how it works on the practice tees. Our tee time is at nine-thirty, so we will have enough time to see how it goes."

"Okay, Coach, I would like that."

I also thought having an English mum who had tea all the time should help me, though I didn't see the connection between tea and golf.

I walked home with Tom and Bill. Now that they had heard my whole story, they were almost in awe of me. We had only met when I moved to this neighborhood, so they didn't know what to make of me.

At dinner, I told my parents about dropping out of football and what Coach Crowley had recommended. They were okay with me meeting Coach Stone on Saturday. I asked what tea had to do with golf. After some confusion, I found out what a golf tee was.

I am glad I had asked my parents. It could have been embarrassing on Saturday. Maybe my parents knew more than I thought.

Dad told me he had to work the third trick on Friday night but would like to take me with him back to the old house on Saturday afternoon to see what had to be done to rent it out.

After dinner, I rode my bike to my Scout meeting. I handed my merit badge card to Mr. Geist. He said he would turn it into the council in Springfield, but we would have to wait until the first of the year to hold the Eagle ceremony.

There were elections that night, and I stepped down from Patrol Leader. If I made the golf team and couldn't make the meetings until November, I would even have to skip the camporee. No one got excited. In Scouts, someone was always moving on, and others stepped up.

Even Denny and Eddie hadn't fought when I got home, so I knew we were all tired. It was an early night at the Jackson house.

After a good night's sleep, my morning exercises, a brisk run, and a full breakfast, I felt like a new person. I took my shower. Even toweling my hair as dry as possible still got me, "You will catch your death if you go out with wet hair."

I had to figure something out. The shower was so easy and refreshing in the morning. It was a shame that the shower head was pointed straight down in the ceiling. If I didn't have to stand directly under it, I could wash up and not get my hair wet.

It was like a lightbulb went on. Why were shower heads built into the ceiling? Why not into the wall?

I thought about the shower construction as I walked to school. None of the other kids were walking this morning which was odd. Some would ride with their parents some days or be late, but neither

Tom nor Bill was walking today. I saw Eleanor run out of her house and get in a car with an older boy. So much for those romantic hopes.

I made it to school early, so I stopped into the shop and asked Mr. Donaldson why showers were made to dump down on the person. He thought for a moment.

"I guess that is the way they have always made them. The first showers were buckets with small holes suspended over the top of the tub. Why do you ask?"

"We have a shower at home, and I have to get my hair wet every time I use the shower."

"I bet your mother tells you 'You will catch your death going out with wet hair!'"

"How did you know that?"

"It is what my mother told me."

"It must be in the Mother's Handbook."

"Remember, when I was a kid, antibiotics weren't available. You could die from a cold."

"Wow, that's hard to think of."

"How long ago did you get your polio shot?"

"I got the Salk shot in the fifth grade like everyone else. Then I took the Sabin sugar cube in the sixth."

"Medicine has come a long way in the last few years. So don't make fun of your mother!"

"Yes, sir. I better hurry, or I will be late for class."

School was kind of strange that day. Some kids were all over me, wanting to talk and hang around me. Others would turn their heads when I came into the classroom.

At lunch, I saw Tom and Bill sitting at our usual table. When I sat down, they both got funny looks on their faces.

"What?" I asked. "Do I have a booger hanging?"

Tom spoke without raising his head, "My parents say you are too wild, and I can't do things with you anymore."

I looked at Bill. He just nodded his head and said, "Me too."

"Can I sit here?"

Tom replied, "I am supposed to leave when you show up." He and Bill took their trays and moved to another table.

I was shocked. I just ate my lunch and left. To this day, I have no idea what I ate.

The other side of this coin showed up in my last study hall. One of the guys who we called a juvenile delinquent, Tom Hamilton, said, "Hey, Killer, do you want to go riding around with our group after the football game?"

"No, Tom. I have other plans. Thanks anyway."

"Anytime. We could use a tough guy like you when we go to Urbana."

Urbana was in the county south of us, and there was a rivalry between the two towns on every level. And this rivalry extended from the sports teams to the gangs.

We knew Tom and his friends were juvenile delinquents because they wore leather motorcycle jackets and wore their hair greased back in a DA, which stood for Duck's Ass, but we couldn't say that.

They also smoked across the street from the school and bragged that they drank beer. The beer was three-point two percent alcohol by weight. You could get drunk, but you had to drink a lot.

I didn't want to be like them. It was neat to wear a black cowboy hat, but not a black motorcycle cap with a short bill. I was happy to get home to my family that night.

My Dad asked the usual, "How did school go today?"

I almost gave the ritual, "Fine."

Instead, I said, "Not so good."

"Why?"

I then explained how good kids couldn't associate with me, and the bad wanted me to go with them. Mum went through the roof when I told her I had been called a "Killer."

Dad told me, "Rick, this is one of those things that time will have to take care of."

"How?"

"When you don't get in trouble, things will calm down, and people's attitudes will change. We know you are a good kid, but Tom and Bill's parents haven't known you for years. All they know is what they read in the paper.

"You don't come across as running from trouble when it comes to you. Those poor rustlers minded their own business doing what rustlers do until you jumped in. Now, how would you feel if you were a parent?"

"It's not fair."

"What has that got to do with anything?"

That stopped me cold. I could almost hear machine-gun bullets rattling off the door of that ship. Life wasn't fair. I would do well to remember that and learn to live with it.

"You're right. I will try not to get into trouble, which will bore the bad guys, and maybe the good guys will be allowed to be near me."

"Sorry, son. That is the way it has to be. I could knock on their door and talk to them, but it wouldn't change anything."

I had a lot to think of before I fell asleep that night. Doing exciting things appeared to have some cost to them.

Chapter 18

Saturday morning, I cleaned up after doing my run and exercises and was at the school five minutes early. Coach Stone pulled up as I got there.

It was only a fifteen-minute drive to the country club. Once there, we went into the pro shop. Coach had me hold various clubs and finally settled on a set to rent for the day.

He paid seventy-five cents for me. From there, we went to the driving range. He handed me a tee and showed me how to tee up in the tee box. Thank you, Mum, for explaining the difference between tea and tee. I would have been so mortified I could never have come back.

Coach took me through what he called the mechanics of the swing. He explained I didn't have to get under the ball. That was why the clubface was slanted. He explained how a swing must be repetitive and smooth.

He showed me power by rotating the hips into the swing as the arms came down and turning the wrist through the swing. He explained how follow-through was important.

He had me do several practice swings without a ball. Next, he showed me how to tee one the proper height. Then he told me to take a swing without thinking of all the things he had just told me.

Of course, I thought about them as I slowly did my backswing. When I started moving forward, it happened too quickly to think about. The ball went straight, but it barely made it past the 200-yard sign. I would have to work to get it out to the 300-yard sign.

Coach just said, "Do it again."

I must have hit twenty balls, they all cleared 200 yards, but none made 300. I figured Coach would tell me I had no future in golf. I turned around and realized that over a dozen adults were standing there.

I asked Coach, "Do you think I might be able to make the team?"

For some reason, everyone started laughing.

One guy said, "The question is, kid, when are you going to turn pro?"

That's when I realized I must have found my sport.

In no uncertain terms, Coach Stone let me know that the fact I could drive was wonderful. However, I needed to take to heart the old pro golf saying. "You drive for show. You putt for dough."

We went over to the practice green, and he demonstrated how the slightest hill or depression in the green could change the ball's path. He called it "reading the green." It was a combination of visualizing the ball's path and the speed needed to follow it.

Putting was harder than driving. I would miss some if my ball was fifteen feet or more from the hole. Coach didn't get on me about it, so I guess it wasn't a total disaster.

Finally, Coach slowly said, "I've seen enough, let's play an 18-hole round and see how you do."

The club pro joined us. They both worked with me on what club to use and why. The course had a par of 72. Mr. Collins, the club pro, had a 76, Coach, a 77, and I had an 82. My problem was that the ball would fly over the green on par 3s. I had to keep using a higher number of irons.

I understood that I was doing pretty well for a first-time golfer by this time.

When I expressed this to Coach, he replied, "More than pretty well. Your timing is perfect. That is why you did so well bull riding."

Coach continued, "There are many things you don't know about the game, like the rules. Are you interested in going out for the team?"

"Yes, I am."

"Good because our fourth man is moving. His dad has taken a job in Lima at the tank factory. We will have to get you some accelerated lessons. State rules are that I can only work with students for so many hours during the season."

"Can Mr. Collins work with me?"

"Yes, he can, but he is a golf professional, which means he gets paid for teaching."

"Mr. Collins, how much do you charge?"

"It would be five dollars a lesson. I can give you two lessons a week for the next six weeks so that would be sixty dollars plus forty dollars for a good set of clubs and a bag and another ten dollars for shoes and balls. That is a lot of money for someone your age. Can your parents afford it?"

"They can, but I will be paying for my lessons. Do you want the money for the lessons all at once?"

"In advance, each month will do."

I gave him twenty dollars for the rest of September.

"Since you are joining in the middle of the season, Coach Stone will tell me what I should teach each week."

We agreed on back-to-back lessons on Sunday morning starting at seven o'clock. This timing would fit in with Mr. Collins's other weekend appointments. If the weather was too bad and we couldn't use the outside, we would go over the rules and things like golf etiquette. It seems the golfers were very polite. I shook hands with Mr. Collins.

My coach was kind enough to drop me off at my house. He asked if Dad was at home. He had just gotten there. Coach and Dad had a private conversation. I don't know what was said, but Dad encouraged me to play golf. He even volunteered to drive me to the golf course when he could.

After lunch, Denny and Eddie kept their squabbling down to a dull roar, and Mary only spilled her Kool-Aid once. Dad and I went to our old house on Detroit Street.

Twyla was outside, so Dad talked to her for a while. She was ten years older than me and was newly married. She and Mum had become good friends while they lived next door. I think Mum helped her understand and put up with her husband, who could be demanding and unthoughtful.

I knew this because you could hear her explain this to him on summer nights with all the windows open. The neighbors, three houses down, probably heard it all.

He drove in the drag races, and that was all he talked about. After Dad made nice, we opened the old house up. After living there for years, it seemed strange. It also felt lonely sitting empty.

I had never noticed how beat up the walls were. The house had been built in 1890, so it had aged. Every wall had been papered. With it empty, you could see every smudge and smear. I noticed that the paper was torn in several corners in the rooms.

I realized that the paper didn't fit squarely with each corner. It made a curve around the corner. Not much, but someone had taken their finger and broken the paper at the curve. Hey, what else do you have to do while standing in the corner?

Dad had the grace not to point this out to me. He did observe that all the paper would have to be replaced. We would have to steam the old paper off and then repaper the room. We went through every room in the house. The rooms were all smaller than I remembered. It was amazing that we all fit in that house.

The biggest expense was taking the old coal-fired furnace out and replacing it with a new gas furnace. Also, the bathroom tub would have to be taken out, as the floor under it was showing signs of rot. I asked Dad if he planned to put a shower in the new bathroom.

"I haven't given it a thought. Why?"

"If you do, could we have the plumber install the showerhead coming out of the side of the wall instead of the ceiling?"

He asked me why I wanted that. I explained how nice the shower was but that I had to get my hair wet every time. Dad smiled and said, "My mom would always say I would catch my death."

He wondered why I laughed so much at that.

He made notes and assigned me the chore of mowing the yard and neatening things after Sunday's golf lesson.

Sunday was another quiet day at our house. Dad drove me out for my first golf lessons. The lessons went well. I practiced "chipping, plus pitching and running."

After this, Mr. Collins took me into the pro shop and helped "fit me" for a set of clubs. He told me this was my starter set and that I would probably own many sets of clubs in my playing days. The fitting made certain that the clubs were the right length for my reach.

I ended up with a set of Wilson woods and irons. It didn't include a sand wedge, so I bought a McGregor. These, along with the shoes, balls, and tees, came to ninety dollars.

The pair of shoes felt comfortable. However, it sounded and felt weird to walk around with the metal spikes hitting the floor. Mr. Collins told me never to wear them anywhere other than golfing or in the clubhouse.

Even I could figure out Mum would kill me if I tore up the carpeting. The new house had wall-to-wall carpets, and she loved them. I liked them because they were soft, and I wouldn't have to take them out in the spring, wrestle them over the clothesline, and beat the dust out of them.

Mr. Collins gave me a tour of the clubhouse and the locker room. He showed me a locker I could use and loaned me a combination lock so I wouldn't have to haul my equipment back and forth.

He explained that having a locker was standard for the school golf team. I asked how one joined the country club. He explained that you had to have a sponsor, be voted on at a member's meeting, pay a two-hundred-dollar initiation fee, and fifty dollars a year.

I said, "Wow, you have to have a lot of money to play golf!"

"Money helps, but you have to be known in the community to get voted in. They are a little snobbish. Since you will probably be on the golf team, you will have a standing invitation to events. They have a monthly dance, and the dining room is the best in Bellefontaine."

"As long as I don't have to pay for it," I remarked.

"Oh no, it is free, as long as you are on the team and only in season."

After that, Mr. Collins took me home.

I had done all my school reading ahead, so I just had to mow the lawn on Detroit Street, and I was done for the day. I towed the push mower behind my bike to Detroit Street to do the yard. It was easy going downhill and a lot of work coming back up.

I spent the rest of the afternoon outside as the weather was still holding. I was reading one of the classics I had inherited from my Aunt Merle. I thought being sent to prison and ending up a galley slave was harsh for stealing a loaf of bread.

I want to bed early and wondered if anyone would speak to me at school.

Chapter 19

Monday started clear, but it looked like it might rain later. I was able to do my exercises and get in my run. But I wondered how much longer I could do this. It was still September, and I should be able to run till Thanksgiving. How was I to practice golf all winter? I needed to talk to Mr. Collins about what could be done.

No one was there on my walk to school. I didn't even see Eleanor. The best description of Monday is that I just went through the motions. I didn't want to cause problems or embarrassment at lunch, so I sat at a table by myself. Even the delinquents left me alone.

The previous Friday, we had several exams. They were returned to class today. I had straight A's going, so something was working right.

It was like I was invisible. Last week everyone wanted to know me. Now no one would speak to me. They weren't rude, they would say excuse me or thank you if I did something for them, but it was like I didn't exist. I was glad when school let out.

I boarded a school bus with the other members of the golf team. There were four of them: John Scott was a senior. Gary Matthews and Tim Green were juniors, and Phil Thompson a sophomore. Phil was the boy who was moving. He was the fourth man. That was a polite way of saying he was the fourth-best golfer on the team.

The guys asked what my handicap was. I told them I had no idea since I had only played one round in my life. I told them that I had an eighty-two last Sunday at the country club playing with Coach Stone and Mr. Collins.

Phil was the one who got excited, "I am doing good with shooting a ninety-two out there. You will help the team."

Coach Stone was already at the club. We spent the day practicing our putting.

Later at dinner, I told my parents about my day's experience. They had no answers other than to be patient. I did tell them that the guys on the golf team treated me well.

I started reading a new book that evening. Some old guy talked about shadows on the wall and tried to decide, "What is truth?"

It was pretty interesting.

Tuesday was more of the same. Golf practice was more putting. I got the impression that the coach thought this was the most important part of the game.

Tuesday evening was better. Mr. Weaver stopped by the house to drop off a new story he had written. It was about how our family had changed and reacted to my summer vacation. He also wrote about the high school assembly where I explained that I wasn't a hero. People like Bill Samson who landed on Omaha Beach, were the real heroes.

He was funny when describing my singing experience. My down-to-earth interaction with people like Elvis and John Wayne impressed him by the fact that I didn't let it go to my head. Capturing the rustlers was what any red-blooded American boy would do if he didn't realize the inherent dangers.

My family having the cookouts to answer all the questions impressed him. He even described Mary answering the phone. About the only thing left out was Mum's broom. I wonder why?

He presented us as an ordinary family thrown into some extraordinary events. Reading his logical presentation of events, my family and I hadn't any choice in how we reacted. We all liked the story and told him that we would confirm everything he had written if asked.

He could have left out the part where none of the girls rushed the stage to date a rock star.

Mr. Weaver then told us it would run in the *Examiner* on Thursday. They would build it up in Wednesday's edition to increase

Thursday's circulation. Thursday was the day all the weekend ads appeared. They were paid for ads on a sliding scale. The more papers they sold, the more they were paid.

Wednesday was more of the same at school. I was glad to get it over with. Golf practice was more interesting because we spent time in the driving range. No one else could hit the ball past the 225-yard marker. I was now booming them out close to 300 yards. Now I can understand why the adults were impressed last weekend.

Thursday was just another day of walking to school alone and having empty chairs next to me in the cafeteria. I tried not to think about it because I felt lonely, rejected, and plain mad at it all.

I had taken to carrying a book with me all the time, so I would appear to be busy. I read about a guy who rode around thinking he was a knight and charging at windmills. What a loon.

Golf practice was fun that night as we got to play nine holes. I did better this time, shooting a thirty-eight on the front nine. My thirty-eight was the best score. John Scott had a thirty-nine, while the others had a forty-one and forty-two.

I had thought they would resent me scoring better, but they were all excited that we might beat our archrival Urbana on Saturday. Phil's last day was Friday, so he wouldn't be able to play.

We all wished Phil luck at his new school. We weren't in the same league as the Lima schools, so we didn't know how well they played. His dad had brought a Lima paper home, and it didn't look like he would get to play anymore this year. We all made positive sounds about next year but the bigger the school, the harder it was to make the first team.

Here at Bellefontaine, we could barely field one team. Schools like Lima Public would have three or four. Private schools would have six or seven. That put us at a huge disadvantage in the district tournaments.

But as Coach said, "It doesn't matter how many golfers you have, just as long as you're better than the other guys."

That sounded good, but the lessons on statistics, which we were covering in Algebra, said otherwise.

Thursday evening, the newspaper came out with our family story. The phone started ringing again. This time after the first hour, my parents allowed Mary to answer the phone and tell people, "No one is home. Call back later, please."

That kid will have some strange telephone habits when she grows up.

I had finished the book on the Spanish guy in the study hall. I was getting so far ahead in my classes I had to slow down, or I would have forgotten what that day's lesson was on.

Now I was reading about a whaling ship with a crazy captain. He was going to get them all killed. I just knew it. I fell asleep and dreamed of a huge white whale.

Friday morning came with me twisted in all my covers. I think I wrestled that whale half the night. I was still there, and he wasn't, so I must have won. I was still doing my daily exercises and running starting at six in the morning.

My showers were getting longer each day as my dreams were more vivid every night.

When I went out to walk to school, Tom and Bill were waiting for me. Tom in his usual ivy league look and Bill in his blue jeans. Now what? Both of them looked embarrassed, but they were there.

"Hi, guys. What's up?" I asked.

"We are allowed to walk and have lunch with you again," Tom almost whispered.

"That's great, guys. I have missed seeing you."

That broke the ice, and we started the walk downhill to school.

"What changed your parents' mind?" I inquired.

Bill told me, "That article in the *Examiner* last night; my parents realized you weren't the wild man they thought you were."

"Yeah," Tom added, "my dad was in the 101st Airborne, and he liked how you stepped up for true heroes in that assembly. Even though he said he wouldn't be brave enough to get on the back of a Brahma bull."

Several thoughts were flashing through my mind. *Thank you, Mr. Weaver.* The written word does have a lot of power, and people sure can reach wrong conclusions if they don't have all the facts. Riding Brahma bulls isn't so bad. Now those rodeo clowns are the brave ones. I didn't voice any of these. I just enjoyed the company of my friends.

Eleanor came out of her house just in time to walk in front of us. She was wearing a tight skirt. Bill changed the subject to football. "Look at that backfield in motion!"

I started to look around when it hit me what he meant. I snickered and said, "I would like to sack the quarterback."

That got both guys laughing, and we enjoyed the view as we walked to school. By the time we got there, I wondered if I should go home and take another shower.

Chapter 20

Friday was a good day at school. We had several exams, but they all seemed easy. I think any exam is easy if you know the answers. There was a pep rally for the football team. They had a good start to the year, even without my being on the field.

It was an away game at Findley, so I didn't go to the football game. The youth center was open as usual, and I went there to look around and see what was happening.

Eleanor Price was there, and I about fell over when she came up to me and got right to the point.

"Ricky, next week is the homecoming game and dance. Do you have a date?"

"No, I don't," I said cautiously.

"Janet Huber doesn't have a date and would say yes if you asked her."

That is how I learned how the world of first dates worked for us. An intermediary who knew both parties would make the first overture. That way, there would be no outright rejection. I could choose not to ask her, and she would not be publicly rejected. If I asked her, I knew she would say yes unless it were some cruel trick.

Janet had been a classmate for years, so I wasn't worried about a cruel trick.

I told Eleanor, "I think I would like to ask her."

"Oh good. She is sitting in the booth on end."

I had gone to school with Janet for years, but I had never really looked at her in a while. My image of her was short and skinny with knobby knees. They really ought to send out updates to us guys on every girl.

Janet was now tall and thin and filled out on top. Her hair was down to her shoulders, and she had short bangs. The most important thing, she was cute! Even though I knew this was supposed to be a sure thing, I was still nervous walking over. Give me a Brahma bull over this any day.

I asked Janet if I could join her. She scooted over so I could sit next to her. The booth would hold six, three on each side. There were four other girls with her. Oh great, a public performance.

I figured I'd get it over with, "Janet, I don't have a date for the homecoming dance. Would you be interested in going?"

She opened her mouth to say something, then changed her mind and gave me a simple, "Yes."

"Great, now what were you going to say?"

"My friends dared me to tell you I had to wash my hair that night."

"Oh, if you did that, you couldn't go to the dance. You would catch your death."

This small joke got all the girls giggling. We then got into the mechanics of the date.

I would pick her up at her house on Friday before the game. We would go somewhere for dinner, then return home to change for the game, go to the game, and return to her home so she could change for the dance. I could drop some clothes off at her house to save time on my changing.

Oh, and buy a wrist corsage from the juniors. They were selling them to raise money for the prom.

I don't think General Patton had such logistic issues.

I was asked what I was going to wear.

"Is a tux required, or is a suit okay for the dinner and dance?"

"A suit would be fine. What color is it?"

"Grey with gold edging."

"You have a suit with gold edging?"

"It is the one I wore on *American Bandstand*, a modern cowboy suit."

As luck would have it, the jukebox started playing "Rock and Roll Cowboy". I thought the girls were all going to have a cow the way they squealed.

I had a brainstorm. "For dinner, would you like to go to the country club?"

"Are your parents members?"

"No, I'm on the golf team and have membership privileges during the season."

That I was on the golf team was news to everyone at the table. You could see my social status going up quickly.

"That would be wonderful."

"I will ask my dad if he could drive us around, or we can take a taxi."

"That would be good because my dad is on duty at the fire station that night. That reminds me, he wants to meet you before we go out."

"Okay, but he has known me since we were in the first grade."

The girls promptly educated me. It was now an official date and had to be properly looked at. It was in the Dad's Handbook! I would have to ask my dad to borrow his copy.

We talked for a little while. I told the girls how my golfing career had just started and that my first match was tomorrow at Urbana. I then spent time asking the various girls questions about themselves.

I had watched Elvis and Tab Hunter get to know girls this way. They were successful until the boyfriends showed up. I kept a look out of the corner of my eye to see if any boyfriends were charging my way. At least I had bail money on me.

None came. We chatted for a while, and then the girls had to leave. I got Janet's phone number and gave her mine. We agreed to stay in contact during the week.

I stopped at Eleanor Price's table and thanked her for the nudge on the way out.

She grinned and said, "All you kids need a kick start."

Well, I already knew where I stood with her.

It was up the hill and home before curfew. I think I was beginning to worry my parents about getting in early. I told them that I had asked Janet Huber to the homecoming dance and asked dad if he would drive?

He told me he was already scheduled to work. I may not have mentioned this before, but my Mum had never driven in her life, so that was not an option.

"I will call a taxi then."

Dad brought up, "Rick, you may want to call them early in the week and get on their schedule because it's probably a busy night for them."

"Good thinking Dad. I will do it tomorrow afternoon."

I was up at my normal time on Saturday and went through all my routines. Now, thinking of Janet Huber was included in my morning routine. I was at the school at eight where a bus was waiting. Coach and my team members all got there at about the same time. The bus took us to the country club to collect our equipment. Then we continued south to Urbana.

We got to the Champaign County Country Club, called the 4Cs, by nine o'clock, so we had plenty of time to hit the driving range and practice greens before our ten o'clock tee time.

Before we started, the coaches went over their list and matched players by handicaps. Since I didn't have an official one, I was the fourth rated on our team.

Coach Stone told Coach Yeager, "Bill, I don't want you to think I'm sandbagging you. Rick doesn't have a handicap, but he is rather good."

"We will see shortly," replied Coach Yeager.

We were split into two foursomes; the strongest players went first. The team captains stood facing each other. Coach Yeager threw a tee up in the air, and it came down pointing to the Urbana captain, so they had the honors. It meant they hit first. It also meant I would be the last player to hit, with plenty of time to get nervous.

Except I didn't get nervous, this wasn't like a Brahma bull might throw me off and stomp me to death. It was only a game.

The first foursome got off okay with everyone staying in the fairway and hitting at least 200 yards. When they had moved up enough, it was my group's turn. Bob Turner, the Urbana player, ripped one almost 250 yards. Tim Green from our team groaned, as he was playing him directly.

Tim let one go straight up the middle for 220 yards despite groaning. That left the first two in the perfect position to hit around the slight dogleg to the right. The Urbana player Jim Unger was up. He shanked it off the tee about 50 yards down the fairway to the right.

Now it was my turn. I tried to blank everything out and just prepare for the shot. When I made my swing, I knew it was good. I followed through completely rather than trying to watch the ball. I think it was my best golf shot to date. It didn't go 300 yards, but it went every bit of 270, drawing right into the center of the dogleg. I was now left with 50 yards to the green.

The first foursome was still on the green, and one of them saw my ball come rolling up towards the green. Two of the players were waving their clubs back at me. I bet it was John Scott and Gary Matthews doing the waving.

After the other players had hit near the apron of the green, with poor Jim Unger hitting twice to get up with us, I had an easy pitch and run to the green. It went exactly as it should. The ball was in the air to the green, hit, then released, and rolled within three feet of the hole. When everyone was up on the green and in the hole but me, I was able to roll the ball into the center of the hole for a three and my first competition birdie.

The entire day went like that. I was relaxed and joked around with Tim as we played. We were all nice to Jim because we knew we could have bad days.

As I played better, he played worse. His coach talked to him, trying to get him settled down. On the par 74 course, I got a 79. Jim got a 97. I not only won my match, everyone on our team had won as well. My score was the low player score of the day.

Chapter 21

My day hadn't been perfect. I proved once again that the devil invented sand traps. They added seven strokes to my score. I knew what I would be practicing with Mr. Collins on Sunday. We finished the match and were on our way home by three o'clock, arriving at the country club to drop off our equipment by four.

I checked with the reservation desk about dinner for two at six o'clock next Friday. This was the time Janet suggested. There wasn't any problem. The lady there told me that it was a good thing I was doing it now because there were always a lot of requests for seating on homecoming weekend.

I asked Coach if I could be dropped off at the cab company downtown, as I had to arrange a ride for next Friday for homecoming.

He said, "Run in and take care of business. We will wait five minutes for you."

Coach was smiling on the way home. We had won all our matches to clean Urbana's clock, which had not happened since 1949.

We stopped at the taxi company, and I explained that I needed several rides for homecoming. Pick me up, and then my date at her house. Then go to the country club. Pick us up at the country club, take us to her house, wait while we change, then take us to the game. Pick us up after the game and go to her house to change for the dance at the youth center. Then pick us up and take her home. Lastly, drop me off at my house!

The dispatcher John Sullivan said, "That makes me tired just hearing about it. I have a suggestion. All of that riding around will come to about twenty-five dollars. Why not rent a car and driver for the evening for forty dollars, including a tip? The car will always be ready and waiting for you."

"That sounds wonderful."

"Even better, we have just obtained a new vehicle. It is called a stretch limousine or limo for short. You will be our first customer to ride in it. It will hold three couples."

The bus driver started honking his horn about that time, so I went out and waved them on. I wanted to see this new car before I put my money down. It was shiny black, gleamed, had chrome everywhere, and it was big. What was not to like. It was a Cadillac Coupe De Ville that had been modified or stretched out.

Mr. Sullivan told me they had it for a week and were anxious to get it out on the street in front of people. The homecoming was perfect. It might even become a tradition of kids taking limos to big events. I asked him why they had bought it.

He looked around and told me, "I don't think we bought it. I think the boss won it in a card game from some big wig in Columbus."

I agreed to take the car and driver for the evening and paid twenty dollars upfront. The rest would be due when they picked me up the night of the dance. I had another brainstorm. Since I just rented this, could you guys give me a free ride home now?

The redheaded Mr. Sullivan laughed and told me his shift was ending. I waited five minutes while he wrote me a receipt and turned things over to the night dispatcher, and he then gave me a lift.

I intended to take a brief nap before dinner, but there was mail. The Conair Company had sent me a catalog. I immediately looked up industrial dryers. They had one similar to what I had seen at the gold mine in California.

It was eleven dollars, which I thought was expensive, but it would be worth it if it worked in drying my hair. I didn't want to "Catch my death!"

They had an order form in the back. Nonbusiness payment could be by check or money order. I didn't have a checking account and didn't know what a money order was. I asked Dad, and he explained about money orders. I could get a money order from our bank.

Mum was the guardian of the family checkbook, and I didn't want to have to explain spending eleven dollars on a device to dry my hair. Mum was tight with a dollar, and I didn't think this would pass her "need test". So, I would have to go to the bank on Monday after school.

It had been quite a day. It was neat telling my parents about the golf match stroke by stroke until Denny and Eddie started squabbling at the table. Dad made a light swat towards Denny when he wouldn't shut up. Denny overreacted, jerked away, and managed to chip his tooth on the edge of the table. Mum got mad at Dad.

My parents contrasted when they each got angry. Fair-haired dad got very red in the face. Mum had jet-black hair and was pale. When she gets mad, she gets paler, to the point you would think of a vampire. I retreated to my room, skipping Mum's rice pudding for dessert.

When the noise died down, I went back downstairs and called Janet Huber. She wanted to know all about my golf match. It felt good to tell her we had all won. I got to the main reason for my call. I told her about talking to the taxi company and ending up with a car and driver at our disposal for the evening.

She was ecstatic, but I opened up a can of worms when I told her it would hold three couples. That led to many questions about the limousine. Being the worldly person I am, I referred to it as the limo as the conversation progressed. She adapted quickly.

She told me that she and a friend would be checking out this limo tomorrow. I was able to tell her our dinner reservations were confirmed at the country club. She told me to reconfirm for a party of six. I asked her who the others would be. She countered with orders to find out if my friends Tom and Bill had dates and let her know by noon tomorrow! What am I getting into?

That night I was reading a story about families who moved to California from the dustbowl of Oklahoma during the 1930s. It was a hard-working life, but it seemed simpler and easier than mine.

Sunday morning, after getting my exercises out of the way and cleaning up, I rode my bike the half-hour ride out to the country club. It didn't take long because I could roll down the hill on Sandusky Street. Coming back up would be different.

Coach Stone had talked to Mr. Collins about my problems with sand traps. After several hours of work, I no longer felt they were the devil's work, just one of his lesser demons. Every time I hit one buried in damp sand, it felt like I would send it a mile. Instead, they plopped nicely on the green.

I also learned to hate the way sand spreads when you hit the ball and ends up in your eyes, nose, and ears. I decided to quit hitting the ball into sand traps right then and there. I'm sure many other golfers made the same decision and failed as miserably as I have.

I stopped at the restaurant front desk and told Kathy I would like to increase my party to six. That wasn't a problem. The fact her name badge said "Kathy" is the only reason I knew her name. She asked how I would be paying for all the dinners. I told her cash after dinner.

She explained that the club host (me) was responsible for the check, and they weren't set up to take cash. It would normally be billed to the member's account. Since I was a courtesy member, I didn't have an account.

This information was surprising to me. I thought it would be like a regular restaurant where you paid after meals. She suggested I talk to Mr. Hastings, the club manager.

She led me to his office and explained the situation. He was helpful. He first congratulated me on the victory over Urbana. He had already called his counterpart at the 4Cs to rub it in.

He told me that a party of six with no alcohol could expect to spend about four dollars a person. If I could pay fifteen dollars upfront, I could pay the balance later. Fortunately, no tips were allowed in the restaurant, so the math would be simple.

At this point, I didn't think I had any choice, so I gave him the money, and he wrote me a receipt. I asked him if something happened and we couldn't make it, what would happen? He told me that I would get a complete refund. If not all of us made it to dinner, I would be charged only for what was on the check.

As I was pedaling the long ride home, I considered how great it was that I had stopped in today to make the reservations. It would have been an embarrassing disaster to have the payment question brought up after dinner. This social stuff could get complicated, and I would have to check things out before committing to it in the future.

While I was on the subject of payment, I added it up and realized that I had spent almost two hundred and fifty dollars since school started. I hoped that reward money from Texas would come through before I was broke. I was so busy thinking about it that I hardly noticed the long bike ride uphill.

Chapter 22

I walked over to Tom and Bill's when I got home. Tom and I talked on his front porch. I asked him if he had a date for homecoming; he said, "No, but I would love to go with Tracy Gallagher."

"Did she say no?"

"I haven't asked her."

"Oh, then she probably won't go with you."

"I know. I am a real Melvin when it comes to girls."

"If you found out a girl would like to go with you, would you ask her?"

"Well yeah, I would ask her if she wasn't a skag."

"That's what I needed to know."

"Wait, what's going on?"

"I am just following orders from Janet Huber, my date for homecoming."

"Wow, you have a date with Janet, you lucky dog."

Bill's house, it was different. I was invited in by his mom, a big change from a week ago. I think she was trying to make up. When it was apparent that she wasn't leaving, I asked Bill if he had a date for homecoming, but before he could open his mouth, his mom said, "No, he hasn't. Is there some girl who wants him to ask her to go to the dance?"

There must be a Handbook for Girls.

"Not yet, ma'am. I was supposed to find out if he had a date. I think things are in progress."

In the way of Mom's and Mum's everywhere, she got the details out of me in short order. She thought it would be a nice evening if it could be brought together. Poor Bill just sat there.

His mother decided she had all the information available, and I was allowed to leave. After I was out the door, I realized that Bill had never said a word.

After lunch, Dad and I went to the house on Detroit Street and worked for several hours. We managed to move the bathtub to take the rotten floorboards out. Dad now knew what he faced. He would buy the lumber to repair the floor and new linoleum. He intended to do it tomorrow, Monday, if he didn't get a call to work.

We had moved the bathtub an inch at a time. Those cast-iron tubs must have weighed three hundred pounds. It didn't help that the clawed feet on the tub kept catching and hanging up on the rotten floorboards. While moving it, I thought about putting a shower attachment on the tub. It would have to attach to the current faucet. It would go straight up for about four feet and then have a curved neck so the showerhead would spray out at an angle instead of straight down on your head.

There were several issues to overcome. There would have to be a framework to hold a shower curtain around the whole tub, like at our new home, or there would be a mess.

Also, the showerhead needed to be aimed exactly right. I wondered if anyone made adjustable showerheads. I know the one at home wasn't.

I had got home just in time for a call from Janet. She wanted to know why I hadn't let her know yet about Tom and Bill's date status. I had forgotten all about calling her.

I let her know that neither had a date and that Tom would like to go with Tracy Gallagher but didn't have the nerve to ask her.

She thought for a minute and said, "That will work. I will call Tina, who knows Tracy pretty well, and find out if she would go with him."

Now I know why men don't have a chance.

I thought I had gotten away with forgetting to let her know about Tom and Bill's availability. But I quickly understood the old joke: "You're right; I'm wrong; I'm sorry, dear." She wasn't angry but it had gotten to the point that she had to make a lot happen in a short time to bring everything together. All I wanted to do was go to the homecoming dance.

She let me know that she and Nancy Sparks had gone to the taxi company and checked out the limo. They both thought it was really neat. I thought that I knew who Bill's date would be.

Dinner was a lot calmer than last night, and there didn't seem to be any friction between Mum and Dad. Denny and Eddie both kept their mouths shut while they ate. Mary was funny.

She offered to save one of her teeth from the tooth fairy so that Denny could replace his chipped tooth. It was so sincere that no one cracked a smile.

Mum wanted to know where we were with the homecoming dance. When she found out about Tom and Bill, she said she had better talk to their mothers and Janet. I swear Patton had it easier.

That night I finished up the story on the migrant workers during the depression. After finishing it, I realized that I had it rather good. I dozed off thinking about getting a money order, checking out showerheads, doing whatever Janet required, and golf practice.

I had just about dropped off when I realized I needed to get my suit down to Uncle Gene's dry cleaner's tomorrow. Belle Cleaners was next to our bank, but I had to come home tomorrow before going to the bank.

Cripes, it struck me. I had golf practice after school. I wouldn't be able to get to the dry cleaner's or the bank. I would have to ask dad to do it. The easiest thing I had going was my schoolwork.

Chapter 23

My mind started racing as soon as my alarm clock went off. My life was getting so complicated. There were so many details to handle, but none of them were hard. I raced through my morning exercises, running then showering. I had a busy day ahead. Dressing in my normal chinos and cotton plaid long sleeve shirt, I got ready for a busy day.

At breakfast, I bit the bullet.

"I need to get my suit dry cleaned and buy a money order, but I have golf practice. Could you do it for me, Dad?"

After taking a sip of his black coffee, he replied, "I have time. I have to go downtown and rent a steamer to peel a lot of the old wallpaper off the living room walls on Detroit Street. How much do you want the money order for?"

"Eleven dollars," I said while looking at Mum out of the corner of my eye.

She was busy buttering toast, but she turned around quickly.

"What is the money order for?" she asked quietly.

"For an industrial dryer for my hair, I saw one at the gold mine in California. It will prevent me from catching my death."

"Is it like the ones at the beauty parlor?"

"Oh, no. It is handheld. At least the barrel is that the hot air comes out of. I didn't get a close look at the mine, so I don't know how big the heater and motor are. It gives the RPM of the motor and watts of the heater, but they don't mean anything to me. The total weight of the unit isn't included."

She surprised me with, "Well, it will be a Godsend around here if it works."

I didn't push my luck on the subject any further. I had the money ready and gave it to dad. My suit was rolled up in a bag for him to take to my Uncle Gene's Belle Cleaners.

"Thanks, Dad. This will help a lot."

He smiled. "We have to have you looking good for your first date."

He just had to say that. Mum now followed up.

"I have talked to Janet's Mum. Today Tom and Bill's dates will be made tickety-boo."

Sometimes Mum talked funny. I think she meant everything was coming together.

On our walk to school, Tom and Bill pressed me for what I knew about their dates for homecoming. I told them not to do anything until I heard from Janet.

Today was noticeably cooler than it had been. It was getting near the end of September, and we were due for the first killing frost. We would have to start wearing coats to school soon.

I heard lots of "Go, Bellefontaine" as I walked through the hall. They were directed at me! This cheer was traditional whenever we beat our arch-rivals in Urbana. I suspect if our trash men could pick up garbage faster than theirs, it would be, "Go, Bellefontaine." Still, it was neat.

Janet, looking fine in a navy-blue skirt and white blouse, cornered me on the way into the cafeteria for lunch.

"Ricky, tell Tom to ask Tracy and Bill to ask Nancy to homecoming and dinner. They will both say yes."

I walked over to the two guys and gave them their marching orders. Tom got an enormous smile. Bill looked worried.

Just then, Janet came walking up with Tracy and Nancy. The two girls standing side by side looked like Mutt and Jeff. Both were good-looking.

Tracy was tall, maybe five foot eight inches, and slender with brunette hair and brown eyes. Nancy was considerably shorter, a little over five feet tall, blonde with blue eyes and a fair complexion. She was built like you wouldn't believe it.

Several inches taller than Tracy, Tom couldn't ask her out fast enough, knowing that she would say yes. Bill stuttered at the much shorter Nancy but managed to ask her out.

Both girls seemed to appreciate the pressure the boys were under and responded with a simple, "I would love to go with you."

The girls had their lunch trays with them and joined us.

They started going over the details with the guys. I thought I knew all the arrangements. But I found out all the women had been talking back and forth. The girls and all our mothers were in on this operation.

Tom and Bill were informed they had to wear suits to dinner, bring a change for the game, and then back to suits for the dance. All the changes would be at Janet's house. Also, the moms would be meeting at Janet's for pictures.

After the general order of suits and changes for the game, the color of suits, ties, shoes for dinner, and dance was discussed. After several hesitant starts, Bill confessed he did not know how to tie a necktie. I volunteered to tie his tie around my neck in a Windsor knot that could be loosened and slipped over his head.

That would make a quick change from dinner to the game to the dance. I had learned to tie a Windsor knot at church, of all places. A neighbor took me as our family wasn't the church-going type. One of the men saw my sloppy four-in-hand knot and taught me how to tie a Windsor.

The girls told Tom to go to Wolfheim's and get Henry's help in selecting a narrow Vic Damone tie, preferably in blue.

The really good thing was that the costs would be split between us three guys. That meant my share of the limo would be thirteen dollars. I would only be on the hook for two dinners, a corsage, and tickets to the game and dance.

The corsage was only two bucks, the game a buck fifty, and the dance two dollars. My share would be about twenty-five dollars for the whole night. Almost half as much as a grown man-made in a week.

My friends' moms had taken their suits to the dry cleaners and ordered their corsages. I just had to order a corsage. Janet and I stopped at the junior class table outside the cafeteria after lunch and took care of that.

She liked pink baby roses; and thought they would go well with her cream-colored dress and my grey suit. The girls decided they didn't need to wear hats and gloves to the dinner or the dance.

Now, all we guys had to do was formally meet the parents of our dates. At lunch, we were told it would be after dinner this evening. We were to go to our girl's house and meet the parents, and don't worry, the dad's bark was worse than their bite. Our parents would be driving us over. I think I said it before. Guys didn't have a chance.

I wondered if, after the dance, Janet would be my girlfriend. I'm not quite certain what being a boyfriend would mean. I know it might get me a chance to kiss her alone, but what a boyfriend's other duties were was a mystery.

I kept one or two chapters ahead of each class and completed most of my future homework during the class. What I didn't get done in class, I could finish in study hall. I found some of the subjects so interesting that I was doing ten and fifteen handwritten pages when three would do.

One problem with all the writing was ink pen leaks. I had several Shaffer pens, and they would all leak after I put them in my shirt pocket. I gave up and would wear the shirt with an imperfection on it. Mum hated it but refused to buy new shirts when they still fit and didn't wear anything except a little mark.

I was hoping for new shirts at Christmas. Turns out I was like Mum. I hated to waste money when I had these perfectly fine shirts, except for a little flaw. Maybe I should start using a pocket protector like the geeks.

There still was time to read books from my inherited collection. I had just finished one about a huge plantation before and during the Civil War.

I thought it was so neat when he said, "Frankly, I don't give a damn."

If I tried that, I would be in so much trouble.

Chapter 24

The golf lessons after school were fun. Coach put a bushel basket in the center of a practice green, and we had to try to put the ball in the basket from 50 yards. I did the best on the golf team, making one out of four, but I thought I could do better with practice. Even the ones I missed stayed within a few feet of the basket.

At dinner that night, I related the day's events to Mum that involved dating. She expressed her opinion that things appeared to be under control but that no doubt there would be a snafu. I asked what a snafu was; she blushed and said it meant things would go wrong. Somehow, I think there was more to it than that. I would ask Dad later.

Dad ignored that conversation and showed interest in my schoolwork, but I had been bringing home the A's from my exams, so they were mild questions, not the inquisition.

Mum was satisfied with my answers, and Dad had dropped my suit off at the dry cleaner's, so all was on schedule. Dad had also stopped at the bank and picked up a money order for me. I immediately placed it and the order form into an addressed stamped envelope.

We had to drive by the post office to Janet's house, so I put it into the new drive-through mailbox.

On the way, Dad asked me if I was nervous. I told him I was a little. He laughed and told me he was scared to death when he had to meet Mum's dad.

His full name was Ernest Thomas Smyth Butler. He had been a regimental sergeant major in the British Army during World War I. Dad told me that granddad Ernie was probably the hardest man he had ever met. This statement was made by a man that had been through the Battle of the Bulge.

I was brought to America when I was three in 1947 and hadn't been back, so I didn't know my English grandparents.

Dad's story was interesting enough to get me to Janet's house without throwing up. I think that's why he did it. When I went in, Mr. Huber was waiting. I remembered him as a nice friendly man. But the person I met looked like he wanted to tear my head off.

Dad gave his moral support by waiting in the car. Thanks, Dad.

Mr. Huber took me out to the kitchen for a Man-to-Man talk. When we got there, suddenly, he relaxed and was Mr. Huber the smiling, friendly man I remembered. It was weird that I was now taller than him.

He said, "Ricky, I had orders to scare you to death so you would treat my daughter with respect. You will, won't you?"

"Yes, sir," I replied.

"Good. Now that is over, tell me about beating Urbana in golf."

I described the match as best as I could.

Her Dad then said, "Okay, let's join the women, and please try to look a little frightened. Maybe hang your head down till you get out the door."

I did and was glad to escape.

When dad asked, I told him how it went.

He snorted and said, "Just be glad you weren't any older, or he would have been cleaning a gun while he talked to you."

I wondered if I would ever be issued a handbook on life. It sure would help.

I cheated on my reading; I reread an old favorite, *A Study in Scarlet*.

Tuesday, I woke up to a downpour. It was the nasty, cold, fall-type of rain. There would be no running today. Dad hadn't been called to work for several days, so he loaded us kids into the car and drove us to school. Having an attached garage was neat that day. The garage on Detroit Street wasn't attached and was so stuffed with junk you couldn't park a car in it anyway. We would have drowned getting to the car.

Thinking about that garage made me wonder. There was a stout workbench there. Were we going to leave it? I asked Dad during the drive, and he told me he intended to move it to our new garage. There was plenty of room in the garage as we had only one car.

He was just waiting for the time and a nice day for him and Uncle Jim to move it. My Dad has four living brothers, all local, Ross, Gene, Jim, and Wally. Dad fell between Ross and Gene. Jim and Wally were half-brothers. I have a lot of cousins, but I'm the oldest, so I don't have much to do with them.

The school smelled of damp wool as the radiators heated up and dried all the wet coats. It was cool now, but it would be roasting before the day was over. Mr. Harper, the school janitor, continuously mopped the floor as we brought mud in. He normally wasn't the most cheerful person; today, he wore a large frown.

Since they couldn't wait outside today, sneaking a smoke or just talking, students were milling around in the halls. Fortunately, I was large enough to push my way through to my locker. Some of the smaller freshmen just seemed to push in place, getting nowhere.

I took pity on a classmate, Linda Harvey, and helped her and two friends through the crowd at the door. A quick "thanks," and we separated.

Homeroom was full early and noisy. My homeroom teacher Mr. Watkins stood by the door and watched the class while doing hall monitoring. Soon, announcements came over the school PA; among these, no golf practice today. After the announcements, we all stood for the pledge and prayer.

The bell rang, and it was time to go to our first class. I was caught up as usual on all my work, so I spent time keeping ahead. The day seemed to take forever; I think it had to do with the rooms getting warmer all day long. Those radiators kept putting out heat. After lunch, everyone appeared sleepy, even our teachers!

It had stopped raining by the time school was out, so I walked downtown, intending to get something to eat at Don's Hamburgers. It was a general hangout for kids after school who could afford it.

Only freshmen and up were seen there, and this was my first visit. I wanted to see how the elite of Bellefontaine lived. Somehow, I don't think John Wayne or Elvis would be overwhelmed by the ambiance.

The busiest intersection in town was Main and Sandusky. US 33 and US 68 meet there. If you were passing through Bellefontaine, you used these roads. Travelers didn't know how dangerous crossing this intersection could be. I saw near misses several times a week when I was the paperboy on this route.

I was waiting for the traffic light to change. This was the only light in town that people who walked waited for before crossing. I watched as a long-distance truck slid through a red light. He came down Sandusky Street with its long hill. He applied his brakes, but the road was wet, and he just slid into the intersection.

It collided with a southbound car and tore it up pretty badly. He had hit the front end and spun the car around, so it was now facing north. The engine compartment was open with the hood bent right over the car's roof. Smoke was starting to curl out; a fire could start at any moment.

I ran over to the car to see if I could help. There were two people in the car. I later learned they were a married couple from Kenton, Ohio. They were John and Marge Sutton. That didn't matter at the time.

He had hit the steering wheel pretty hard, and she had broken the windshield with her head. They were both unconscious. Flames were coming out of the engine as I was looking in the window. In Scouts, we were taught not to move injured people if we could avoid it. But it couldn't be avoided. I got her out of the car, carrying her to the library on the corner. I laid her on the grass and ran back for her husband.

The car was starting to burn, but I could get him out. Seat belts weren't required and were only used on racing cars. So, I could get them both out of the car without any problems.

I put him in a fireman's carry and got him away from the burning car. As I carried him, I saw people standing there like they didn't know what to do.

By the time I got him to the library lawn, his wife was coming around. I looked back, and the truck driver had gotten out of his truck but wasn't moving away. He was too close to the flames, so I led him to the others. He must have been in shock. Dr. Costin's office was across the street, so he and his nurses had come out and were just starting to examine the Suttons.

Chapter 25

There was nothing more for me to do, so I walked downtown, intending to go to Don's. I wondered if I would go into shock as I did after the Colorado bank robbery, but I guess only killing people did that to me.

Walking by Winger's Plumbing, I had a thought and went in. I asked Mr. Winger at the counter if they carried adjustable showerheads. He didn't know what I was talking about.

After explaining what I was looking for, he pulled out catalogs from Moen and Delta. They didn't have anything like that. All shower heads were made to send out a stream of water straight in front. The direction you aimed it when installing was where it went.

Mr. Winger laughed and said, "That sounds handy. You should invent one."

I thanked him and left.

There was one good thing at Don's. "Rock and Roll Cowboy" had been removed from the jukebox. That thing had run its course.

I had a hamburger, fries, and a Coke. While eating at the counter, several kids talked about the big wreck downtown. Two people were hurt, but no one was dead. A car caught fire and burned completely. Some guy ran into flames ten feet high and got the people out. The fire department had put the fire out, but traffic was a mess.

I thought about what those kids had said. There were no ten-foot-high flames when I carried the people out. If it got out that I did it, would I have to go through the hero-worship and then shunning that occurred after my summer vacation? Neither the hero worship nor shunning was an experience I wanted to repeat.

There weren't any of my classmates to talk to at Don's. All the tables and booths were filled with juniors and seniors. Eleanor Price was there but didn't say "Hi." I'm not even certain she noticed me.

I went on home. I had already read my chapters ahead and worked on the problems in the back of the book, so I didn't have much to do till dinner.

So, I started to read another book about the injustice of being wounded in World War I while being an ambulance driver. The main character makes many bad decisions and ends up alone. A sad, useless story with no point other than life isn't always fair, and war is bad. Bill Samson had taught me that lesson.

At dinner, Dad told Mum about a big wreck downtown. They were looking for the person who had pulled the passengers out of the burning car. He made it sound like fifteen-foot-tall flames and a gas explosion. The hero had just walked away, and they didn't know who he was.

I had the decision to make, but I didn't want to talk in front of Denny or Eddie. They would blab it all over their schools. After dinner, I helped with dishes. The other kids had moved to the TV, so I let Mum and Dad know I was the one who pulled the people out of the car. I also told Dad the flames had just started and weren't that strong, and the gas tank hadn't blown up, at least while I was there.

They asked why I had left, and I explained they were being cared for by professionals, so there was nothing to do. I explained that I had time to think about it and that my last brush with fame had some problems that I would prefer to avoid. They weren't really happy but were willing to let it all go.

That lasted for about two minutes; then, the doorbell rang. It was the police.

Dad answered the door, and they asked if Richard Jackson was home. He called me to the door. They didn't look like they were here to sell me a ticket to the policemen's ball. When I identified myself, they asked if I was at the scene of the accident. There wasn't any way I could get out of this. Someone had recognized me and given them my name.

"Yes, I was."

I had been told by Elvis and Tab in Mexico when dealing with the police to only answer their questions and don't volunteer anything. I didn't know if that only held with Mexican Police, but I decided not to take any chances.

"We know you pulled the Suttons out of the vehicle."

"I didn't know their names."

"Did you see the accident occur?"

"Yes, I did."

"What happened?"

"The truck was trying to stop for the red light, but the road was so wet, he just slid into the intersection."

"Did he appear to be speeding?"

"Not really. It looked like the truck had enough clear distance to stop if the roads weren't wet."

One of the policemen was taking notes as I was speaking.

"Why did you leave the scene?"

"I had helped all that I could. The team from Dr. Costin's office was there, so there was nothing else I could do."

"You certainly saved their lives. For your information, both will live. The woman has a lacerated scalp and is being kept under observation for a possible concussion. He has broken ribs, a dislocated shoulder, and a concussion. They would never have gotten out before that fire if you hadn't helped."

"I'm glad I could."

"You shouldn't have left the scene, but since we have been so busy, and this has been our first chance to interview you, there is no problem. If something like this ever happens again, please stick around."

The cop then relaxed his demeanor, "Rick, you are a hero here. I know about your notoriety recently and understand why you are trying to keep a low profile. However, the law is pretty sticky about leaving the scene, so please be careful in the future."

"I will, Officer Wilgus," reading it off his name badge.

They thanked me for my time and turned to go. The officer whose name I had missed started laughing.

"At least we got here and are done before George turned up this time. Half the time, he beats us to the person."

Reporter George Weaver had just pulled up. As he came up the walk, Dad invited him in. He was now a friend of the family.

"George, took you long enough. There should be some coffee on."

George said, "I have been at the hospital checking on the accident victims, the Sutton family from Kenton. The truck driver is being charged for going too fast for conditions. Can I have milk instead?"

George spits this out all in one breath.

"So, you've heard about Rick's latest?"

"Yep, you might have to keep that boy locked up at home."

As this banter went on, we moved to the kitchen and sat down. Mum got busy with the coffee for Dad and milk for George. I was on my own. As I was mixing a glass of Tang, I asked, "How did they know it was me?"

"Ricky, you have been going to Dr. Costin's since you were five years old. How would they not know it was you?" There went the last thin chance of keeping things quiet. I patiently answered Mr. Weaver's questions.

When he asked me how I knew what to do, I credited my Boy Scout training. It then came out from a proud Mum that I had my First Aid Merit Badge, completed my Eagle requirements, and was just waiting for the award, which would be after the first of next year.

We talked about my leaving the scene. George thought for a moment.

"I will present the truth. The police knew you were the hero. They didn't have time to talk to you, so they interviewed you at home later."

That was interesting. What Mr. Weaver was going to write was correct but far from the whole story. I wondered how many other things I heard and read were like that.

That night I couldn't get into reading. I kept wondering about what I had read in my history books. Were they telling the truth, but not the whole story? I had read somewhere that the winners write the history books. This thought put a whole new perspective on what I was learning at school.

Chapter 26

Wednesday, I had a preview of what school would be like when Tom and Bill said, "Hello, Hero," as I came out the door.

At least they were being nice about it. My recent experiences have taught me that everything wouldn't be seen in a good light.

"Hi guys, all I did was help get them out of their car before the fire spread. The fire was just starting, and I was never in danger."

Tom said, "How can you be so calm about that? I would have stood there too long, wondering what I should do. I probably would've run into the library and called the fire department."

Bill helpfully added, "I would've crapped in my pants."

"Not a pleasant thought, Bill," I replied.

That started an argument between Tom and Bill about when it was acceptable to crap your pants. Finally, they asked my opinion. I considered it for a minute and concluded, "I guess it is okay when there are no other options."

They wanted examples. "Well, if the guy has a gun and you don't, and he is pulling the trigger, and your feet are set in cement, so you can't move...why are we talking about this anyway? It's plain stupid!"

This high-toned conversation got us to school.

Of course, by the time I was in my homeroom, the car had not only burned and exploded, but the library was half gone. There was even damage to the Kennedy Funeral Parlor across from the library. Before lunch, the exploding car would probably be launched high enough to be spotted by the radar station on Campbell's Hill.

The word had spread that I was the one who pulled the people out of the car. I tried to explain that it wasn't that big of a deal to everyone who would listen. The story just kept going around and around reaching its peak at noon in the cafeteria.

People kept coming up to me asking questions about risking my life. I couldn't take any more. I stood up on a table and got everyone's attention. I started talking before the teachers on duty could get to me.

Once I said the whole story was wrong, they slowed down to see what I would say. I gave the story as it occurred. The flames were just starting, and I was never in danger.

Yes, they would've been in trouble if I hadn't gotten them out. I wasn't some superhero, just a guy that moved two people from point A to point B at the correct time. Now let it rest, please.

When I shut up, silence reigned. I started to get down from the table. Then the applause started. It kept going and going. Then someone started chanting, "Go, Bellefontaine." Even the two teachers were clapping. I left my lunch and walked out the door. Kids were touching me as I went by. I walked up the hill and went home. These people were crazy.

Mum wanted to know what I was doing home so early. I didn't even know what to tell her. The world didn't seem real. I just walked by her as the phone started ringing.

Mary was in the front room and saw me. "Oh good, Rick, you're just in time for tea."

She had a tea party set up with her dolls. I spent the rest of the afternoon at the party.

Dad got home at about three o'clock. I could hear him and Mum talking in the kitchen. Mary was tired of playing tea party, so she told us the royal audience was over, and we commoners could now leave.

Not wanting to be thrown into a royal dungeon, I bowed to Her Majesty and took my leave. Mum has to quit reading the stories in that magazine to Mary. Some are facts, and some are fiction. I can see the future queen on the phone now. "Off with their heads!"

Dad was waiting in the kitchen and gestured for me to sit down. Mum was nowhere around.

"Rick, I hear it was rough for you at school today."

"It was Dad. They don't see the real me. They keep making things greater and better than they are."

"That happens, Rick. It is human nature. You are learning one of the hard lessons of fame. So far, you haven't bought into it, and I can't tell you how I am about that. Let me ask you a question."

"Okay."

"Is John Wayne the greatest cowboy who ever lived?"

"Of course, he...no, he is an actor who plays cowboys."

"Did Mr. Wayne come across to you as someone who believed he was a great cowboy?"

"No, he was just a nice guy doing his job."

"But many people want to believe he is a great cowboy, the embodiment of the American dream of the West. He has learned to separate what people think he is from what he is. If anything, that is what makes him great.

"You haven't come to terms with that. It sounds like you are scared that you have to be what people think you are rather than the person you are."

"Dad, you have no idea what it's like when people chant like you are some God or something. I wanted to smile and wave and let my subjects bow down. But that would be a fraud; I am just Ricky Jackson, a kid from Bellefontaine. That's all I want to be."

"And that is all you should be; however, you have to realize that you have done some special things that most people will never have a chance to do. They look at you as living their dream. Just don't believe for one moment that you are their dream."

"Then what should I do?"

"Be yourself. When people applaud like they did today or chant "Go, Bellefontaine," remember they are voicing their dreams, and don't let it affect yours. Please take it in stride; don't expect it; don't reject it. Go on being Ricky. As you have already seen, you can be a hero one day and a bum the next in the public eye."

"Again, what should I do?"

"Damned if I know, Rick. It's your problem to sort out, not mine."

My mouth dropped open; this was my dad, and he wouldn't help me. Then I closed my mouth. He wasn't going to help me because he couldn't. I had to learn how to handle this myself.

"Thanks, Dad. If I hurry, I can still make golf practice."

"Mum and I have talked to the school. They don't expect you until tomorrow. Mr. Gordon understands that the last two days have been hard for you. Tom is bringing your assignments."

"Thanks, Dad. I think I am going to read until dinner time."

Even that plan didn't work out. Denny and Eddie had just gotten home from school. They pestered me to shoot some baskets with them. It turned out to be fun. They were both better shots than me. I just never cared for the sport. Eddie was the real surprise. He was now taller than Denny. For his age, he was quite tall.

We played horse until dinner time. For some reason, I felt better when we were done. I had forgotten about everything except trying to beat those two little monsters at the game. They kept calling me bad eyes when I would miss a shot. Insult to injury, I was first out every game. No chance of me being a superhero here.

Dinner went like nothing had happened. The two boys hadn't been told of my leaving school. They hadn't even been told about me pulling the people out of their car. Queen Mary deigned us with her presence. I know she did because that is what she told us.

Mum had got some magazines mailed from England that had news of the royal family. She had read it aloud to Mary, and I guess Mary crowned herself. No messing around with being a princess. She went right for the top job.

The *Bellefontaine Examiner* had the correct information about the wreck. Mr. Weaver wrote that the Scouts trained me on what to do, and I had done it. No big deal. He didn't say that, but that was how he wrote it.

Tom had dropped my school assignments off, but I had already done them. They were all problems and questions from the end of the chapter. That guy at Berkeley was right.

My reading that night had difficult language, but it was a hoot. Back in the seventeenth century, Tom Jones had quite a life of his own. It was certainly more interesting than mine.

Chapter 27

Tom and Bill were waiting as usual Thursday morning. It was a cool but clear day, so I had done my morning run. Today, the conversation was about Elvis being in the army; Tom had a picture of him as they cut his hair. We wondered if they saved it or just swept it away.

Bill figured some barber saved it and was selling it. From there it was, well, he could sell all the hair cut that day or any day and say it was Elvis's. Tom said, "I can just see him selling a bag of blonde hair or, better yet, red hair, as Elvis's."

The way we told it, you would have thought we were teenagers.

Waiting at the school front door was Janet. She wanted to make sure everything was okay for the dance. I thought that was a little odd. She didn't ask how I was. She just wanted to know if everything was still on for the dance. Of course, it was.

Once she heard that, it was, "Great, C' ya."

No one said anything about my speech in the cafeteria or how I left school. At the same time, I got a lot of "Good mornings." I felt so much better today than yesterday. Being treated like I was normal was much better than being some fake hero.

Classes went well, except the teachers gave us an early homecoming present. They knew that homecoming day wasn't the day to give tests, so they all gave them today! What a present.

Golf practice was fun. We did the front nine and I got a 32. Coach told me the course record was 64, so if I kept it up for nine more holes, I would have tied it.

After practice, I stopped at the restaurant and confirmed that my reservations were still correct. They were.

Kathy got me good. She asked me if I was so nervous about things because I would pop the big question.

"What big question?"

"Propose to her."

She burst out laughing.

"You should have seen the look on your face. I wish I had a picture."

I was blushing and feeling pale at the same time. I swear my life flashed before my eyes.

Kathy grinned, "I was just teasing."

"I know, but it was a shock. I won't be fifteen until next month."

This took Kathy aback.

"Are you fourteen? I thought you were seventeen going on eighteen. You are certainly big for your age."

I just nodded, not knowing what else to do.

The fact that Kathy had even looked at me was astounding. She was an extremely attractive twenty-something, way out of my class. I retreated from this minefield as quickly as I could. The bus was almost ready to leave to take us back to school.

Dinner was cheerful. Mary had decided she would rather be a pony. Not have a pony, be a pony. She talked Denny and Eddie into taking rides but took one look at me and said, "Some people are too big to ride ponies. They ride horses."

I continued my nightly reading and finished the adventures of *Tom Jones*. Now there was a life.

School Friday was a complete waste as far as learning went. All the talk was about homecoming. The biggest issue was that the captain of the football team, Tim Jefferson, was black. The captain of the team was always the homecoming king.

He would crown the homecoming queen and then kiss her. This created potential problems, but the senior class elected Connie Hastings. Connie was the only black girl in the class.

That solved the racial issue nicely. It was politely ignored that Tim and Connie were first cousins. I always wondered later how their families felt about that.

Right after the second lunch period, there was a big pep rally. The football team and coaches were introduced, and we were told how they would beat the Kenton Wildcats. Many cheers were led, and we were dismissed for the day. I picked up the corsage from the junior class. They had set up in the cafeteria. And from the number of corsages being picked up, they would have a nice prom. Not that I was old enough to go.

There wasn't golf practice that night, but we did have a match against Sidney on Saturday, so Coach Stone asked us not to stay out too late. Luckily, it was a home match for us, so we didn't have to be at the course until nine o'clock for a ten o'clock tee-off.

My suit just fit me. It was tight in the shoulders, and the pants cuff should have been let down. The pants weren't embarrassingly short, but I would have to have the cuffs turned down if I tried to wear the suit again. When the limo pulled up, I was about to walk out the door when Mum reminded me of the corsage in the refrigerator.

"Thanks, Mum; that would have been a bad start to the evening."

"I would've brought it with me."

"Brought it with you? What's going on, Mum?"

"Sue Ellen, Belinda, and I are going together to Janet's house to take pictures. You didn't think we would let our boys go on their first dates without pictures."

Pictures never entered my mind even though we had discussed it at lunch.

"Oh, then see you there."

The limo gleamed it had been shined so much. There was discreet lettering on the driver's door that said, "Maverick Taxi Service". The driver, who turned out to be John Sullivan, was wearing an old-fashioned driver's uniform with buttons. He even had the hat.

He jumped out and opened the door for me. This was going to be neat. I told him so.

Mr. Sullivan said, "This is our big night, our opportunity to show this thing off and make some money. Speaking of, you still owe twenty dollars."

I had the money ready. He had a receipt already made out, so it was an easy exchange.

My parents took pictures of me in the limo. Neighbors were coming out to take a look. Tom and Bill, who only lived a few doors down, walked over, dressed, and ready to go. They were both awed by the limo.

Our mums took pictures of us and the limo; our dads checked the limo out. After a few minutes, Mr. Sullivan opened a back door for us and said, "Gentlemen, your chariot awaits."

We boys were pushed aside by the mums who had to check out the car's interior. The dads followed them. After the proper amount of oohs and ahs, we were allowed to get in. I started to apologize to Mr. Sullivan, and he laughed.

"This is exactly what we were hoping for."

There was a small refrigerator in the back. It was loaded with soda pop, but we didn't have time to open any, and besides, we didn't know if we had to pay separately. When we arrived at Janet's house, Mr. Sullivan again jumped out and opened the doors. I asked him about the soft drinks, and he told me they were free.

We walked to the door and rang the doorbell. Mrs. Huber opened the door and invited us all in for a while, telling us how nice we looked. I guess we dress up pretty well. Tom had on a dark blue suit with a thin red stripe; Bill, a dark brown suit with a light cross-check pattern in it.

Both their ties were the snazzy thin Vic Damone style. The singer sure had set a fashion trend. Even Frank Sinatra had followed his lead in the super skinny ties.

I went with the full Western rig. The fancy suit was fit for the Grand Ole Opry, with boots, and a black cowboy hat. I wore a bolo tie with a turquoise slide. This would be a sight to see for staid old Bellefontaine. We had also pre-staged our clothes for the football game; we all had jeans and long-sleeved shirts.

It was cool, so we also had light jackets. I was going to wear one of my silver Western belt buckles with the jeans and still had a hat and boots.

We only had to wait five minutes for the girls to finish getting ready. Nancy's mom told us that this was almost record time for an event like this. I tried to picture what they were doing upstairs, but I couldn't imagine it. I imagined girls in garter belts, and nothing else would come to me after that.

They came down the stairs together. I must say our dates were lovely. All wore beautiful dresses with crinoline underskirts which their moms had starched, so they stood out. I knew this because Mum would starch hers. There was a corsage presentation ceremony. Thank God I didn't have to pin one on Janet. I just knew I would draw blood.

Then there were the pictures: a boy with his date, the boys as a group, a boy with his mum, then a boy with his date and his mum, the girls as a group, and finally all of us as a group. The Kodak Brownies were clicking like crazy. I had spots before my eyes because of all the flashes going off. I kept looking at my watch because we were getting close to our dinner reservation. We finally broke free and went outside.

We were greeted by the sight of half the neighborhood looking the limo over. You would think they had never seen a car before. Of course, the limo set off a new round of picture taking with all the various groups. There was the obligatory examination of the interior of the car. Finally, we were ready to go. Mr. Sullivan was all smiles as he held the car door for us.

You could hear all that starched crinoline crinkling as the girls got in the car. It sounded like a small rainstorm. The girls had all changed their minds and were wearing white gloves and small pillbox-like hats. They also had silk stockings which renewed my vision of garter belts. The Sears catalog had given me an extensive education on garter belts.

The trip to the country club went quickly as the girls recounted the trials and tribulations of getting ready. Who knew that so many disasters lurked in the closet, on the makeup table, and with curlers!

We arrived at the country club a few minutes late, and our table was ready. Mum had coached me on such refinements as holding the chair for my date, putting my napkin on my lap, and using the silverware from the outside in. Also, I wasn't to slurp my soup or belch. I promised not to slurp; the belch would take its chances.

The waiter took our drink order. Of course, we all had soft drinks. I went with a Dr. Pepper to keep up the Western theme. The rest had a Coke. I cringed at the drink prices, fifteen cents each! I wistfully thought of the free drinks in the limo but knew it would be gauche to bring them in. I loved the new words I was learning from all my reading.

We looked over the menu. Nancy mentioned there was lobster, and she had never tried it. I told the group I had it in a restaurant in Philadelphia and that it could be so messy you had to wear a bib.

She looked down at her dress and changed her mind. Bill heaved a sigh of relief. There wasn't a dollar amount mentioned on the menu for lobster, just "Market Price".

We all settled on some form of steak. I hadn't eaten many, so I wasn't familiar with things like filet mignon or ribeye. I ordered a T-bone medium-rare. Luckily, I found out that I liked it that way. As the meal progressed, we talked about school, but it quickly centered on my summer vacation. The other kids asked questions about the people I had met and the places I had been to.

It was so pleasant that I couldn't tell you what I had for dessert. This was the first time I had a normal conversation with kids my age since I got home. It was wonderful.

Chapter 28

Other kids were at the club with their dates, as a couple or in groups. Their parents must be members. During the meal, kids would walk from table to table to say hello. Our table was treated the same as the others.

Well, other than the fact that one of the guys in every group thought he was a genius by calling me "Tex." I took it in the fun it was meant. I think my companions got tired of it before I did.

I was in such a glow that I told the guys I would take care of the check. I signed my name, and away we went. The girls exchanged looks, and my social status went up another click. I would pay Mr. Hastings what I owed the club in the morning.

Mr. Sullivan was waiting in the car at the entrance to the restaurant. He took us back to Janet's house, where we changed into jeans and shirts with light jackets. I could wear one of my belts with the large silver buckle. Everyone asked about it. I explained it was for the National Junior Championship in bull riding this year and that it was 100% silver. You could hear my status click up again.

The game was great; we beat Kenton in a close game, 21-20. At half time the homecoming queen was crowned and kissed. After the game, we headed back to Janet's to change. Getting in the limo, I mentioned to Mr. Sullivan that this was the only way to travel and that he would see me again.

He chuckled, "Not in this car. The cards went the wrong way last night. We were allowed to keep this commitment and then turn it over to the new owner. Easy come, easy go."

"That's tough!"

"I've had this job for ten years; this is how it is. We always end up ahead, but sometimes the road gets bumpy. After tonight I suspect we will buy one."

It was chaos at Janet's house as we all changed back for the dance. Bill had managed to mess up the tie I had pre-tied for him, so I had to stand in front of a mirror and tie it, then slip it off and slip it over his head. Okay, so I pulled it a little tight. He lived.

The girls said we would only be a little late, which was okay as it was only "fashionably late". I wish someone would explain that to my teachers.

The dance was okay. The youth center had been decorated for the occasion, and every table had a centerpiece. Tom had a chance to shine here. His older brother told him about past dances, so Tom had paid extra and reserved us a table.

It was a table for eight, and only six of us were there. Linda Harvey and her date Jason Robertson joined us. None of us knew them. The only interaction I had with Linda was to help her get through a crowd at school. It turned out that Jason was visiting from Louisiana. It was a town I had never heard of, Monroe. He came with his dad on business with Mr. Harvey. He seemed nice enough, but I bet he had to shave twice a day.

There were more kids than seats, so other girls would leave their purses at our table when they danced. This allowed us to talk to many people without walking all around. It was good because Tom Humphrey and some pals were kicked out because they tried to take another freshman's table.

Janet and I danced a lot and had fun. While she allowed me to hold her close, it was not too close, if you know what I mean. I guess I had secretly been hoping for more.

Towards the end of the evening, she broke it to me.

"Ricky, I have had a lot of fun and appreciate you being my date tonight. I have to let you know that I'm not ready for a boyfriend yet, and my parents won't allow me to go on real dates until I'm sixteen."

I'm proud to say I took it calmly but was crushed and upset inside. As she accepted a dance with another boy, I thought about it.

I had taken her to the country club. I had rented a limo.... Oh wait, I did that. She didn't ask for any of that. All she had wanted was a date. Maybe I better slow down before I said something really stupid.

The more I thought about it as Janet danced, I hadn't been hunting for a date to homecoming. It was suggested to me that Janet was available if asked. I hadn't been looking for a girlfriend. I just started assuming she would be because I was taking her to dance.

Heck, I didn't know what having a girlfriend meant other than trying to neck. Another point to consider was her parents wouldn't let her date until she was sixteen.

What was my parent's position on when I could start dating? Last summer, I was given a lot of freedom, so maybe I made some poor assumptions. I should talk to my parents before I make myself look foolish. In the meantime, I would be nice to Janet, as she had done nothing wrong. Enjoy the evening for what it is, a dance, not a romance.

When the boy I knew from gym class brought Janet back, I smiled at them and asked, "Are you going to dance again, or do I get a turn?"

Janet gave me a curious look and said, "If you don't mind, I will dance with Roger one more time."

"Okay, I will ask someone else."

I danced with a dozen different girls during the evening, and Janet danced with many different boys. We both were smiling and overly warm when the evening ended.

The limo took us back to Janet's home; the girls had a sleepover. So, it was three couples that walked to the door. Tom and I got a good night kiss from our dates. Nancy laid one on Bill. When they came up for air, he told her, "I will call you tomorrow."

Someone had a really good time!

John Sullivan drove us home and dropped us off at my house. Tom and Bill made their way home on foot. Each was carrying his bag of clothes. I chuckled. They looked ready to go on the road, except they would be hitching in suits.

Mum was waiting up when I walked into the house. She wanted to know all about the evening. I shared all of it with her, including Janet's comment about being too young for a boyfriend.

From her face, you could tell Mum was happy to hear that.

"Good, we have never really discussed when you could start dating for real. Sixteen when you have your driver's license seems good. You can go to special group events like this, but no dates alone."

Well, that took care of that, I thought. Now it was either sneak around or wait. Since there was no one in sight to sneak with, I guess no dates.

That night I read about a young farmer fighting stobor. That would be an adventure!

Chapter 29

As usual, my alarm went off at six the next morning. After my exercises and morning run, I had what according to Mum was real breakfast. Bacon and two eggs over easy, hash brown potatoes, wheat toast, and orange juice. I was ready for my golf match with Sidney!

As Coach requested, I was at our meeting spot at the school's front door at nine. The bus was on time, so we arrived at the country club in short order. My first stop was to see Mr. Hastings. I asked how much I owed. It wasn't too bad, nine fifty. I thanked him; he said anytime.

If I wanted to come back again, I would be allowed to sign in since I now had an account set up. It had to be during the season, though. I told him I doubted that would happen.

"I don't know, Rick; some of those girls gave you the eye."

I would love to quiz him on who they were, but I had to get ready to play.

Our team loosened up on the practice tees and then putted to see how the greens would feel today. I was starting to appreciate how much the weather and time of day could influence a putt. This time Bellefontaine won the honors. I waited for John to tee up. Everyone just stood there.

"Hey Rick, you were low man last week. You're up first."

Wow, from last in the lineup to first in one week!

I sent it a country mile in the air, then it rolled and rolled. The ball had to have gone 275 yards up the middle.

One of the guys from Sidney said, "It's going to be a long day."

Tim cracked, "Or a short one; depends on how you look at it."

Tim lost his match, but we won overall. Tim had a long day as those sand trap demons got even with his smart remark.

I set a course record of 63, and word went around the club like wildfire. Men I had never met were shaking my hand. Pictures were taken, and golf balls were signed. It was amazing.

I had never thought about what would happen if I were good at this game. After everything else I had been through, it was easy to bask in the attention without getting carried away.

I had just packed my clubs away when the inevitable happened. There stood George Weaver and a photographer.

George shook his head and said, "I told your parents they should keep you home."

So now my picture would be in the *Examiner* again. At least I hadn't killed anyone.

George asked, "How does it feel about setting a course record?"

"It feels great, but I couldn't have done it without the training Coach Stone has provided and the support of my teammates."

You could have knocked Mr. Weaver and Coach over with a feather.

"Where did you learn to give answers like that?" Mr. Weaver inquired.

"How soon we forget. I have won three rodeos, including a national title, and have hung around with John Wayne and Elvis while they were interviewed."

Both Coach and Mr. Weaver looked at each other and shook their heads.

"Precocious," said Coach.

"No, that's my sister Mary."

Mr. Weaver let out a great laugh, "That she is."

"Does she play golf?" Coach asked.

"Not yet, Coach, but any day now."

After everything settled down and we had shaken hands with a demoralized Sidney team, we boarded the bus for the ride back to school.

I decided to have some fun when Dad asked how the golf match went on the way home.

I replied, "Our team won, but I didn't do as well as I hoped."

"Well, there is always next week unless they decide to drop you from the team."

"Dad, I didn't do that bad."

"I know you, scoundrel. George Weaver called and wanted to know how we felt about you setting a course record."

Note to self: you can't do anything in this town without your parents finding out immediately.

I kicked around with Denny and Eddie for the rest of the afternoon. They were passing a football back and forth. Both were better than me.

Dinner was spaghetti, a family favorite. Mary ended up red-faced. Not embarrassed. Sauced! I shared that funny remark and was surprised at my parents' silence.

Dad finally said, "When you said sauced, I thought you meant drunk."

"Oh no, Dad, I meant sauce all over her face."

"This is a good time to tell you. I have been going to AA for three months now and haven't had a drop to drink."

"Dad, that is great. I'm happy for you and Mum."

It was awkward until Mum suggested a family game of Monopoly after dinner. We all played, Mary and me a team, Mum and Dad a team, with Denny and Eddie each on his own.

No one threw a tantrum on the board for a change, so we had a good time. Mary and I were the winners. I suspect it was because Mum and Dad seemed more interested in each other than the game.

Sunday, I helped Dad with the Detroit Street house. It was almost ready to rent. He had steamed all the wallpaper off the living room walls. He counted fourteen different layers of paper in the last sixty years. He had to replace some of the laths and put up new plaster.

While he cleaned up the mess, I used the push mower we had brought. Tapp Realty was ready to rent the house out; ads would run next week in the *Examiner*.

In bed that night, I reflected on the past week. It had been so busy; I just hoped next week would be calmer.

That night I started a book about a Russian family during and after the Napoleonic Wars. It didn't take me long to go to sleep.

Chapter 30

Monday, I crawled out of bed feeling a little dizzy. Last week had been a busy week, and I didn't feel rested even after a good night's sleep. By the time I had performed my morning exercises and finished my run, I was ready for the day. Mum switched breakfast over to porridge since the mornings were cooler.

The round box said, "Quaker Oats Oatmeal."

If Mum wanted it to be porridge, it was porridge. No matter what you called it, it was warm and filling. Put enough brown sugar on it, and it even tasted good.

Tom and Bill were coming down the walk as I came out the door. The conversation was about the dinner and dance. Bill bragged about the way Nancy kissed him. He made some other comments about what they had done that hadn't any relation to reality.

Tom and I both tried to tell him to tone it down. If he spread that sort of stuff, the girls wouldn't go out with him. Bill didn't seem to get it as his story got bigger.

Classes were back to normal after the hectic homecoming week. While classes may have been normal, the rumor mill was working overtime discussing who broke up over the weekend and what new couples had emerged. The limo was considered the neatest item of the weekend. Already girls were talking about a limo for prom.

What interested me was that Janet was getting credit for dinner and the limo. She had managed her date well.

As far as I was concerned, the best thing about all the conversations was that my name didn't come up alone. Tom and Bill would get equal billing with me even when talking about the limo.

A few people said to me "Go, Bellefontaine!" for beating Sidney in golf, but nothing was said about a course record. That would appear in the Monday edition of the *Examiner*. On Sunday, there wasn't a paper, so that the record wouldn't be common knowledge until Tuesday.

Going from Algebra to Latin, I met Janet in the hallway. She gave me a cheerful "Hi," but didn't stop. I returned the greeting and kept moving. This established that we were now friends and nothing more.

Lunch was more of the same; but one of the seniors stopped at our table.

"Hey guys, I saw you at the country club with your dates and then getting out of that limo at the dance. You are making it hard on us normal people."

Since this was said with a smile, we took it as a compliment.

Bill had to add, "It was worth it for how the girls treated us." He leered as he said it.

Tom and I just shook our heads.

Tom added, "Well, how some of us *thought* we were treated."

When the senior left, Bill took Tom to the task.

"I'm trying to build up the gang's reputation. All the girls want to be with real men."

Bill found out how much his reputation had built up right after lunch. As we left the school to take a walk, a very sore Nancy Sparks caught up with us. She started to berate Bill for all the lies he told about her. Tom and I looked at each other and took off walking, leaving Bill to his fate.

Golf practice was different. All the other guys could talk about was the course record. They had to replay every stroke while we practiced putting. Coach Stone had us putting more and more. He would add in some little tricks, like how to hit the ball around a tree.

He had us point the clubface where we wanted to hit the ball. We would then line our bodies up where we wanted the ball to start. Next, we would swing along our body line.

The ball would then curve around the tree and end up where we had aimed the clubface. The same principle would work to draw the ball right or fade it left around a dogleg, gentle curves, but not a sharp turn.

Practice went well. Various members of the club stopped to congratulate me on the new record. After his congratulations, Doctor Costin gave me an update on the Suttons.

They were expected to recover.

"I know that your club membership only extends for the school golf season. If you want to join the club, I would be proud to sponsor you."

I replied, "Thank you, Doctor. It's expensive. How old do you have to be?"

"Hmm, good question Rick. I don't know, and I'm on the board of directors. I will look into that."

I had a small surprise when I got home. My industrial dryer had arrived. A special mail truck dropped it off at the house and I had never seen a one-dollar stamp on a package before. It must have weighed forty pounds!

I took it into the garage and opened the package on the workbench that Dad and Uncle Jim had moved it from the Detroit Street house. I opened the package and realized it wouldn't work as I thought.

The motor and heater were in a unit that weighed thirty pounds. The handheld dryer portion was connected by a heavy rubber hose and weighed over ten pounds. That was just too much weight to handle comfortably.

I found an extension cord and plugged the dryer in. The air on the one-speed unit was too hot and too fast. I would either burn myself or blow away. What a waste of money.

At dinner, I related how the unit wasn't as I thought.

My brother Denny asked, "Well if it is too hot and too much air, can't you make a smaller one?"

"I don't know, Denny."

Dad spoke up, "What do you need to know to make it work?"

"How hot the air should be and how fast the air should blow. I could determine what size of motor and heater I would need from that. From there, I could tell if it could be made light enough to use."

"There you go then."

Mum spoke up, "You could ask Sharon Bailey about her hair dryers."

Sharon Bailey owned a local hair salon.

Thanks, Mum, "I will do that after school one day soon."

I continued my slog through the Russian novel that night. Before it was over, I was cheering for Napoleon, though I knew he wouldn't win.

At breakfast, I told Mum I would try to see Mrs. Bailey after golf practice. Mum told me she would call her about expecting me with questions about her hairdryers.

Chapter 33

I started taking the industrial hairdryer apart after dinner that night. I was interested in how it was wired. In my notebook, I drew a schematic of the electrical wiring. I also noted the model numbers of the fan, motor, and switches.

The switching was the most interesting. It looked like it would be right at home inside an old vacuum tube radio I owned.

I wondered if the on-off, fan speed, and heat controls I was thinking of could be transistorized.

I would like to have a high and low-speed fan, and the same for heat. That would give four combinations for the user.

I remembered the movie set makeup artists who dealt with many hairstyles needed options. They called themselves artists, and at first, I laughed. After seeing what they had to achieve, I quit laughing.

The current would run through a basic dipole switch, either on or off for the on-off. The current would have to be directed through a transistor that would send it to one of two resistors. This would then regulate the current sent to the nichrome wire, which would control the heat generated. There would be a similar arrangement to the fan controlling the speed.

I knew I probably didn't have the circuit completely correct, but I knew someone to help me. My electricity merit badge counselor Mr. Robinson would be the man. Mr. Robinson was an avid HAM radio operator and built stuff.

I had a HAM license, but he was far ahead of me in the actual building of electronics. He was my Elmer when I first started.

Later I went in for some lighter reading. That Russian novel, or whatever the author wanted to call it, had just about done me in. I went back to one of my old favorites from my bookshelf. The two brothers doing detective work was exactly my speed tonight.

Saturday, we met at the school at seven o'clock for the one-hour bus trip to the Northmoor Golf Club near Grand Lake St. Mary's. I had to remember to tell Mary she had a lake named after her; she would like that. I hoped we weren't spoiling her.

The match was never in doubt. Gary Matthews was the only team member who lost to his Celina competitor by only one stroke. I tore the course up.

When I got to the dreaded 613-yard sixteenth hole of the Red Course, I hit a drive that rolled on the flat hard fairway. It ended up being a 305-yard drive, my best.

Then my second shot with a 3-wood was another 300 yards ending up two feet from the hole. I never did understand how it went so far. Coach said I must have been charged up. I was never able to hit a 3-wood like that again. It was an easy putt for my first-ever Eagle.

Our team lead was so great that the Celina boys were even excited for me by this time. After the match, while having a soft drink at the refreshment area named the Nineteenth Hole, the club pro told me that only happened once or twice a season. I ended up with a 67, which was four under par for the course.

Dad had good news at dinner that night. We had rented out the North Detroit Street house for seventy-five dollars a month. With this start, he now intended to start looking for duplexes in town that he could buy, repair, and rent out.

I wondered if they could buy, repair, and sell them quickly, making a good turnaround profit. I brought this up to Dad, who turned the idea down after thinking about it for a moment. He would rather work towards long-term income.

I continued reading old favorites, this time with a young inventor and his flying machine. I chose the original stories; they had been redone with the inventor's son, but I liked the original better.

Reading the story reminded me of my decision to learn to fly one day. I needed to check into that. I would go out to Tanger Field and see what lessons cost when the golf season was over.

Sunday was a lazy day at the Jackson household. My dad drove down to Jackson's Newsstand and bought a *Columbus Dispatch*. The newsstand owner was no relation. The George Weaver piece wasn't in the paper, which disappointed Mum and Dad, but not me. I was glad for a rest from the recent notoriety.

Later, Tom and I walked downtown to Isley's Restaurant. It was a combination of a cafeteria and an ice cream parlor. It was a Sunday destination for the high school crowd. None of the kids we ran around with were there, so we bought a cone and walked to the Holland Theater. Nothing was playing that interested us, but I got excited to see that *It Never Happened*, the movie I was in with John Wayne and Elvis, would be showing next week.

We walked home, taking the long way through Mary Rutan Park. We both agreed that life in Bellefontaine could be boring. That boredom lasted until we ran into Sue Barton and the dark-haired, full-figured Pam Schaffer walking back to the "Heights," as our neighborhood was called.

Pam walked with me, and Sue with Tom. We talked about nothing and everything. Pam got very animated when she talked about the Drama Club. They were getting ready to start cast selection for the spring play they would be putting on in early May.

"Rick, you should try out!"

I didn't commit immediately. I told Pam I would think about it.

She countered with, "I wish you would. We would have fun being together."

Now I was interested. It had gone from being in a play to spending time with an extremely cute girl who was showing interest.

I asked, "When are tryouts?"

"The casting call is next Tuesday immediately after school," replied the veteran actress.

"I will talk to Coach Stone and see if I can miss practice. When will rehearsals start?"

"We start memorizing our lines immediately but don't get together for our first rehearsal until November."

"Great. Golf season will be over. I think I would like to do this and spend time with you."

"That would be great, Ricky," responded Pam with a voice that would be described as sultry when she grew up.

"What do we do at this casting call?" I inquired.

"You will be given some lines to read. Our Drama Coach Mrs. Hadley looks for people who can give the proper inflection, then selects the best person for the part."

"What is the play?"

"*Our Town* by Thornton Wilder, I bet you will get the role of George, and I will be Emily. The story revolves around their lives."

"I will give it a try. Where do we meet?"

"We meet after sixth period in the auditorium."

We arrived at a corner; the girls went one way and us boys another. When they were a little way down the street, I looked back at Pam. She was looking back at me. This was a good sign!

When I got home, I rummaged through all the bookshelves in the house, but they had nothing by Thornton Wilder. The encyclopedia did describe the play with its plot and roles. I made a mental note to look it up in the school library.

That night I reread an old favorite about some really little people followed by giants and intelligent horses. When reading this time, I tried to understand what the author was trying to say. I got the political satire part and loved the peeing to put out the fire. The intelligent horses meant nothing to me. Luckily that night, my last thoughts before drifting off to sleep were of Pam rather than horses.

Chapter 34

Monday was a windy day, and I didn't want to run, but it wasn't raining, so out I went. I still couldn't do my five miles faster than thirty minutes, but I wasn't winded at the end. I also increased my sit-ups and pushups to one hundred each. I felt like I was in fairly good shape but decided to look for other exercises.

Breakfast was quiet except for a little bickering between Denny and Eddie. They did that so much that no one even noticed. Mary was still asleep. Dad was deep in thought as he drank his coffee.

Mum asked me, "Rick, what are your plans for this week?"

"Golf practice every day, but I have to ask Coach if I can skip Tuesday for Drama Club tryouts. I have to call Mr. Robinson to see if he would review the electrical circuit for the hairdryer."

"So long as you keep dinner open on Saturday."

I knew exactly what that was all about but said, "Our golf tournament is in Columbus; we leave early but finish late so we will have to stay overnight."

"Richard Edward Jackson, you will be home for your birthday party on Saturday!" Mum exploded.

I just grinned.

She realized I had gotten her and started laughing, "You little so and so; you will pay for that."

Birthdays at our house had always been small private parties. Not even cousins were invited, just our immediate family. We had always given each other gifts, even if Mum and Dad had to take us shopping and pay for them.

"We play Marysville on Saturday here, so I should be home by three o'clock at the latest."

"I'm still considering Tam Tattler's Tart for your dessert," threatened Mum.

"Oh, not that!"

There is no such thing as Tam Tattler's Tart. Mum always threatened us with it. She swore that she and her sister Mary had been acting up at dinner once, so my Grandmum had told them they deserved Tam Tattler's Tart. After dinner, they sat at the table expectantly, waiting for their dessert.

After a while, they went to the kitchen and asked where the Tam Tattler's Tart was. Grandmum told them there was no such thing, and they were getting what they deserved. Mum never did that to us, but we knew we were on thin ice when it was offered.

"Pax. I surrender."

I learned Pax in Latin. Mum learned it in school, Pax Britannia.

I watched Tom and Bill coming down the walk before I went out the door. Tom and I had been going places together, but we hadn't seen much of Bill lately. Bill calmly pulled out a pack of Lucky Strikes and a lighter as we walked along.

"Bill, what are you doing?" a shocked Tom asked.

Every kid I knew had tried a cigarette at one time or the other, but to light one up on the way to school put you in another social class, and it wasn't a move up.

Bill belligerently told Tom, "I'm tired of being seen as a little kid."

"Now, you will be seen as a stupid kid," I replied. "Have you read in the paper how they can cause lung cancer?"

"That happens to old people. I will have stopped by then. If you guys don't like it walk with someone else, I'm heading down to Wilcox's anyway."

Wilcox's is the corner grocery store that is just far enough from the school that teachers ignored the kids hanging out down there. It is a rougher crowd, not bad as in delinquent, usually the guys taking shop class and their girls. Most of them smoked, and it was well known that girls who smoked were wilder than those who didn't. I have no idea how this was established, but it was regarded as gospel.

"Bill, do you think that is such a good idea?" I tried to reason.

"You guys can still get dates. I can't. That skag Nancy Sparks has told everyone I have a big mouth, so none of the girls I ask out will date me."

"How many did you ask?" inquired Tom.

"I asked about twenty girls in our class if they would like to go to the movies with me. They all said no, and the last couple just laughed at me."

Tom and I looked at each other; we had no idea what else to say but knew Bill was going down a bad path. It wasn't just the smoking. It was the whole attitude he was developing.

Tom and I walked to school while Bill headed to Wilcox's. Talking while we walked, Tom and I admitted that we had tried a cigarette when we were thirteen, and it was terrible.

Tom also wondered what his first taste of beer would be like. I kept my mouth shut. Beer was also terrible. I had one with Tab Hunter and Elvis Presley down in Mexico and didn't care for it.

Classes were all reviewed for our six-week exams, which would be given on Thursday and Friday. To say I was bored was mild. The only interesting part of the day was Algebra. Sue Barton told me that Pam Schaffer was excited about the play and liked me.

I tried to slow this down. "Sue, I have to try out for the part and get it. Before I can even do that, I have to get Coach Stone's permission to skip golf practice. I'm glad Pam likes me, and I like her, but we really don't know each other that well and have just begun to talk."

"Oh, she knows she will like you very well. You take girls on the neatest dates."

At that point, the bell rang for class to start. I was glad it had; I didn't like the feeling that I might be being used.

Tom and I met for lunch, but Bill didn't show up. He must have gone to Wilcox's to buy lunch, smoke, and be with his new friends, whoever they were.

Pam Schaffer and Sue Barton stopped by our table as we were finishing. Pam was all excited about the Drama Club tryouts. I told her I had found a copy of *Our Town* in the school library.

"Rick, you will know the story but not the lines. The book is different from the script. Your reading will be from the script, not the book."

"Since I can read, that shouldn't be a problem," I told Pam.

"It's harder than you think, Rick. You have to know the person's mood and inject that into the reading."

"Okay, I will keep that in mind as I read."

"I wish I had a copy of the script so that we could practice, but they don't hand them out until you have the part."

During my study halls and classes, I started reading ahead and working on problems for the next six weeks. If I kept this up, I might have the year done by Christmas. That was a nice thought, but I was only running a week ahead of my classes.

On the bus going to golf practice, I asked Coach about missing one practice. You would have thought I was asking for his firstborn.

That was until he started laughing. "Rick, I think we can let you off just this once."

The practice was putting, sand traps, sand traps, and putting for variation. I would complain if asked, but I could see an enormous improvement in these areas since I had started playing.

When I got home, I called Mr. Robinson and asked him if I could come over some evening to review a control circuit schematic I had laid out. He was enthusiastic in his response. He liked anything working with electricity. He asked if I could come over after dinner. Mum said okay, so I told him I would be there around six-thirty.

Dinner was Swiss steak and mashed potatoes, one of my favorites. Halfway through dinner, the phone rang. Mum answered it. She kept saying "yes, yes, yes, that is me." She was still on the phone as I was leaving to see Mr. Robinson. Whoever it was, they were asking her a lot of questions.

I was at Mr. Robinson's for over an hour. After he was satisfied that he knew what I was trying to achieve, he went through my circuit in great detail and suggested several changes.

Once we both agreed on a finished diagram, he redrew it for me. He then signed and dated it; he also printed his name, with Electrical Engineer behind it, and his license number.

"Rick, when you sell your hairdryers, I expect five hundred dollars for this work."

He appeared to be joking, but I treated it very seriously.

"Yes, sir, I will do that. Do you want your name on the patent as a co-inventor?"

He laughed and said, "No, most inventions don't make any money for the inventor, so I will just take the money."

I asked for a blank sheet of paper and wrote down the terms of our deal. He was to receive five hundred dollars for consulting on the electrical portion of this project but wasn't a co-inventor. I had just read about doing this in a Tom Swift book.

"Rick, I am glad to see you are serious, and I wish you the best of luck. You know, having the idea is only the first step. You have to manufacture the product and then sell it. That is not easy, my lad."

"Yes, sir, but I am determined."

"Good for you."

Chapter 35

When I got home, Mum was still on the phone, talking a mile a minute. Dad had made her a cup of tea. She had been crying with tears from her eyes and had wads of handkerchiefs, but she was happy now, almost to hysteria.

She talked for another half hour and finally wound down. When she hung up, she told Dad that it was Bets. He told her he had figured that out. The other kids were in watching TV.

Mum poured boiling water over another teabag.

"That was my friend from the war, Betsy. She was my ambulance driver."

We all knew Mum had been a first aider in the British Women's Land Army during the blitz in World War II.

She continued, "Betsy and I were great friends and had a good time together. Then I was transferred to Grays in Essex, where I met your father. She's your godmother Ricky.

"The last time I saw or heard from her was on VE Day. Our wartime duties prevented us from contacting each other. After the war, I came here, and she was busy.

"She saw that article in the *Daily Mail* about our family. All the names matched, so she had someone check on us. When it was confirmed who we were, she called."

Mum then went into the front room to the glass-faced locked cabinet where she kept her mementos, such as our bronzed baby shoes. She came back with a small, framed picture. It was a picture of two young women in shapeless coveralls. They had their arms around each other's backs and smiled for the camera. It was two beautiful young ladies in a horrible time.

"Rick, this is your godmother, Elizabeth Windsor."

She had a second picture that I had never seen before.

"This picture was taken at your baptism by the Church of England at Gravesend. This is the same church where Pocahontas is buried."

My dad was in uniform, Elizabeth Windsor in a nice hat and dress. Mum was holding me in her arms. There was also a man dressed as an American general.

"Mum, why is Eisenhower in this picture?"

"He was the only one they could get to balance Betsy."

"Balance Betsy?" I asked.

"Your father was going to ask his captain to do the honors, but when they found out Princess Elizabeth would be your god mother, they thought someone of higher rank should perform the duty."

As Mum would say, I was gobsmacked, "You mean to tell me that Queen Elizabeth and President Eisenhower are my god parents?"

"Yes, and ten cents will get you a cup of coffee."

"Wow!" was all I could say.

"When Betsy read that article, she had her embassy in Washington check us out to see if we were the same Jacksons she knew. She originally knew me as Peggy Newman, my maiden name."

"Wow!" was all I could still say.

Mum went on to tell stories of some of the things she and Betsy did during the war. One night they were on a train to Grays. A Canadian soldier, a good-looking young man with very curly hair, was passed out drunk. There was no one else in their car, so they clipped all his curls using their nail scissors. They didn't brush the curls off so that when he stood up, he would shed hair everywhere.

They exited at the next stop. In Canada, a middle-aged ex-soldier tells his family about the night he got so drunk his hair fell off.

"Wow!" was all I could still say.

That night I had a hard time going to sleep. I couldn't even settle down and read. Trying to imagine my Mum as a young lady and running around with a princess doing crazy things was insane. This was nothing I could share with my friends, but it was so neat!

It was raining too heavily in the morning to run. My running days were coming to an end until spring. I would miss that. Breakfast was a slight rehash of last night. Mum and Dad impressed upon us that this wasn't to be shared outside of the family.

Denny nodded solemnly. Eddie and I both said, "Yes, Mum."

Mary didn't understand what had gone on, but she proudly told Mum, "I won't tell anyone you and the princess cut the soldier's hair off."

Mum and Dad exchanged looks. We were all glad that no one would know what Mary was talking about. Talk she would.

Dad loaded us boys into the Buick Roadmaster and dropped us off at our schools. The car was big enough he could have hauled the whole football team. It was cool looking though, blue and white with portholes on the sides of the engine cover. The tires were huge white walls. It was spiffy.

The school was half empty today; the flu had started going around early this year. I heard one teacher tell another that thirty percent of the students were absent. It would be a mess with so many kids missing their six-week exams.

After school was the tryouts for the Drama Club spring play. I went to the auditorium and there were quite a few kids there. Actors mustn't get sick.

A senior student-directed all aspiring actors and actresses to sit in the front row. The Drama Coach and tenth-grade English teacher Mrs. Ramsey sat several rows behind us in the auditorium center. She had a clipboard to take notes and a copy of the script.

After sitting there for a few minutes, she stood and announced, "The first person at the end of the row will be given a copy of what they are to read on stage. There are two parts. The first is male; boys are to read this part. The second is marked female; the girls are to read that part.

"When the first person goes on stage, they hand the pages to the person sitting next to them. There will be another copy to read from when they get on stage. Announce your name and then start reading the lines.

"After reading, leave the copy on the stand where you found it. Then take a seat anywhere but the front row. In the meantime, the next person will have a chance to read over their lines while waiting. Is this clear?"

I thought it was clear as mud. I was really glad I wasn't first. Once it started, it went smoothly. Well, as far as getting kids up on stage with a script in their hands. I couldn't believe how poorly some read, not in acting, just in their ability to read.

I was finally the next to read, so the pages were handed to me to study. I read them to myself, trying to understand the scene's emotion. I had also listened to others deliver the same lines. It sounded like the person I would be playing was raging against the injustice of his wife dying.

It was time for me to walk up on stage. Boy, that was a different feeling, all eyes on me, waiting for me to say something. I stood there.

Finally, Mrs. Ramsey said, "You may want to announce your name, then pick up the script and start reading."

I wished l could sink into the stage at that moment.

I managed to read the lines, putting all the passion into the lines I could. I then went to sit with Pam, who had already read her lines. She nodded but didn't seem excited to see me.

I whispered that she had done great and was certain she would get the lead. She nodded her head in thanks or agreement but said nothing about my reading.

Finally, all had read. Some students had left, but most had stayed to see if they would get a part. Mrs. Ramsey spent about fifteen minutes with her notes and finally stood.

She announced, "The cast is as follows, Pam Schaeffer will play Emily. Sam Shepard is George."

She went on to name the rest of the cast.

My name wasn't read as an actor.

Mrs. Ramsey told us, "If your name wasn't readout for the cast, we still need stagehands. Please see me if you are interested."

I turned to congratulate Pam, but she was gone. She was on the other side of the auditorium, speaking to Sam.

I approached Mrs. Ramsey; she asked if I wanted a stagehand position. I told her no. I just wanted to know what was so bad about my reading. She asked my name and looked at her notes.

She smiled and said, "That was the most over-the-top reading I have ever heard. Please don't take offense, but I don't think the stage or screen is in your future."

I managed to nod my head and walk away.

Chapter 36

I was humiliated. I was fuming mad; I had to get out of there without opening my mouth. What would come out would get me in big trouble. I wanted to cry. I wanted to get even. I wanted to run away.

How could I ever face the world again? As I walked home in the rain, I had visions of taking Mrs. Ramsey to the Holland Theater this weekend to see me on the big screen in *It Never Happened*.

Of course, all she would see was me falling off a horse. Okay, I would get her to watch *Spin and Marty* when it was on the air. But she would see me riding a bull, then trying to force myself on Annette the first time she talked to me.

If I took her to see *Hell Fighters*, she would briefly glimpse me working on an oil rig. Okay, I would join the Marines; that would show them!

By the time I walked home, I had figured out how ridiculous I was being. It started to strike me as being funny. When I walked into the kitchen where Mum was working on dinner, she asked me what I was smiling about. I told her everything about how I tried to inject passion into my reading.

How badly it came across, the stupid thoughts I had on the way home. Then I realized that it was no big deal, and I should forget it just like Pam appeared to forget me.

Mum's face looked like a lightbulb had come on.

She said, "I'm so glad I'm not your age. I would never want to live through that again."

"Live through what?" I brilliantly asked.

"Being a teenager with all those hormones running amok," she replied.

She then changed the subject.

"Wait here. I have some things to show you." She went into the front room where her cabinet was and returned with a spoon and a cup.

These were special items. Both were made out of silver. The spoon handle was engraved "To my Godchild Richard Edward Jackson from HRH Princess Elizabeth of Great Britain" on the back. The cup was engraved "To my Godchild Richard Edward Jackson from Dwight David Eisenhower, Commander in Chief Allied Forces, General of the Army USA."

"These are yours, but they should be kept locked up. One day they may be of great value."

"Mum, would you keep them for now? And I don't care how much value they may have. They belong with the family forever."

"I'll keep them for you, Richard. When I see the fine young man and how you behaved today in the face of great disappointment, I am almost ready to forgive you for how you were born."

Mum had never forgiven me, no matter what she said, about my timing in being born. It was in the middle of an air raid. She couldn't be moved while in labor, so I was born in her bed upstairs as the bombs fell. They destroyed the house across the street, blew our door open, and broke all the windows. You would think she would get over it.

At dinner that night, I shared with the rest of the family how I had stunk up the stage. Denny and Eddie thought it was funny. Mary wanted to punch the old meanie who didn't like my acting. Dad laughed about it but didn't make a big deal about it, so that was good.

Dad had news to share with the family. It was several pieces of news. First of all, he had made an offer on a duplex through Tapp Realty, and it was accepted. He hoped to complete the purchase by Thanksgiving and start work on renovations.

His second news was that we were getting a TV antenna! The installers will be here tomorrow to erect a tower for the antenna. It would connect to a box on top of the TV. By turning a knob, you would be able to change the direction of the antenna and improve the picture.

It would be so much better than the rabbit ears that we had to move around all the time. The ears worked better when Dad wrapped them with aluminum foil, but they still had problems. Mum thought it would be great if we could watch all three channels just by turning the antenna.

The events of the day left me very tired. I went to bed and fell asleep without reading.

Wednesday, I was up and at it. The rain had passed through, and we had another beautiful fall day. Mum had the radio on when I came in from my run. They were interviewing Ohio State Coach Woody Hayes.

Woody was predicting they would beat Illinois this Saturday at Champaign.

He said, "It will be fullback Bob White in three yards and a cloud of dust," when asked his strategy. We will bring the Illibuck Trophy home again."

When asked if there would be a repeat trip to the Rose Bowl, he replied, "Of course, after beating Michigan."

(Ed. Note: They beat Illinois that week and brought the carved wooden turtle home. Bob White had another good week running. They did beat Michigan but didn't go to the Rose Bowl.)

I went out the door and I saw Tom coming. We hadn't seen Bill for a while. I didn't know when or how Bill was getting to school.

Tom's first words were, "Did you hear about Bill?"

"No, what happened?"

"He and a couple of other guys got caught by the police in Mary Rutan Park Saturday night. They were drinking beer. Bill was drunk and took a swing at one of the cops. He didn't hurt the cop when he hit him, but the cop hit Bill with his nightstick and broke his arm. His parents are talking about sending him to a Military Academy to get him out of town."

"Where is he now?"

"At home. He is not allowed out until after his court date. The police wanted to put him in jail on the assault charge, but his Uncle Tom Patterson, the County Prosecutor, was able to get house arrest."

"That's too bad, but he is having some problems."

"Yeah, I tried to call him, but his parents wouldn't let me talk to him. They said they didn't want him to associate with anyone who helped him get in trouble."

"That's not fair! You had nothing to do with it."

"I know. Some blame a woman, Nancy Sparks, but it's his own damn fault."

Of course, Bill was the talk of the school. Before the day was over, I heard he had tried to shoot a policeman but shot himself in the arm instead.

It was also a day of review for the upcoming tests. I kept working ahead on the next six weeks.

Chapter 37

Golf practice was a surprise. Putting! We did spend some time on the driving range, but most of it was putting. Coach also started talking about the Sectional Tournament at Bowling Green, Ohio. It will be played at the Stone Ridge Golf Course.

Stone Ridge is 7054 yards from the gold tees. So, while not a long course, it is still within the range that professional golfers play. There would be one team from each school.

The team that wins the tournament will advance to the Districts. The four top individuals will also advance. At the district level, it is the same advancement to the state.

That way, if the team doesn't make it to the State Championship, the top individuals still have a chance of competing and winning. Coach was looking straight at me when he said that. No pressure here.

Dinner was spaghetti which we all loved and to top it off Mum had made a trifle. Her version was a biscuit base covered by a can of fruit cocktail topped with vanilla pudding. She let the canned fruit juices soak into the biscuit before she poured the hot vanilla pudding, then it was allowed to set up. This was my favorite dessert of all time.

That night I read about a guy who didn't age but had a picture in his attic that did. It was creepy but kind of neat.

Thursday was cool but clear so I could run once more. The radio this morning was talking about Bobby Fischer winning the United States Chess Championship at age 14. I hadn't paid any attention to that, but that explained why the Chess Club at school had gotten so popular. I played, but nowhere near that well.

The six-week tests were a yawn. My biggest problem was with American History. There were one hundred and fifty questions. They were all fill-in-the-blank questions. I finished one hundred and forty-nine of them in thirty minutes and sat there for the next fifteen minutes to remember who wrote *Uncle Tom's Cabin*. Of course, right after turning my test in, I thought of Harriet Beecher Stowe.

Golf practice was on the front nine. It was fun since there were few people on the course. The fairways and greens were pretty beat up from the summer, but the rough's condition wasn't too bad. It was rough as usual.

It certainly added a dimension when my putt would take an unexpected bounce or change direction because of a previous ding in the green. I would have to pay special attention to this on Saturday.

At dinner Denny announced he would try out for the junior high basketball team. We thought he would do well; his accuracy was incredible. Eddie was chomping at the bit for his time to play. He was just as accurate as Denny and would be taller.

Mary was noticeably quiet. Mum asked her why she wasn't talking.

Mary asked, "Mum, do they have teams for princesses in school?"

Mum thought and told her, "Yes, they do. They are called cheerleaders."

"Then I will be a cheerleader."

We all agreed she would be the best cheerleader ever. What sort of monster were we creating?

After dinner, I went to my room and brought out a set of pom-poms for Mary. They were the stick type with long thin slices of paper, half the paper black, half red, the Bellefontaine High School colors.

They were handed out in the stands at every football game. I proceeded to teach Mary several simple cheers. She may end up a monster, but she will always be my baby sister.

That night I read some funny stories by an old Englishman who spoke weirdly. Some words did not even seem to be English. They were tales about a group of travelers on a pilgrimage to a town. They named a ghost after the town later on, or maybe the town was named after the ghost. I saw that in a movie on TV.

Friday was nice, but we had a hard frost that night. Dad called it a killing frost as the bugs would all die. It made running a pleasure once I warmed up.

School was okay. More tests. During the morning walk with Tom, I asked him if he knew anything more about Bill. He didn't. The only time they saw anyone from the family was Bill's dad as he went back and forth to his job as a supervisor at Detroit Aluminum and Brass.

Golf practice was the back nine today. Again, it was laid back and easy as we had the course to ourselves. I did run into Dr. Costin in the clubhouse when we were finished. He told me he had checked, and there was no age limit on membership. Just have a sponsor and the money.

I told him I would think about it. It would be good to be able to play here when the school golf season is over. However, I didn't plan to stick around next summer.

I didn't know where I would go yet, but I had some thoughts percolating. I didn't even have a girlfriend to bring to the restaurant for dinner. All in all, I wasn't certain there was a need.

I talked about it with my parents at dinner. Dad thought for a while.

"If this rental business goes well, I could see it as a useful business tool for the contacts. That would mean I would have to be a member and have a full family membership. Why don't you hold off till next season, and we see how things go?"

That made sense to me.

That night I finished up the *Canterbury Tales*. I also figured out that it had nothing to do with the Canterville Ghost. Maybe I shouldn't believe everything I watched on the TV.

Before I fell asleep, I thought about Bill. After his rejection by the girls in our class for his loudmouth and exaggeration about Nancy, his reaction was to reject us all. His smoking, running with a different crowd, drinking beer, and attacking a police officer was certainly a rejection of our high school society.

How was that different than my initial reaction to not making the play? The only difference was I didn't act on my first impulse. Bill did, and now he was in a mess. Taking that together with Mum's comment about hormones running amok, I better watch my reaction to disappointment. The first action should always be to shut my mouth and think it through.

Chapter 38

Saturday morning, I was up bright and early as usual. I doubt if I could sleep in anymore, even if I wanted to. Dad was drinking his morning coffee as I came back from my run.

My cheerful "Good Morning" received a grunt in return.

I interpreted that to mean, "Shut up and leave me alone, you horrible cheerful person."

Taking this hint, I took my shower. I still couldn't figure out how to make the showerhead adjustable without leaking.

We met at the school for the bus to the country club. The whole team was up for the match with Marysville. We loosened up on the practice green and driving range.

The Marysville team started at the same time we did. In all the other golf matches we played, everyone was polite to each other. The Marysville group was different.

They started making comments about how they were going to kick our butts. Then they got personal about our appearances and how we hit the golf ball. If a ball went slightly wrong, they laughed and pointed out what losers we were. Our respective coaches were drinking a cup of coffee inside the club, so they heard none of this.

I hadn't hit anything other than my irons. I decided to keep it that way. I felt limber enough that I wouldn't use my driver until I teed off. My actions would be my statement. One by one, I pulled my teammates aside and explained my plan. We wouldn't respond to their taunts other than to beat the crap out of them.

Our team went from looking frustrated to almost smug. This got to the Marysville team, and they redoubled their efforts. The more they did, the less we said and the more we smiled. When we lined up for the tee toss to see who had the honors, we won with the tee pointing towards our team.

Since I currently had the best handicap, I was first up. The first hole was a three hundred and fifty-four dog leg to the right. I had tried the shot on Thursday, so I knew I could make it. I drove the ball, and it landed curving into the dogleg.

The ground was hard enough it rolled almost to the apron of the green. After my follow-through, I turned to the Marysville player who was up next and said, "Talk is cheap."

Even that comment was enough to get me taken aside by Coach and told to watch my sportsmanship.

My plan worked; the Marysville player badly shanked his shot to the left. It cleared the lady's tees enough that his teammates didn't have to tell him to wear a dress, but it was close.

John Scott from our team was up after that, and he hit a career distance line drive approaching 240 yards. That was the end of the day for Marysville.

Marysville never got its act together. Their coach started berating them to the point that we were embarrassed for the other team. At least we were learning where their speech habits were formed.

The icing on the cake was when we walked up to the first green. My ball had rolled directly in front of it. The hole was nicely centered in the front of the green that day, so I had an easy hit and ran up a slight slope for a two-under eagle.

My opponent had a double bogey. I want to say I set another course record that day. I didn't; I only tied it.

All four members of our team won our matches. What I found interesting was when we were shaking hands after the match, the Marysville team captain, who was looking down at his shoes, quietly said, "I'm sorry about the early talk. We were told it would mess your minds up and get you off balance for the match."

I took that to mean their coach had told them to use that garbage. Was garbage talk going to be the way games were played in the future? What lesson would that teach young athletes?

How they talked didn't matter. We won!

The ride back to town was loud and cheerful. John Scott filled Coach in on how Marysville had talked on the practice green.

Coach told us that he was proud of our reaction. He even forgave me for my comment on the first tee.

"Rick, at least you only made a general comment. It wasn't personal to anyone there."

Then he burst into a big smile and told me, "Good team leadership."

I hadn't told the team about my birthday, so I escaped without any big scenes. That all changed when I got home.

It started quiet with soup and hotdogs for lunch. After that, the house started smelling good as Mum baked my birthday cake. As usual, it was my favorite white cake with lots of icing. Of course, there would be ice cream with it.

While Mum was baking, Denny and Eddie were putting up streamers. Mary was already practicing pinning the tail on the donkey. She would need a blindfold and a tail to pin when it was time. In the meantime, Mary was nailing it with her finger. She never missed.

Dad was having another one of his thousand or so cups of coffee a day. It may not be that many, but it seemed like it. I was a disappointment to both Mum and Dad. I didn't like coffee or tea. Just don't get between me and a Nehi grape soda.

After lunch, it was time for the annual height measurement. I would be the first to be measured in this house. We would go to a closet at our old house and stand in the doorway, and Mum would mark off our height on the edge. She would then measure our height with a tape measure.

Our names, dates, and heights would then be written on the mark. My birthday was the first at our new home, so my mark was the first up in the hall closet.

I painted over the measurements on Detroit Street and remembered feeling funny about painting over our lives. Now a new tradition was starting. I started it out right. I had grown another inch.

I was now six foot three inches tall. That immediately got Dad dragged into the fray. We were placed back-to-back, with Mum holding a yardstick level. I was now taller than my dad. He reminded me he could still kick my butt. I didn't doubt that for a second.

Not to be left out, Mary showed us how she had grown. Since her birthday was in June, she wasn't eligible for official measurement. She showed the whole family that she could now sit at the table and eat using only the Sears & Roebuck catalog.

She had removed the thinner J.C. Penney catalog from the stack and was able to reach her plate simply fine. She would be able to remove the four folded brown paper shopping bags from under the Sears catalog very soon!

When the thundering herd went outside to play for the afternoon, Mum gave me two letters. This was unusual because we always opened and shared birthday cards at the party after dinner.

"I thought you should see these without the other kids present. What they don't know they won't talk about."

One was in a cream-colored envelope, and it was made of the fanciest paper I had ever held. I didn't know how to describe it, but you knew whoever used this paper was rich. Seeing the British stamps gave me a clue. The royal coat of arms of the United Kingdom on the back put all doubts to rest.

Mum handed me a letter opener. I didn't even know we owned one. I slit the envelope open, and there was a handwritten letter inside.

It was from Her Majesty Elizabeth the Second, by the Grace of God, of the United Kingdom of Great Britain and Northern

Ireland, and of Her other Realms and Territories, Queen, Head of the Commonwealth, Defender of the Faith.

At least she did not use her full title: Her Majesty Elizabeth the Second, by the Grace of God, of Great Britain, Ireland and the British Dominions beyond the Seas Queen, Defender of the Faith, Duchess of Edinburgh, Countess of Merioneth, Baroness Greenwich, Duke of Lancaster, Lord of Mann, Duke of Normandy, Sovereign of the Most Honourable Order of the Garter, Sovereign of the Most Honourable Order of the Bath, Sovereign of the Most Ancient and Most Noble Order of the Thistle, Sovereign of the Most Illustrious Order of Saint Patrick, Sovereign of the Most Distinguished Order of Saint Michael and Saint George, Sovereign of the Most Excellent Order of the British Empire, Sovereign of the Distinguished Service Order, Sovereign of the Imperial Service Order, Sovereign of the Most Exalted Order of the Star of India, Sovereign of the Most Eminent Order of the Indian Empire, Sovereign of the Order of British India, Sovereign of the Indian Order of Merit, Sovereign of the Order of Burma, Sovereign of the Royal Order of Victoria and Albert, Sovereign of the Royal Family Order of King Edward VII, Sovereign of the Order of Merit, Sovereign of the Order of the Companions of Honour, Sovereign of the Royal Victorian Order, Sovereign of the Most Venerable Order of the Hospital of St John of Jerusalem.

And that does not count the titles for seventeen other countries like Canada and Australia.

The handwritten note boiled down to birthday greetings from my sovereign. If I was ever in the area, pop in at Buckingham Palace or wherever she resided. There were so many castles and so little time.

The letter was much more formal and nicer, but that is what it said. I was to let the Palace know in advance. I suspect that was so I wouldn't be sent directly to the Tower and have my head chopped off. She also extended an offer to provide help where she could if I had problems. I can see it now, skipping school, getting caught, and having the Queen of England intercede. I had to share that thought with Mum.

"Richard Edward Jackson," she started.

Then stopped, "You little so and so, you have got me again. You are going to pay. Now, where is that chocolate icing?"

"No, Mum, not that, anything but that!" I cried!

I didn't mind chocolate icing; it just wasn't my favorite. It is not as though she had threatened to put ketchup on my hot dog. Only mustard will do.

I gave her the queen's letter to read. She handed me the other letter. It was a bright white envelope and easy to figure out.

It had a seal that said, "The President of the United States".

Carefully using the letter opener, I opened President Eisenhower's letter. I read it through completely. Dad wanted to know, "What does that strike breaker have to say?"

I handed him the letter to read.

President Eisenhower took the time to write. He explained that he barely remembered my baptism as he had many things on his mind (think the European Theater of World War II).

Somehow a follow-up note for my first birthday was never put on file. Because of this, no cards or greetings were sent. As the years went by, he had forgotten. Only a message from Queen Elizabeth and a search by an aide-de-camp had found a record of the event.

He wished me a happy birthday, and if I was ever in the area, pop into the White House after advance notification. I could see J. Edgar Hoover hauling me off to Alcatraz if I showed up unannounced. If there was anything within reason that he could do to help me, please let him know.

All in all, nice letters, but I doubted I would have the chance to pop into Buckingham Palace or the White House. Well maybe.

After a wonderful roast beef and mashed potato dinner, we had the ice cream and cake and did the usual butcher job singing "Happy Birthday".

I opened and shared the birthday cards from Dad's side of the family. Then the ones from Mum's side with exotic postage stamps. England, New Zealand, Trinidad, India, and Singapore included. After the war, Mum's brothers, sisters, and cousins spread worldwide.

When it was time to open presents, I first opened those from my brothers and sister. They bought me two new shirts. Mary told me I needed them because my others had ugly ink stains. Mum and Dad took care of the ink stain problem.

They presented me with a Gold Cross ballpoint pen and pencil set with my name engraved.

"These were expensive."

When I started to object, Dad said, "Ricky, we are sitting in this home because of you. We are working towards a more stable income because of you. I think we can afford it, and you deserve this."

That ended all my objections.

I was now officially fifteen years old.

Sunday, the whole family went to the movie to watch *It Never Happened*, starring John Wayne, Elvis Presley, and, if you looked fast at the end credits, Ricky Jackson. The family had been prepped for my big scene. I fell off the horse like a sack of potatoes, nothing graceful about it.

The horse dragged me along, bouncing my head off the ground. It was painful to watch even though I didn't get hurt. My siblings made so much noise other people sitting near us shushed them.

Mum took umbrage and told them her son was the one that had been dragged by the horse, and they would make noise if they wanted. We almost got asked to leave by the usher when he came down to see the commotion.

After things were explained in a low whisper, we were asked to see the manager after the show. The manager wanted me to sign the poster advertising the movie. They had heard a local was in the movie but weren't sure who.

We saw the marquee being changed as we left the Holland Theater with its moving clouds and turning windmills. My name was being added.

That night, I read about a deformed guy who rang bells in a church.

Chapter 39

Monday, I was ready for school and the week. This week was the start of the Ohio State Golf Tournament for boys. I practically flew around my five-mile run. My time was within seconds of normal. The day was bright and clear.

I was excited about going to Bowling Green; though I was born in England and traveled from there, it didn't count as I didn't remember it.

I had hitchhiked to California and gone coast to coast, but I still was excited about going someplace new to me. We would leave Thursday after school.

Breakfast was the normal chaos. Denny and Eddie argued over the better superhero, Saturn Girl or Lightning Boy. They had just recruited Super Boy to the Legion of Heros.

Dad wasn't there. He was working a freight train to Cleveland. He had left late last night and wouldn't be home till late tonight. I always thought it would be fun to ride in a caboose until I had the chance several years ago.

They are dirty, cold, and uncomfortable. I had to pee and use the toilet. When I flushed it, I realized the pee and anything else was dumped directly on the track.

I had asked Dad about that, and he told me that was why he hated passenger trains. Setting the airbrakes on a Pullman car was nasty as it had stuff all over the bottom of them. I would be glad when we owned enough rentals that he could quit the railroad.

I walked to school with Tom as usual. Neither of us had heard any more about Bill. He was being kept home until his case was resolved. We hoped he would be sent to a military academy rather than juvenile hall.

We then argued the merits of Culver Academy vs. Howe Military School. We had both done in-depth research by reading their small ads in the back of *Boy's Life*. I had the advantage of reading *The Black Horse of Culver* to win my argument easily.

I did wonder how the fiction I had read related to reality. I thought back to the winner's write history lesson, which I had learned. That didn't matter; I wouldn't let the lack of hard facts get in the way of winning such an important argument.

The school was busy, and the flu had run its course, so now we had almost a third of the school in a panic about taking makeup exams for their six weeks' grades. Mr. Gordon, the Principal, announced that all students needing to make up exams should report to their regular classroom where the tests would be administered.

Those who had taken their tests were to go to the auditorium and bring their books. I wondered how many who hadn't taken their tests would end up in the auditorium.

The auditorium was a mess. Everyone sat where they pleased and did nothing but talk. The monitoring teachers kept it to a dull roar. It was successful. There was only one pushing, shoving, and shouting match. I never did find out what it was about or who was involved. I spent my time reading. We were dismissed for our usual lunches and told to report back to the auditorium.

If we weren't taking exams, we didn't have to come to school the next day. However, for those children that hadn't anywhere else to go and their parents both worked, they could come and spend the day at the auditorium. I could think of three kids who might do it. They obeyed every other rule to the point of pain.

Golf practice was spent on the putting green and reviewing the Stone Ridge Golf Course layout. Coach had a nice large map, and we discussed how to play each hole, depending on our strengths. Coach passed out small notebooks to us that would fit in our shirt pockets.

Coach told us, "Write Stone Ridge Golf Course and October 1958 on the front cover and inside page. Saving two pages for each hole, number them one through eighteen, gold tees.

"Take notes today; add to them when we walk the course on Friday and later during Friday's practice round. Note the clubs you plan to use and update as you play. During the actual rounds, refer to these notes before you tee off. It will save you a lot of confusion in the heat of play."

It was similar to my inventor's notebook.

At dinner that night, I updated Mum on no school tomorrow. I asked if it would be okay to go downtown and shop for some new pants. After my birthday height measurement, I now realized that my current pants were too short.

She thought that would be a good idea.

"That reminds me; there was a call from Bush Electric; your order is here. You can pick it up anytime."

"That's good news. I'll do that."

After dinner, Denny, Eddie, and I played a little basketball, but it was getting dark earlier and earlier. We went in and watched *Robin Hood* on CBS. After that was *Burns and Allen*, but we didn't care for them. Their comedy was for old people. I read until lights out at ten o'clock.

I had checked a book out of the library on time travel. It had Eloi and Morlocks. It was a good story, but I didn't think the future would end up like that. I think the author was trying to make a political statement about class.

His statement was made within British Victorian society. I wonder what he would have made of America in the 1950s?

Dad was at breakfast in the morning. His train had gotten back from Cleveland a little while ago. He was about to get cleaned up and go to bed, but he first had to have a cup of coffee and a cigarette.

I woke up at my usual time even though I hadn't any school today. I told Dad about how the flu had messed up the school schedule. He told me that he had read that this was the worst flu season since 1918, when so many died. Dad's oldest brother died from it when he was a newborn in 1918.

The other kids managed to sleep in. Mum was doing the laundry using her new washer and dryer. That was so neat; the washer would spin water out of the clothes. The dryer would heat and spin them some more.

This beat the old way of hanging the clothes outside to dry after running them through the rollers on the washing machine tub to get rid of most water.

The rollers that squeezed the water out of the clothes were called mangles because they would mangle your arm if you were caught in between the rollers. When it was too cold outside, we would have laundry hanging all over the house.

I went out to the garage to the workbench and made a shopping list to take to Bush Electric. This comprised solid-state transistors, diodes, and resistors recommended by Mr. Robinson.

They would be used to make my control circuit for my hairdryer. I also need solder, flux, and a soldering iron to make the circuit. That Boy Scout Electricity Merit Badge was one of the better awards.

I read till ten o'clock, finishing up the book on time travel. I would drop it off when I went downtown. Maybe the library will have something new.

Tom knocked on the door just before I was ready to leave.

"What's up, Tom?"

"I wanted to see if you wanted to go downtown, maybe catch lunch at Don's?"

"I was about to run some errands downtown. Let me check with Mum about lunch."

Mum said it was fine with her to be back by dinner time.

Our first stop was the library to drop my book off. Mrs. Bush was back in the stacks, re-shelving books, so I checked in my book when I went in. I had this privilege from my paperboy days.

The library was on my route, so I was there every day. They soon got tired of me and taught me how to check my books in and out. Laura said this probably saved her a hundred hours a year.

This was an exaggeration, but I loved to hear her cute southern accent when she said it. There wasn't anything interesting on the new arrivals shelf.

We proceeded to Wolfheim's; Henry was there, as usual. He wouldn't make eye contact, just look at your feet. However, he had the best selection of clothes in town as far as teenagers were concerned.

He showed me a cool corduroy suit; it was black. He also had a red shirt that I could wear to ball games and pep rally days. I had to buy them even though the suit was sixteen dollars and the shirt three dollars. I already owned a black tie, so I was all set.

I think Tom was a little jealous of both the suits and that I had money to buy them, but he didn't say anything. Henry put the suit on a hanger with a paper bag over it.

He agreed to hold on to the items until we were ready to go home. We walked down to DeLong's record store and listened to some of the new releases. I bought a 45 of Peggy Sue by Buddy Holly.

Chapter 40

At DeLong's, I noticed "Rock and Roll Cowboy" had dropped completely off the charts. This was a mixed blessing. I hated the song after hearing it so many times, but I liked the money going to the Leukemia fund; also, this would give us a tax break. I said us on the tax break because, as a minor, everything had to go through my parents.

We stopped at Dee's Department Store. That place made me feel weird. It was mostly women's fashion but had some men's clothes, so I wanted to check them out. They had nothing that interested me. What was weird about the store was they only had one cash register. It was on a balcony that overlooked the entire store.

There was a system of tracks for each point of sale. The clerk would put the sales slip and cash in a little box and on the tracks. The tracks had cords turning that made a big loop.

The cords would take the box up to the balcony, where you would hear the big old brass register ring up the sale. The cords would then be reversed, and a paid-in-full sales slip would come back. There was a whole network of these. I thought of it as a big spider web, with the cash register being the spider in the center of the web.

We left there and crossed the street to Don's. We spent almost two hours there. Every kid who was out of school came and went. We got to Don's at about eleven-thirty to get a booth.

Lunch was hamburgers, fries, and a Coke. Later I had a butterscotch milkshake. Gary and Tim from the golf team joined us.

Half the kids in our high school came there for lunch that day. Unfortunately, no pretty girls asked to join us. I would have kicked Gary and Tim out if they had.

Pam Schaffer came in holding hands with Sam Shepard, and she didn't even look my way. I would have to become a big-time actor before she would notice me. But if I were a big-time actor, would I notice her?

After lunch, we worked our way back up the street. Stopping by Wolfheim's, I remembered my original mission had been to buy several pairs of pants. Instead, I bought a suit and a shirt.

Asking for his help, Henry helped me pick out a light and dark pair of chino pants. My waist size was still thirty inches, but my inseam was now thirty-four inches.

From there, we stopped at Bush Electric. Tom was at the counter and knew that I was there to pick up my order. I also placed a new order for solid-state transistors, diodes, and resistors. Tom suggested I buy the latest silicon transistors rather than germanium because they handled the heat better.

The fixed germanium diodes were still the best. The resistors that worked best for potentiometers were those made by Western Electric. I ended up ordering all Western Electric-made parts.

Bush had the flux, solder, and soldering iron in stock but agreed to hold them till the other parts were in. I ordered enough parts to build ten control sets for the hairdryer. While I was doing this, Tom was listening avidly.

He thought it was cool that I was trying to build something that would be of use. He agreed that anything was better than hearing his mother say, "You will catch your death."

I now had the motor, fan, and parts to build a heating element for my dryer. I could work on proper airflow and temperatures using the Variac controller.

The controller weighed about twenty pounds, so I cheated and paid for a taxi to take us home. The taxi service was only half a block away, so we walked there. John Sullivan was on duty.

Mr. Sullivan remembered me well. He told me they had bought a new limo, and it was booked up with enough weddings, dances, and other special events to pay for the first year. It looked like a money maker. He just hoped it didn't get lost in a card game. The ride home cost seventy-five cents and was well worth it.

When Tom and I got back to my house, Mum asked what clothes I had bought. When she saw the suit, I was ordered to try it on to make certain it fit. I had tried it on in the store, and it fit. But when Mum says, try it on, you try it on or beat a hasty retreat out the door.

The suit fit perfectly well, and Mum approved of its look. She also liked the red shirt that went with it for school spirit. The other pants also fit and passed muster. Once this was out of the way, I took my other purchases to the garage.

I had already collected vital elements; a small cigar box, a toilet paper roll, parts from my erector set, Popsicle sticks, a plugin lamp cord, and an extension cord.

Using my Barlow knife and a pair of tin snips, I cut the Popsicle sticks to make an "X," which would fit inside the toilet paper roll. I made two of these, inserting one at each end of the roll.

I then threaded two feet of nichrome wire back and forth on the "X", careful to leave both ends of the wire at the same end of the toilet paper roll. This would be my heating element.

I then cut a hole as close to the diameter of the toilet paper roll as I could in the short end of the cigar box. The box I had selected was about six inches in length and width. It was four inches high. I did a poor job of cutting and it ended up as a very ragged circle.

That was okay. I used one of Dad's ever-present rolls of duct tape to attach the toilet paper roll and close the gaps left by the ragged edges.

After installation, the toilet paper roll was now known as the barrel with a heating element installed. I sketched it in my notebook and labeled the parts. I also signed and dated the sketch.

Using parts of my erector set, I made a simple framework inside the cigar box to attach the fan and motor. The fan was attached to blow air through the barrel across the heating element.

The ends of the nichrome wires threaded through another hole I had cut in the cigar box at a right angle to the first hole.

I also cut two pieces of copper wire, attached them to the motor, and threaded them through the same hole as the nichrome wire.

I realized that I had bare wires which could touch each other and short out, so I took everything apart and wrapped the bare wires in some of Dad's electrical tape. I also made a note to buy more duct tape and electrical tape.

Dad got bent out of shape when his tools weren't replaced. He wouldn't like it if I used his stuff and didn't replace it.

After reassembling the unit, I attached the loose heating element wires and motor wires to the Variac. Using the extension cord, I plugged it into the outlet near the door to the house.

I took the time to wonder why garages only have one outlet in inconvenient spots.

The moment of truth had arrived. I turned the power on. Nothing happened, at least no sound from the fan running.

Turning the unit off, I saw the fan hadn't any electrical connection to the motor. I hadn't wired it. Disassembling it once more, I installed the wires after wrapping all but the ends in electrical tape.

After reassembling the unit, I turned it on. Success. Well, at least I could hear the fan running. As I stood there basking at the moment, the fan started to increase its pitch. It went from a low humming to a scream. Mum came out of the kitchen to see what was going on.

I had turned the Variac off by then.

Mum said, "I wondered what that sound was. It's like my Hoover when it gets clogged up."

A lightbulb came on. I cut vent holes in the lid of the box so the fan could get enough air.

Trying once more still had an increase in sound, so I cut more vent holes. That fixed the problem. This required more notes in my notebook. I logged each step, mistake, and disassembly required for the fix. I learned logging action while using the little lab notebook as instructed with my Gilbert Chemistry set.

The air coming out of the barrel didn't feel hot enough to dry hair, so I increased the power to the Variac. Two things happened. The air got warmer, and the fan sped up. Since I had them connected to the same leads on the Variac, they acted in unison rather than separately.

After turning the unit off and unplugging it, I disconnected the motor wires from the Variac and spliced them to the lamp cord wire. The motor was made to work off the house current, so this wasn't a safety hazard; I couldn't vary the fan speed.

Once again, reassembling the unit, I turned it on using the Variac. I could change the heat up and down. The only problem was that I did not know what temperatures I was getting or what was needed to dry my hair.

This would require a trip back to Mrs. Bailey's salon to measure the temperature put out by her Sunbeam dryers. I also needed to acquire a thermometer.

It was close to dinner, so I unplugged everything and coiled the extension cord. I remembered Dad's lecture on trip hazards. If there was one thing in life my father could do, it was give a lecture.

I had read that in a speech, you told people what you were going to tell them, you told them, then you told them what you told them. This was called "telling three times." Dad was of the "telling fifteen times" school of speech.

I also left a handmade sign on the workbench, "Please do not disturb. Mad Scientist at work."

Chapter 41

We had pancakes for dinner. Dad's specialty, so Mum got the night off. He would make what he called Silver Dollar pancakes. They were small, close to the size of a silver dollar. We kids would keep track of how many we could eat. I could eat five normal pancakes. These were about a third of the size, so that I could eat fifteen of them. Denny had to beat me with sixteen. I wonder if that had anything to do with his later bellyache.

As we finished dinner, the telephone rang.

Dad answered with his usual, "City morgue, you stab 'em, we slab 'em, some go to Heaven, and some go to Hello."

The person on the other end took it well, as you could hear laughter.

Dad then got serious, "This is the Jackson Residence."

He listened and then turned to me and handed me the phone, "It's John Wayne."

I thought he was kidding.

I answered with a tentative, "Hello."

"Ricky, this is John Wayne. How have you been?"

"Fine, thank you, and how are you?"

"I'm great, Ricky. I'm putting together a new movie, and I have a part that would be perfect for you."

Mr. Wayne then proceeded to tell me about the movie *The Cowboys*, its basis was that all the adult men in town who usually went on a trail drive were off on a search for gold. This left the old trail boss, played by Mr. Wayne, hiring eleven teenage boys to drive the cattle four hundred miles to the train.

He felt I would be good for a part since I could ride bulls, fall off horses, plus behave myself on a movie set. He had to put in that crack about falling off horses.

The movie would start production in January and take seven weeks. I objected that I had school. He countered that they would be running a school on set and coordinating with my school to avoid falling behind. The pay would be twenty-five hundred dollars a week. He then asked to speak to my dad.

They talked for a while; well, Mr. Wayne talked a lot, answering Dad's questions.

Dad finally ended it with, "Send a contract as you have described, and if our lawyer says okay, he will do it."

Dad handed the phone back to me.

"Rick, we will be mailing you a copy of the screenplay once we have a signed contract. You will have to memorize your lines before shooting starts."

Thinking of my recent Drama Club audition, I replied, "I don't know if I can deliver lines."

"That's why we have acting coaches, to teach you how to say your lines naturally."

That was a big relief.

We said our goodnights and hung up. The whole family was excited. Dad asked if Mr. Wayne had said anything about how much they were paying. I whispered to him, twenty-five hundred dollars. He said that it is good for seven weeks' work. I whispered back, no, that is each week.

You would think I had attached those electric wires to Dad. He dragged Mum and me into the front room, where we could talk without hearing from the other kids. When I repeated it was twenty-five hundred per week, they both jumped up and down like kids. Dad was ready to ship me off to Hollywood right then and there.

Mum had the practical questions like school and where would I stay, you know, Mum things. Since I spent the summer on the road, she knew I could handle myself; she just wanted to ensure I would be taken care of.

We went back to the kitchen, where my brothers and sister waited. Dad told them I might be in another movie but to not talk about it yet, as there was no signed contract. Eddie wanted to know when and Dad told him it was being mailed so that it would be soon. Denny wanted to know if he could have my room.

"Not yet."

Mary wanted to know if cheerleading princesses were allowed to ride horses in movies.

Mum told her, "Yes, they are. Watch Annette in *Zorro* on the Disney show."

That night my mind was going a million miles an hour, thinking of all the possibilities, and imagining what being in a full movie would be like. I had been in scenes but hadn't acted. I kept trying to read but would go over the same page several times. I finally put the book down and fell asleep a long time later.

My alarm went off way too early. It was a struggle to get out of bed and do my exercises. I was waking up as I finished my run. The shower finished the job. I still couldn't figure out how to make an adjustable showerhead.

Dad was drinking his coffee when I went down for breakfast. I knew he was in a good mood because he said, "Morning," rather than grunting. Mum had a pot of porridge ready to go.

While I ate, she asked me if I was ready to go to Bowling Green for the golf tournament. I told her I was. When I was picking up my books to leave for school, Mum asked, "Are you going to take any clothes?"

"Sure, Mum, I am going to pack right now. Do we own a suitcase?"

That last question gave me away.

She laughed and said, "Coach Stone has experience with teenage boys. He mailed us a note. I got the suitcase down from the attic. Let's go pack. You are to leave your case in his office in the locker room."

The suitcase was pretty cool; it had stickers from when Mum crossed the Atlantic. They were from the Queen Mary of the Cunard White Star Line, with city stickers from Liverpool, London, and New York.

Tom was impressed by all the stickers on the suitcase as we walked to school. Mum was a real-world traveler. I told him that I was also a world traveler since I was on that trip. He cut me no slack because I was three years old.

For me, the sectional golf tournament had become real. I was leaving town and staying at a college. I wondered what it would be like to stay in a college dorm. Would there be toga parties and food fights? Only time will tell.

School was a blur and all messed up. Teachers were trying to get classes back on track since their lesson plans were two days behind. Kids who had been off yesterday were rambunctious, and kids who had been off ill were trying to figure out if they missed any homework.

Then there were the poor souls who were still sick and had to see about makeup tests. As I said, a blur and all messed up.

After lunch, Coach Stone, John, Gary, Tim, and I met at Coach's office and collected our gear. Coach had prearranged our being out on Friday and had all our assignments for us. He suggested we work on them during the bus ride.

After a quick look, I knew I had already done all the reading and worked on the problems. Since I was over a week ahead, I decided not to take any textbooks.

This, of course, led to a conversation with Coach. He knew I was a straight-A student; he didn't know how far ahead of the class

I routinely kept. During this talk, the other guys stood there and reassured Coach that I was a famous grind in school.

"Okay, Jackson, but if your grades drop this next six weeks, you are off the team the rest of the year."

I wondered why the other guys were smiling; then I realized the golf season would be over for the year in three weeks.

We went out to the club to pick up our clubs and other gear. It took us about three hours to get to Bowling Green State University.

Chapter 42

I read about a sailor who rounded Cape Horn on a sailing ship on the trip. They went to California to trade for cattle hides and visited the Sandwich Islands; it took two years and was extremely hard.

I was impressed with the description of icebergs and the hard life of the common sailor. I was glad that they didn't ship me off to sea when I had measles.

Our bus drove behind the stadium. A row of fifteen steel Quonset hut buildings was sitting there. This is where we were staying. I learned this was called "Tin Pan Alley" for the steel buildings.

It must sound like drums on the roof when it rains or hails. They had been put up in 1946 to house men returning from the war. Students in the last two years had been moved to the two new residence halls.

Bowling Green, or BGSU as it is known, had done a credible job setting the buildings up for us. They had been subdivided into rooms for two. There was a central lounge, a large shower, and a bathroom facility. It was very much like a dorm setup would be.

I had been preassigned hut four, room five. Tim and I were to share a room, John and Gary in another. Coach would be staying with our bus driver.

It didn't take us long to move our gear, including clubs, to our rooms. After that, we all met in the lounge and went to one of the school cafeterias. We said hello to players from Urbana, Kenton, and Celina. We didn't see the group from Marysville, but someone said they were here.

After dinner, we were split into smaller groups and were given a campus tour. While going through the library, I stopped to look at the books and separated from our group. I continued to browse until an attractive young lady named Diane asked me to reach for a book that was on a high shelf. We started talking, and soon I joined her at a study table.

We sat down, and then our tour guide showed up. The rest of the tour was with him. He started giving me grief about keeping up with the tour group and that high school kids were a pain at best.

At this point, Diane asked, "You are in high school?"

"Yes, I am a freshman," I replied.

She blushed a deep red I had never seen, and she couldn't get out of the library fast enough. I had done nothing, but it made my reputation with the guys on tour. From the way they talked in the lounge back at Tin Pan Alley, I was the pickup artist of all time. I wondered what price I would pay for this.

We were all up and ready to go by seven in the morning. Breakfast was in the cafeteria. While eating, I heard that a team had gotten in trouble. They left Tin Pan Alley after lights out and went downtown and tried to buy beer. The police brought them back. The word was they were on their way back to Marysville right now. They were definitely out of the tournament.

We were loaded on the bus and taken to Stone Ridge, where we walked the course from 8 to 10 a.m. The first practice round started at 10; our tee time wasn't until 2 p.m. We had a bad draw for tee times. We would have to hustle to get a round in before dark.

This was the first time I had walked a course before playing. It was interesting. I was making notes in my book like crazy. I had planned an ideal golf round for my shots from the course map. Now I got to see what lies I would have if I hit those shots. Of particular note was the fourteenth hole.

It was a par 5 whose green was guarded by my friends, the sand traps. If I hit one of my longer drives it could roll into a trap on my right which curved out in front of the green. I decided to lay up with a 3-wood at about 200 yards unless things were desperate.

We finished up and moved onto the driving range, where we warmed up for a while, then to the putting green. Next, we went into the clubhouse for lunch. The clubhouse was so much nicer than the Bellefontaine clubhouse.

I wondered what the Ohio State clubhouse would be like if I made it that far. We stopped by the pro shop, where I picked up some tees with Stone Ridge printed on them. I decided to start a collection.

Our tee-off was fifteen minutes late. The course officials kept pushing everyone all day, and it was a miracle that it was only fifteen minutes. It is amazing when you walk up to a tee and know what is in front of you.

Except for the Bellefontaine course, every time I teed off this year was an adventure. Knowing what club to use and the conditions where your ball is landing can be a real confidence builder.

It took us five hours to play eighteen. Sunset was at 6:53 and twilight at 7:21. There were two groups behind us. The last one had to quit at the seventeenth hole.

Our tournament draws were much better; we had a 10 a.m. tee time on Saturday and 11 a.m. on Sunday.

I started with pars on the first three holes. I managed to sink a fifteen-foot putt for a birdie on 4. There were another three pars in a row, then birdies on 8 and 9. I came back with pars on 10 and 11.

At 12, I made an eagle, sinking it from twenty feet. It wasn't only a good putt; it was the best looking. There was never a doubt that it would go in.

I birdied the fourteenth hole, hitting up short rather than going for the long drive. That left me in perfect shape to drop the ball on the green within ten feet of the pin. This must have made me a little overconfident.

I bogeyed 15, rolling a long drive into a trap on the left at the front of the green. I came back with pars to finish the round at a five-under 67. This left me as the leader of the tournament.

John Scott had a 71, Gary Matthews a 74, and Tim Green a 65. This gave us an overall team score of 287. The next team from Findlay was at 292, so we still had to play our best to win.

With our 10 a.m. start we were finished by 3 p.m. Coach accompanied us back to campus, where we went to the bookstore and bought Bowling Green State University sweatshirts.

We then walked around the area and saw all the frat houses. They looked neat, but the closer you got to the buildings, the rattier they were. I wasn't impressed. If they looked like that on the outside, what would the inside be like?

I hadn't given much thought to college until this year, as it didn't seem like we could ever afford it. I had never thought about joining a fraternity and doubted I would now. The other guys talked about the great parties they must have. So far, anything to do with drinking hadn't ended well.

The next day I crushed the course with seven birdies. I was out at 65. A youth course record. It also was enough to pull the team through. Tim went through a rough patch and ended with an 81. Gary and John were both at par, so our team score was 290. Findlay had 291. When you added the two days' scores together, we took the team tournament by four strokes.

It was a little ironic. We were both going to Findlay. Since they lost, we got to play on their home course, and they didn't. I had a very brief conversation with a Findlay team member, and he seemed puzzled about the Districts being played at Red Hawk. He didn't seem to know that course.

He got called away, and I forgot the conversation. All Findlay team members were real gentlemen about losing at the trophy presentation. What a difference from those Marysville jerks.

The bus ride home took forever on Sunday evening. It was a tired but happy bunch that got dropped off at the school. Our parents were all waiting for us, so there was a lot of noise. Mary was there with her pom poms; she had been allowed to stay up late. Our golf team declared her to be our official cheerleader. To heck with those older pretty girls.

Chapter 43

Monday didn't start well; a cold front had moved in overnight, and it was raining. I performed my exercises but didn't even think about running. How is it possible to feel great and terrible at the same time?

I was tired; it felt like I had been on the go for weeks. At the same time, I felt great; we had won the sectional and would be going to the Districts this week. I had an offer to be in a movie. I was making progress on my hairdryer. Everything was good even if I was tired and ached.

I went down for breakfast. One smell of eggs frying in the kitchen, and I ran back to my bathroom to throw up. Mum heard the noise and came to check on me.

She felt my forehead and said, "Off to bed with you, boyo, you have the flu."

I went back to bed and slept most of the day, other than bouts of running to the bathroom. Both ends. My temperature showed no sign of going down. Mum kept bringing cool rags when I was awake. Tuesday was more of the same, so she called Dr. Costin.

He stopped by in the afternoon for a house call and confirmed that I had the flu but that my temperature was down from what Mum had measured. Drink plenty of liquids, and starve the fever was his prescription.

Tuesday night, the fever broke. I felt good enough to get out of bed for lunch late Wednesday morning. By this time, Denny and Eddie had come down with it. Mary was still okay, and Mum was keeping her away from us.

The only good thing was I got all the Nehi grape soda I could drink. It was the only thing I could keep down when I had the flu. This happened at least once every school year.

I could eat and drink anything when I had mumps, chickenpox, whooping cough, German and three-day measles, or a common cold. The flu was Nehi only.

Coach Stone called on Wednesday, and Mum told him she thought I would be back in school Thursday and could go to the district golf tournament. I felt a little weak on Wednesday afternoon but was up and about.

Mum had an appointment with Sharon Bailey to have her hair done, so I was charged with watching the other kids. The boys were asleep, and Mary was playing with her dolls, so I went out to the garage to work with the hairdryer.

The goal was to make a handheld unit. So far, I had a cigar box lying on a workbench. It needed a handle. I tried another toilet paper roll (I had emptied several rolls myself in the last two days) as a handle. I slipped the electric power wires through it and taped them to the cigar box. When I tried to pick it up, the paper rolls broke.

I threaded the wires through an unbroken roll and then put some short Lincoln Logs inside the roll. I then taped it all together and had a sturdy handle. When I picked the prototype hairdryer up, the cigar box lid fell open, so I taped it shut.

I updated a drawing in my notebook. I now had a barrel with a heating element (toilet paper roll), housing (cigar box with erector set parts), and a handle (toilet paper roll reinforced with Lincoln Logs.

Now I only had to find a use for tinker toys, and I would have an all-American hairdryer.

I could pick the dryer up and wave it around. The weight felt good at about one pound, not too heavy but some heft to it. I went in and checked on the boys. They were still asleep. Mary was bored, so I ended up reading Dr. Seuss to her. I love green ham. She told me the story as she had "read" it many times. She also was able to sight-read some of the words.

Mum got home with a present from Mrs. Bailey; she had sent me a bag of hair to test my dryer. She had saved hunks of long hair she had cut. I trapped one end of the hunk of hair between two long tinker toy sticks and duct-taped the sticks together.

I then used the tinker toys to build a framework to suspend the hair. I entered a drawing of my test fixture and its components in my notebook.

The contract from Warner Brothers studio for *The Cowboys* came certified, so Mum had to sign for it.

Dad was switching cars at BN yards today, just at the north end of Bellefontaine. It was where the stockyards were, so Dad would be all stinky when he got home.

Mum opened the letter and let me read it. It was exactly as Mr. Wayne had described from what I could tell. Dad would still take it to our lawyer.

I wetted the hair in the fixture; then dried it. It dried ok but had a burnt smell to it. There was also a roasted smell to the dryer. When I checked it, the toilet paper roll which comprised the barrel was brown, about ready to catch on fire.

Well, at least I knew I could create enough heat. I then disassembled the unit and found that the Popsicle sticks were charred and about to burn.

I asked Mum if I could use the phone. I called Bush Electric, and Tom answered. I explained that my device was about to burn up and asked what he would recommend using.

He told me that they used sheets of asbestos for insulation. It came in a flat sheet that could be cut and even rolled up. I asked him if it could be rolled to fit inside a toilet paper roll, and he told me that it definitely could.

They had it in stock at fifty cents a square foot. I told him it would be next Monday at the earliest before I could stop down, but I needed a sheet.

I watched TV with the kids; *The Adventures of Ozzie and Harriet*, followed by *The Donna Reed Show*. They had to get ready for bed at 9:30, so I changed the channel and watched *Bat Masterson*. At 10, I had to go to bed.

I was allowed to read as late as I wanted, so long as I got up with no trouble. I would read under my covers with a flashlight when I was younger. I thought I was getting away with something. I didn't realize that the light could be seen through the covers.

I was reading a really fun book. It has a guy from New England thrown back in time. He becomes known as The Boss. He destroys the tower of a real grouchy magician and changes a lot of things, but in the end, he can't change history.

Thursday, I was able to go back to school. I skipped all my exercises and my morning run again. I didn't feel that good. They handed out report cards in homeroom.

As expected, I got all A's. By doing everything ahead, I felt less stressed by school than ever. I had yet to run into many problems in the book that I couldn't sort out myself. If I did, all I would have to do is pay attention in class or ask a question.

After lunch we met Coach for our ride to the country club and then (I thought) to Findlay. First, Coach asked me how I was feeling. I told him a lot better, still a little weak, but not ill. He shook his head slightly, accepting my statement. Then Coach made an announcement.

A clown is working in the Ohio State Boys Golf Tournament office. The letter sent out said we would be playing the Districts at Findlay's Red Hawk Golf Course.

There is no such golf course. The guy's uncle wants to build one there with that name, and he thought he would get a plug in for him! He now has the time to help him as he no longer has a job.

We are going up near Toledo to play at the Inverness Club. That is where they played last year's open, won by Dick Mayer. This may be the best course you will ever play in your life. That gave the whole team mixed emotions. Great, we get to play on a world-class golf course; oh crap, it will eat us alive.

Coach continued, "Rick's slacking off turned out good for him. That map we were sent for Red Hawk was the proposed course, so our planning was wasted. I don't have a current map of Inverness, so we will have to take really good notes when we walk the course in the morning."

When we got to the Inverness Club we were taken to a field where tents had been set up. They looked like old army tents. The Ohio National Guard had set them up. They also had a field kitchen, water buffaloes, shower facilities, and portable restrooms. The tents looked like a six-sided pyramid. They had plenty of room for four of us to sleep on cots set up with sleeping bags.

The club may be posh, but we were camping. There was no choice since there wasn't any place to put up thirty-two teams of four plus supporting adults.

After getting settled in, our team walked over as a group to the clubhouse. We were only allowed to go inside the pro shop. I bought some tees that said "Inverness Toledo" on them.

We peeked into the main clubhouse. It was the fanciest place I had ever seen. We also scoped out the practice tees and green, but again weren't allowed to use them.

When we got back it was time for dinner; we had to line up with a metal tray and were served by the National Guardsmen. They were performing their monthly duty, which must have been good as they seemed to be having fun.

I mentioned that to one of them, and he chuckled and said, "No rain, no mud, no middle of the night drills, good duty."

I was glad I had brought that book with knights because there was nothing else to do. They had a lamp in each tent, but it wasn't enough to read by, but I had brought my trusty flashlight.

Chapter 44

We got woken around 2 a.m. by whistles and commotion over at the National Guard tents. They were going on a night march. Not such a good duty.

In the morning breakfast line, I saw the National Guardsman who had told me this was good duty. He didn't look like he'd had a lot of sleep. I nodded to him as I went by but kept my mouth shut.

He surprised me by saying, "You take the good with the bad. It is still good duty."

Now that is a positive attitude if I ever saw one.

I hadn't much experience with the military other than with the veterans in my own family. They all seemed to look at life the same way. They whined a little but kept ongoing. I would try to keep that attitude in mind when things got rough, rather than being what Mum called a whinger.

After breakfast we walked the course. We took many notes as we went. We weren't allowed to do any putting on the green, but the course marshals keeping an eye on things didn't get upset if a golf ball fell out of your pocket and rolled towards the hole on a tricky lie.

These greens were like greased lightning. They were also the smallest and had the most breaks I had seen on any course. The bunkers protecting them would have done credit to the Maginot line. Coach pointed out how 14 and 15 were at right angles, so no matter which way the wind was blowing, you would have trouble on one or the other.

Number 8 hole would be interesting; it is a par 5 and would require a 250-yard drive to clear the bunkers in the fairway. They should be declared illegal on all golf courses. But I could clear the bunkers.

The real problem is that the only way to get a decent putt was to land on the right side of the green below the hole. This would be an accuracy challenge.

The tenth hole was made to cause me problems. It was a par 4 but had a downhill slope with a rough between the 250-yard marker and the green. My normal drive would end up in the rough. I would have to lay up and hit the green with an 8-iron.

The par 4 470-yards seventeenth was a potential problem hole. It was a sharp dogleg left. I could probably position my drive, but if my second shot were long it was a bogey at best, if not a double. It was be below the hole or be in trouble.

The good news was that most of the sand traps and creek crossings were designed to cause problems for the golfer who drove 225 yards or less. I could drive past most of the problems.

After walking the course, we spent time on the driving range to loosen up, but most of our time was on the practice greens. There was no question that I had to be below the hole on every green to have a chance of one-putting. They were just too fast going downhill.

We had a 1 p.m. tee time, so we stopped at an outdoor hotdog stand to get a bite to eat. We had just sat down at the outdoor picnic benches when I noticed a girl who seemed to be having problems. She had her hands at her throat and seemed to have trouble breathing. She was choking.

I took the four steps to get to her and asked her if she was okay. She couldn't say anything, just tried to draw air. Her mouth was open, and I could see part of a hot dog wedged in her throat.

I tried to reach in with my fingers and almost had them bitten off. Not knowing what to do, I slapped her hard in the middle of her back. She spit the hotdog across the table.

She immediately started taking great whoops of air. By that time other people had noticed what was going on. One gentleman came running over and asked, "Judy, are you okay?"

He turned to me and said, "I don't know why you hit my daughter, young man, but I'm calling the sheriff."

Luckily for me, he didn't have far to go because a deputy sheriff was standing right there and had seen the whole event.

The deputy explained that he saw that Judy was having problems and was on his way to help her, but I got there first. He explained that it was lucky I was the first one there because he hadn't any idea how to dislodge a hotdog like that.

Both Judy's father and the deputy looked at me like they wanted me to explain how I knew what to do.

I explained, "I found out quickly I couldn't get it out of her mouth from the front, so I applied force from behind. I hadn't a clue if it would work but had to do something before she suffocated."

Her father, who looked extremely emotional held out his hand. "I'm so sorry I snapped at you. I only saw you hit Judy. Now I know you saved her life. I feel like a fool."

I replied, "That is a natural reaction when one's daughter is hit. No apology is necessary."

By that time, the young lady had recovered her breath. She turned to me and gave me a simple, "Thank you."

I got my first look at her; she was shorter than me with dark brown hair and brown eyes. A nice full figure with well-developed breasts. She looked about my age, and she was the most beautiful girl I had ever seen.

"You're welcome." I managed to stutter. About that time an older woman came up, and there was no doubt that she was Judy's mother. This started a whole new round of questions and explanations.

This whole incident happened in the space of less than a minute. Coach Stone, who had been watching, came over to ensure I was okay. He and Mr. King, Judy's father, introduced themselves.

Judy's Mom hovered over Judy until she heard a "Mom" in that special teenage voice that said, "You are embarrasing me," and also told Mom that she was okay. At that point, Mom joined Coach and Mr. King.

I turned to Judy and said, "That was scary. I hope I didn't hurt you when I hit your back. I didn't know what else to try."

"That's okay; my name is Judy King. What's yours?"

"Rick or Ricky Jackson, I am here for the golf tournament."

"Where are you from?"

"Bellefontaine."

"Oh, that is too bad. I live in Clintonville. That is part of Columbus next to Ohio State."

I asked her, "What grade are you in?"

"The ninth, and I'm fifteen."

"So am I!"

"When is your birthday?"

"October 11; when is yours?"

"May 28."

"That's okay. I like older women." That got me a light slug on the arm. At least she didn't knock me off the bench.

"I see you will be a handful," she said.

Wait, whoa, hold up; what was going on here?

Coach approached me and said, "Rick, it is almost our tee time. We have to go."

Judy pulled out a ballpoint pen and a slip of paper.

She scribbled quickly, "Here is my address, write me. Oh, yes, and win this tournament so that I can see you next week."

"Yes, ma'am," I replied.

Mum hadn't raised a fool.

As we walked towards the first tee for our practice round, I got a lot of "way to go" from my teammates.

Gary Matthews said, "Leave it to Rick. He not only saves the girl, but she also is a pretty girl, and what is that note I saw her hand you?"

"Her address; she wants me to write."

Of course, that got me a lot of grief.

As the other boys limbered up on the tee, Coach took me aside.

"Rick, several things, you were ill earlier in the week. How do you feel now?"

"Fine, Coach, I felt a little weak yesterday, but I am back to normal now."

"I'm glad to hear that. Now the other thing is, Mr. King and his wife Sandra have invited you to have dinner with them and Judy in the clubhouse tonight as their guest. Do you feel comfortable with that?"

"Yes, I do, Coach, though I don't have a coat and tie."

"Did you bring any money with you, and how much?"

Coach didn't even blink when I told him I had about two hundred and fifty dollars. I was running low from last summer's money but still had five hundred left. I sure hoped that reward money would come soon; I lived an expensive life.

"They sell sports coats, ties, and slacks in the pro shop. We will stop there after your round.

"Rick, you should also know that Mr. Robert King is the Ohio High School Athletic Association president. That is a volunteer position. His work job is as the president of the Western Electric Plant in Columbus.

"It has over five thousand employees. His wife Sandra is a vice president of Ohio National Bank. She is Ohio Old Money. She is from one of the founding families. She is descended from Nathan Kelly, one of Washington's officers."

"They told you this?"

"No, Coach Benton from the Toledo Bowsher team did after he saw me talking to them. Right now, you are the talk of the clubhouse."

"Great, what I need is more fame. Oh well, it will pass."

"Right, let's go get you famous for your golf."

Chapter 45

During practice I learned several important lessons about the course. The first was on the eighth hole. You had better be on the right side of the green or you were looking at a bogey.

I came to the left of the pin and when I putted the ball, which was supposed to gently roll into the cup, kept picking up speed as it went, causing it to drift away from the cup and roll right off the green.

The wind on 15 was blowing across the course and what would've been a drive to the middle of the fairway ended up in the rough to the right. I recovered for the par, but this hole would be a chance for a birdie if played correctly.

I would have to watch the wind closely on 14 and 15, and whichever had the crosswind hit a low shot, sacrificing distance for accuracy.

The last five holes were known as "Murderers Row". They would destroy an otherwise good score. The eighteenth had a little valley or swale to the right of the green known as "Death Valley". It was where many good golf rounds went to die. I kept out of it on the practice round, but it lurked there, waiting to grab a careless shot.

After practice, I dropped my gear off at the tent and searched for Mr. King. He wasn't hard to find as he was at the tournament official's pavilion. They had a pavilion as opposed to our tents. It was much fancier, white with doors and windows.

I waited until he finished talking to someone and approached him. He stood up quickly and offered his hand.

After shaking hands, I told him I would be delighted to join his family for dinner this evening.

He asked me, "Rick, do you have a coat and tie?"

"No, sir, I don't. I was planning to buy what I need at the pro shop."

"Rick, now I feel like a fool again. It will cost you over one hundred dollars to buy your clothes in the pro shop. I wanted to reward you nicely for saving my daughter, and here I'm going to cost you a lot of money."

"Sir, that is okay. I have the money on me and can afford it. Besides, I need a new jacket and pants. I have outgrown all my clothes recently."

"You certainly are tall," replied the six-footer.

"I have just got my growth this summer and then again in the last couple of weeks. I don't even know if I've finished growing yet."

"Time will tell. In the meantime, let me go shopping with you. I can get a discount as the club I belong to is reciprocal with Inverness."

"I would appreciate that."

He helped me pick out a pair of grey slacks and a dark blue blazer. He assured me that they would be appropriate for almost any occasion. These with a button-down collar white shirt and a tie with red and black regimental stripes made me look sharp.

When it came time to pay, Mr. King took the clerk aside and talked to him. He returned to me and told me he had got a seventy-five percent discount for me.

I knew that he had told the clerk he would pay the difference, but I didn't want to argue. The clothes still cost me twenty-seven dollars.

I was wearing my ostrich cowboy boots. Mr. King asked me about them. I told him that I had bought them on a trip out West last year. He suggested that I have them cleaned by one of the valets in the clubhouse.

"We aren't allowed in there."

"Come with me, young man."

I dutifully followed him into the men's locker room. They had a regular shoeshine chair there. He had Thomas polish my boots.

Thomas told me he hadn't seen as nice a pair of boots as mine for a long time.

I told him I had bought them at Sheplers in Dallas.

Thomas asked, "What were you doing in Dallas?"

I hadn't told Mr. King the whole story about why I had my boots, but I figured I had better come clean because it would come out anyway.

"I was there for a rodeo."

"Were you in the rodeo or watching it?'

"Okay, you will not quit till I tell you all; I was in the rodeo, riding Brahma bulls. Last year I was the National Champion bull rider for my age group."

"Whoa, young man; that is pretty impressive."

I replied, "Thank you."

I was watching to see what Mr. King's reaction would be. You could see that he was trying to remember something but couldn't bring it to mind. You also could see when he did remember.

"Rick, was it you and your family I read about in the Sunday supplement a few weeks ago?"

"Probably, sir," I replied.

"Oh, Lord, I'm in for it now."

"Why is that?"

"I jokingly told Judy that you were the guy she should marry."

"How did she respond?"

"You are in trouble; she told me she would marry you in a heartbeat."

"But I'm only fifteen."

"I met her mother when she was fifteen. I never had a chance."

I started to say something smart-mouthed but stopped.

"You know, there could be worse ways to go, but I think this is getting way ahead of ourselves, probably five or ten years."

You could see the relief on the young lady's father's face.

He muttered, "Now, if only she looks at it that way."

Mr. King paid and tipped for my shine, and I left to change into my new duds.

I took a very cold shower as the heater was off. That may have been a good thing. I got dressed and slicked down my hair with a little dab of Brylcreem. From the gunk in my comb, I noticed it was about time to change the oil, which meant it was time to wash my hair. It needed washing at least once a week, sometimes even twice, as I got older.

Of course, the guys all gave me a hard time in a fun way. Even the National Guard guys going by jumped in. One said I was bucking to be an officer. He said it nicely, but somehow, I don't think it was a compliment.

I went to the restaurant entrance to the clubhouse precisely on time. The King family was waiting for me. Judy jumped up and hugged me. She also whispered, "Play along."

First, there were thanks again from her parents.

I gave a cowboy, "Ah, shucks, weren't nothing," response.

Then the grilling started. They somehow got a chance to reread that article on our family and my summer vacation since I had left Mr. King in the pro shop. They wanted the details filled in. It was normal curiosity, nothing hostile.

Then Judy dropped her bombshell.

"Daddy, you were right. This is the man I am going to marry."

Daddy's mouth started to hang open, but before he could say anything she turned to me, and said, "Dear, do you want to wait till we graduate high school or get married in the spring?"

Not knowing where this was going, I replied, "We probably should wait until we graduate. It is so hard to go to high school while you have children."

"Yes, dear. I suspect you are right."

You should have seen Mr. King's face. His mouth kept bobbing up and down. He wanted to say something, but nothing would come out.

All of a sudden, Judy and her mother burst into laughter.

"We got you, Daddy."

He took a deep breath and said, "Yes, you did."

Turning to me, he said, "You will pay for this. I expect it from them, but I thought we men were in it together."

"Sir, discretion is the better part of valor, and I had my marching orders."

I'm not certain what discretion had to do with marching orders, but it worked, at least for now.

From that moment on, it was a delightful dinner. Mr. and Mrs. King told me a little about their family. There wasn't any new information, but it was nice to have it confirmed. At the same time, they wanted to know about my parents and what they did. The questions were not rude or too invasive.

My dad bought houses, fixed them up, and rented them out.

Mr. King remarked, "Usually, you hear of people buying houses and renting them, but nothing about fixing them first."

"Dad felt he could get a better monthly rent, and a nicer house would rent out first. In a small town like ours, word gets out which landlord has better houses."

"Your dad has a good head on his shoulders."

When we were finished eating, I paid my respects and got ready to leave.

Judy said, "I will see you back to the camping area."

Her parents didn't object. She only went as far as the picnic tables outside, where we sat down across from each other.

We sat and talked for over an hour. It was a getting-to-know-you type of conversation. We covered a lot of likes and dislikes.

Surprisingly enough, we had more in common than I thought we would.

We were both straight-A students. We weren't in the inner social circles of our class and didn't care. We both were avid readers. She had read everything Heinlein had ever written and could discuss the stories.

She was an only child, so she didn't know the joys of the pests. Her mom and dad both worked hard. She had tried cigarettes but didn't care for them nor beer after a sip, which was terrible. She played field hockey for North High School in Clintonville.

She asked me many questions. What I liked was when I talked about my summer vacation, she wanted to hear about me, not John Wayne or Elvis Presley. She did express the desire to hear me sing. I told her that wasn't going to happen.

It was starting to get too cool to sit outside without a heavier coat. We sat on opposite sides of the picnic table, so we were never close enough for me to try to kiss her. As she walked away, I realized that we had been sitting in front of a window in the restaurant and that her parents were still there and had been able to see us the whole time. I think I had dodged a bullet.

I floated back to the tent area. The guys from the team all wanted to know if I got her alone and how far I got.

"No, I didn't get her alone, and if we had done anything, you would be the last to know."

I remembered Bill's big mouth and the problems it caused him.

That night, I started a book from Aunt Merle's library. It was about ten young adults who went on a retreat, and each had to tell a story a day. Those stories were pretty bawdy. Those old guys knew how to have a good time. They also could get in big trouble, at least in their stories.

Chapter 46

Saturday, I woke up feeling like a new person. I was completely recovered from the flu and did my morning exercises and ran. The National Guard guys who were up and around thought I was crazy. They did a daily run, but only for two miles and not full out. I showered, got dressed for the day, and went to breakfast.

After French toast with bacon and eggs and a large glass of orange juice, I was ready to start my day. The rest of the team had come out for breakfast but hadn't cleaned up yet. Coach Stone was sitting with several other coaches having coffee, so I grabbed my putter and some balls and headed out to the practice green.

It was early enough, there were only a couple of other people there and none of the players in the tournament. While putting, I noticed something a little off. The sun was not up high enough to remove all shadows from the surface of the practice green.

When I put the ball into the shadow, it would slow down, not a lot but enough to make a difference. When I putted from the shadow into the sun, the ball would speed up, again not a lot, but enough to cause the ball to drift off its line.

I was lining up putts to take advantage of this effect when a Mr. Palmer said, "You've noticed the shadow effect here. It's the most pronounced in the spring and fall. In high summer, the greens are hard enough, it doesn't make a difference. Knowing this might save you two strokes."

"Thank you, Mr. Palmer."

"You're welcome and good luck on your round today. I hope to see more of you, Rick."

Now how did Arnold Palmer know my name?

I packed up and went back to the zoo, what we had started calling our area. Scott and Gary were drinking coffee when I got back; Tim wasn't around. I asked about him. He still was asleep the last time they looked. They asked where I had been.

"Over at the practice green, putting and talking to Arnold Palmer about the course."

"Yeah, right, pull the other one," was Gary's response.

Scott just shook his head.

Tim came rushing out looking like he had slept in his clothes.

He grabbed a cup of coffee and said, "Coach wants us to leave now."

Our tee time was not till 11, but there was an opening ceremony we had to attend.

There were the usual opening remarks by tournament officials. Then a genuinely nice talk by Mr. Palmer about the game of golf and how if you played it well and followed the rules, not the official rules, but the unwritten rules of etiquette in your everyday life, they would do well by you.

While Mr. Palmer was talking, I turned to Gary and winked and mouthed, "Way."

After the opening ceremony, we went back to the zoo. Tim went to clean up and change clothes at Coach's insistence. The other guys and I sat and talked. We all had seen a neat movie that was just out, *Bridge over the River Kwai*. We all agreed that the movie was great and the music better; but we didn't like the ending.

We also agreed that just because we didn't like the ending, that was the way of war. We all had heard enough stories from our families to know that fairness and sanity had nothing to do with war. We hoped our generation would never have to fight.

By the time Tim got his act together, it was time to head over to the clubhouse for our start. I had butterflies until I stepped onto the tee box. Then it was time to play, not worry.

The first hole was a 395-yard straight-away hole. It sloped about 285 yards out. If you hit farther, you would be in the rough. I hit a

3-wood with a nice arc landing about 250 yards down the fairway, rolling another 30. It was a perfect placement. I had learned to ignore the other players. I was aware of them being there and taking turns. I didn't pay attention to their game or get emotionally involved with it.

My second shot hit the fringe in front of the green, then released and rolled within five feet of the pin. When it was my turn to putt, I drained it. This put me one under.

The second hole was again a straight-away of 385 yards. They had put bunkers to protect the fairway at 270 yards; a 250-yard drive would most likely roll into the sand trap. My solution was simple; I hit the ball in the air for 280 yards with another 20-yard roll. From there, it was an easy up to the green.

Unfortunately, the green was in two tiers. The flag was on the upper tier. My ball landed on the green and released. It rolled just enough to start up the slope to the second tier.

Halfway up it lost momentum and rolled backward, almost off the green. It took two putts to get it in, so I was still 1- under.

The third hole was a 200-yard par 3 and simple to get there. A pond on the right parallels the fairway, but it is no problem if you keep the ball in play, which I did.

My ball landed on the dance floor and rolled within fifteen feet of the pin. This green was not flat and level. It had undulations that required a good read.

When I got up there, I realized that the small rises and drops in the surface of the green were leaving some of it in shadow. This would slow the ball down.

I made the putt look easy when I took this into account and how the slight rise and drop would affect my putt. It was like the ball had eyes. I was now 2-under. As I walked away, a gentleman in the crowd winked at me.

The next hole was a 466-yard par 4. I laced the driver and then put the ball on the green with a 7-iron. I misjudged; I should have used a 6-iron. I ended up on the fringe of the green, and it took two strokes to get the ball up and down. I was still 2-under.

The fifth hole was a 450-yard par 4. It's a slight dogleg to the left. I was lucky because there had been a slight breeze, but it now had died down. I would've been hitting into it, but with just enough angle to cause a problem with drift.

I moved the ball 270 yards down the fairway and then got on with a 3-iron. Again, the tight green had enough slope to take me two putts. I was still 2-under for the day.

The number 6 hole was a 231-yard par 3. My 3-wood came up short, and I took another par to remain 2-under.

Next was a 481-yard par 4. It was 240 yards to the creek. Again, I took the easy out and just hit over it. I was on in two, but the green was so contoured that I 3-putted for a bogey. This left me 1-under.

The eighth hole was a tricky par 5 with a dogleg to the right. I carried the bunkers, which were at 250 yards. I managed to keep the ball on the right side of the green on my second shot. This position left me an easy two putts for a birdie and put me back to 2-under.

Nine was a 468-yard par 4 with a slight dog leg to the left. I was on in two, but the sharp slope fooled me, and I ended up short of the hole requiring a tap in for par.

The day was going nicely; it was a sunny day with almost no breeze. I felt comfortable on the course. There was a little backup on the tenth tee. Many of the guys were scarfing hotdogs, but I chose to have a cup of water. No sense in taking a chance on indigestion on the course.

As we were getting ready to tee off, I noticed an extremely pretty girl in the crowd. This was the first time enough people were watching to be called a gallery. Judy gave a little wave; I waved back but kept my mind on the game.

Ten is a 363-yard par 4 that rewards an accurate drive. I used a 3-wood to put it out 245 yards and a 6-iron to lay it on the green. It was an easy putt for a birdie. I was now 3-under.

Number 11 was a 378 par 4, and that is exactly what I did, a par. There was a bunker at 270 yards, but my long drive took it out of play.

A par 3 at 172 yards, the twelfth hole was a simple 5-iron shot. I should have had a birdie but left it on the lip for a par. I was still 3-under.

Thirteen was a 516-yard par 5. I cleared the sand trap at 245 yards and got on easy with a 3-iron. I then 2-putted for another birdie. I was now 4-under.

You must understand. I was not dwelling on my score. I was playing golf and having fun doing it. While I wasn't paying attention to the other golfer's game, I would say, "Nice shot, etc."

It was all light banter, certainly no grief. Nobody else in my foursome had a birdie all day, so I knew I was leading my foursome. The only leaderboard was at the clubhouse. There weren't large galleries to make a lot of noise on good shots.

So, I played golf without the pressure of knowing how the competition was doing.

Fourteen was the first hole of what they called Murderers Row. It was 480 yards with a narrow fairway. I walked away with a par and felt good about it.

The fifteenth hole was almost my undoing. It's a 468-yard par 4. The wind is right in your face. There had been no breezes all day. Just as I hit a booming drive, the wind kicked in and carried the ball to the right cutting its distance down.

The ball rolled into a sand trap about 310 yards out. Adding to the pain, the ball rolled right up to the lip of the trap nearest the green. So, I had almost 160 yards to go and had to hit the ball sideways out of the trap. I put it on the green and 3-putted the hole for a double bogey in a poor position. I was now 2-under.

Suddenly, I went from an exceptional round to a good round. I didn't realize how much pressure that had put on me. I thought I was just calmly going around the course.

That wasn't the case at all. It was like the weight of the world came off my shoulders. I would do okay, but I didn't have to be superman.

I then parred the rest of the holes to 2-under for the day. After signing my card and checking the leaderboard, I found I had the lead. The closest player would probably end up with an 81! A local reporter asked Coach if he could talk to me. Coach sat in for the interview.

Chapter 47

The reporter started with, "How do you feel about having a score the same as Dick Mayer, who won the US Open, playing on this course last year and beating Cary Middlecoff's score?"

This was all news to me.

"I feel good about having a nice round of golf on this excellent course. The club and the Ohio State High School Athletic Association should be complimented on putting on such a fine tournament."

This local reporter was an amateur compared with the Hollywood sharks that interviewed John Wayne and Elvis Presley.

"Do you care to comment on how much better you did here today than Jack Nicklaus did last year? The young sensation from Columbus didn't even make the cut with an 80."

"No, I don't care to comment. No course is the same from day to day, much less year to year."

"Well, Rick, what will you do tomorrow?"

"Is that a trick question? I will play golf tomorrow."

The reporter grimaced, and I was sure he would have liked to smack me.

Coach had to cover his mouth with his hand.

I never saw what that reporter wrote, but my guess is that he wasn't a fan.

Coach told me I had handled the interview well until that last question. I might want to tone it down.

It was now 4:30 in the afternoon, and I had had nothing to eat since early morning. The hot dog stand had closed, so it looked like I was stuck until dinner, which would be at 6 p.m. Judy King rescued me. She happened to be near the press tent when I came out.

I asked her if there was any place I could get something to eat. She went into the clubhouse and ordered a cheeseburger, fries, and

Coke. She came out and sat with me at a picnic table while waiting for it to be ready. Judy played golf though her school didn't have a girl's golf team.

She wanted to know about my round today, shot by shot. Rather than bore her to death with that, I gave the highlights and what I thought of each hole. That helped. It was like lessons learned from the day. She liked my story about Arnold Palmer and the shadows on the golf green.

I pulled out my notebook and started taking notes on the course. Judy asked me if I referred to it at each hole. I laughed and told her.

"I never look at it; it helps my memory if I write it down. You just helped me discover that it also helps if I talk about the round and what went right and wrong."

"What went wrong today, Rick?"

"The sand trap on 15 caught me, or I caught it."

"What have you learned?"

"Not to play on a course with sand traps," I said with a straight face.

"But, but...oh, you rat."

I was saved by the waitress bringing out my sandwich. Judy had signed for it, but I gave a fifty-cent tip. I know, a big spender, but I wanted to show off a little.

"Will you be able to eat dinner after eating this?"

"Sure, that is not for at least an hour from now."

"If I ate like that, I would be like the Goodyear Blimp."

"Well, obviously you don't because you look very good to me."

"Oh, you say the nicest things."

"Yes, he does," said a voice over my shoulder, "I'm sorry to break this up, but we have to get back to the zoo."

It was Coach.

Coach remarked, "She is an attractive young lady on the way back to camp. It's a shame she lives so far away."

"Yes, it is," I replied.

We sat down and talked about our day's experiences as a team. Coach made his notes. I had my notebook out and made some entries based on what I heard. The other guys had their books out, but nothing was being written.

I made eye contact once with Coach after we had written down that the green on the fifth hole had seemed slower to all of us. The other guys just sat there chatting whenever Coach didn't involve them in the recap.

Coach gave a sad little smile and said quietly, "You can lead a horse to water."

Our dining hall had spaghetti for dinner. The National Guard guys congratulated me on my day's score. After dinner, I walked up near the clubhouse. Unfortunately, there was no one to talk to. In other words, Judy wasn't there.

I retired to our tent for the evening and started reading. It was about a man who was an ivory transporter down the Congo River. It was one of the more futile stories that I had ever read.

The Europeans were as brutal as the natives in central Africa. The whole story was a sad commentary on mankind. My sleep was restless that night. I'm certain it was the story.\

Chapter 48

The next morning, I awoke at my normal 6 a.m. and was glad that the night was over. By the time I had finished my exercises and daily run, the world looked better. Breakfast was bacon, scrambled eggs, home fries, toast, and orange juice, which set me up for the day.

There was a bowl of apples set out. I snagged a couple for the course. Our foursomes tee time was 9 a.m., so we would be out on the course at lunchtime.

I limbered up on the driving range but only did a dozen balls with each club. I spent most of my time on the practice green.

Soon enough, it was time to tee off. The first hole was kind to me again. I played it the same as yesterday and had the same result, a birdie to start me out at 1-under.

The second hole was also a replay of yesterday. I landed on the lower portion of the green and took two shots to get the ball in the hole. So, I was still 1-under.

I had a birdie on 3 yesterday, but today it was par. The uneven greens surface was too much for me to read correctly, and I left it six inches past the hole. A simple tap-in left me still at 1-under. I was glad that Mr. Palmer wasn't there to see my poor showing.

I made up for it on the fourth hole. Yesterday I had a par, today a birdie. I landed the ball in the center of the green, and it had enough backspin to roll back to within two feet of the pin.

The fifth hole played exactly as it did yesterday. The green was small and so fast that I didn't want to take any chances. I walked away happy with a par and being 2-under.

On the 231-yard par 3, I hit the ball sweet this time. Yesterday I had been a little fat, getting under the ball too much, so it ended up in a high short arc, landing on the fringe. Today it wasn't fat and left me a birdie opportunity, which I sunk to make me 3-under.

Yesterday I bogeyed the number 7 hole. Today it was par. Again, on in two, but it was a 2-putt for par this time.

The eighth hole was becoming my favorite on the course. Last time I had a birdie. Today my approach shot to the green went where I wanted it to and left me three feet from the pin. That left enough distance to think about it, but I didn't overthink it. Well, the real truth is, I quickly addressed the ball and drained it like I knew what I was doing. This eagle put me 5-under.

Nine was the same as yesterday. I was on in two. Then I ended up long and had a nervous twenty-five-foot putt to get the ball next to the hole, then tapped in for par.

At the tenth, guys were scarfing hotdogs. I was satisfied to have my two apples with a drink of water. I looked for Judy, but neither she nor her parents were around.

It would be nice to report that I cruised through the back nine, setting a course record. Instead, it got real ugly quick.

Ten must have given me a false sense of security because I birdied it in the same fashion as yesterday. I was now 6-under for the tournament and on course for a 66. Last year at the Open, the best round recorded by a professional was 68. I wish I hadn't put that together.

I promptly bogeyed number 11 by a poor putt. There was no other way to put it. It was sloppy. So that was one stroke I had given back. It wasn't to end.

It looked like things were back under control on 12. I came back with a birdie and got the stroke back.

Today I didn't clear the sand trap and was happy to get away with a par 5.

Yesterday I was light-hearted at this point. Today I was tense as all get out.

Now I know why they call it Murderers Row.

The only problem with the fourteenth fairway was that it was narrow. The narrowest on the course. Yesterday I stayed in the fairway. Today the wind pushed me into the rough. It left an extremely poor but playable lie. That is how I played it, poorly. I came out of the rough low and fast and rolled across the fairway to the rough on the other side. I was playing army golf: left, right, left. That cost a stroke.

On the fifteenth, I came back with a par.

Sixteen was a par, looking good.

Seventeen another par, only one to go, sitting at a 67. Just keep cool and par on 18.

My second shot on 18 went into Death Valley. I plain pushed it there. Getting out was horrible. I hit it right over the green. So, I was laying three and not even on. That was a first for this tournament.

I attempted a pitch and run, but the ball didn't release and roll. It just landed on the fringe and sat there. That was embarrassing. But embarrassed or not, I had to putt out. I then promptly 3-putted for a triple bogey.

I looked at the gallery and was thrilled that Judy King wasn't there. My course record all of a sudden had turned into a mundane 70.

It is amazing what your mind will do to you. I had just matched the two-day score of the winner of last year's U.S. Open, and I was mildly depressed. Coach Stone got me out of that mood quickly. He told me to get my head out of my rear end and act like a gracious winner.

Well, I didn't have to pretend to be gracious for long. Enough people congratulated me that the act was soon dropped, and my mood improved. I also felt so tired!

It was a shame our team wouldn't be advancing to State. As an individual low score, I would advance, but we came in second behind Toledo Bowsher as a team. The closing ceremonies were held, trophies were handed out, and we were ready to head home. I took one last look around for Judy King, but none of the King family was in sight.

We picked up our packed suitcases from where the tents had been. The National Guard had removed everything and was long gone.

Scott, Gary, and Tim were all nice to me and were happy that I won, but they were also depressed that their golf for the year was over.

We got home to our adoring fans. Our families were led by our personal cheerleader Mary, pom poms, and all. I don't know who she worked with, but she even memorized our official high school cheers.

When I got home, it was lights out, with no reading. I was exhausted. I wondered if I would see Judy in Columbus.

Chapter 49

Monday came quickly. To make matters worse, it was raining buckets, cold, nasty buckets. A cold front had come in during the night with a loud thunderstorm. I did my indoor exercises, but there would be no running this morning.

I went ahead and showered, again thinking about that darn shower head. There had to be some way you could adjust the direction of the showerhead, but how? It was all metal.

I had seen shower heads with a rubber hose attaching them to the water pipe. The problem with those was it took a hand to aim it in the correct direction. I wanted to point the water where I wanted it and let it flow.

Having no inspiration on that front, I went down for breakfast. Since I couldn't run, I was there a half-hour earlier than usual. It was just Mum and Dad sitting with their coffee and tea. I sat down at the table and must have looked like I was still asleep. Dad said nothing; he just got up and poured me a cup of coffee.

I had tried coffee before and couldn't stand the taste. I knew that caffeine would wake you up, so I decided to try it again. It was steaming hot from the pot, so I saucered some like I saw Dad do previously.

I poured some from my cup into the saucer, then blew on it to cool it down. I then sipped the cooler coffee. It still tasted terrible. I kept at it anyway. I needed to wake up.

While we were drinking our morning beverages, the radio was playing. The national news came on. One of the stories was about the conviction of the ringleader of the West's largest modern cattle rustling operation last week.

The story mentioned that the Texas Rangers captured them and had a brief interview with Mr. Walker. Thankfully, my name didn't come up.

I said, "Thank goodness I wasn't named."

The local news reported that the Bellefontaine High School Golf Team had won second place in the district tournament. Local golfer Ricky Jackson had a low individual score and would advance to the state championship this coming weekend in Columbus.

"This is the first time anyone from Bellefontaine has ever made the state playoffs, so let's show support for Ricky this week."

I groaned.

Dad chuckled, "Well, Ricky, you are a big frog in a small pond, but you don't even count as small when you're in the big pond."

He seemed to think he was funny.

Once he quit chuckling over his misguided wit, he continued, "I took the contract from Warner Brothers to our lawyer on Friday. He called a friend out in California who works with movie contracts. This is a standard contract they use.

"There are no hidden tricks. You are being hired to perform in one movie at a given rate of twenty-five hundred dollars a week. They will provide transportation, food, and lodging.

"As a minor, they will ensure your education by providing a tutor who will work with your school. They will also provide a chaperon as needed for going off set, as you will be in Hollywood for seven weeks.

"Rick, it almost seems too good to be true, but it is true. Now all you have left is to go out there and do the job."

I thought about what Dad was saying. I would be in a movie that sounded great, but I was being hired to work. So, I would be working full time for seven weeks plus carrying a full school load. Suddenly, this didn't sound like the good time I thought it would be.

"So, Rick, do you want me to sign this on your behalf?"

"Yes, Dad, I do, but I can see that I will have to work for that money."

"Speaking of the money, I suspect it will be expensive. Your check will be mailed here. I will deposit it in a new savings account for your money only. Our bank has agreed to set it up so that you can draw two hundred dollars weekly from a branch in Los Angeles while you are shooting the movie.

"The studio wants me to sign the contract and nondisclosure agreement, mail them today via certified mail, and let the school know that your tutor will contact them to see what you need to study.

"They will be administering your tests on-site, so you won't be behind when you get home. They seem to have it together on this, but they have been working with child actors for a long time."

"Dad, what is a nondisclosure agreement?"

"We agree in writing not to tell anyone what the movie is about or share the script with anyone other than our lawyer, Eugene Burke.

"Say if you had to share something about your hairdryer with someone you didn't know well. If they then shared your idea with anyone else, you could win a lawsuit since they agreed not to share."

"That's good to know."

"Rick, you will now have more money than I have ever had at one time in my life. What do you plan to do with it?"

"I'm not certain, Dad. I will need to use some for my hairdryer invention, and I bet it will be more than I think before I have a product. Other than that, I would like to see it used to better the family. "What am I going to do, buy a limo and hire a driver to take me wherever I want to go? That seems stupid in Bellefontaine."

A sudden thought of a girl in Columbus made me rethink the limo and driver.

My thought must have shown on my face because Dad asked what was going through my mind. I had never had a problem sharing things with my parents. Of course, some guy stuff would forever remain private, but mostly I talked freely.

When I started, "Well, I met this girl."

Mum, sitting quietly, suddenly sat up and paid close attention. I described Judy and how I met her. Dad had to interrupt with Tom Mix and a damsel in distress.

Mum shushed him and asked more questions about Judy and her family. After she had every bit of information available, was she satisfied? She should work for the FBI.

The conversation ended, "No, you may not hire a car and driver to take you to Columbus, at least not without our permission. I would suggest that you two write to each other as planned and see if you even like each other!"

I noticed that Mum hadn't closed the door completely; they just had to be consulted first.

Mum then went upstairs to begin the morning ritual of nagging Denny and Eddie. I noticed that somehow, I had woken up. This coffee stuff must work. It still tasted bad. Mum had a porridge pot on, so I helped myself and poured a glass of orange juice.

Dad would run us to school, but I had at least half an hour, so I went out into the garage and reviewed my hairdryer project to see if anything was missing. I couldn't see anything I was missing, but I think that was the definition of missing something.

I needed to experiment with the temperature and fan-forced air. I was sort of stuck until the parts for the controller arrived. They should be in soon.

School was the usual Monday morning zoo. The poor janitors were mopping like crazy but falling behind. Everyone was bundled up. Even Eleanor Price didn't stand out as she wore so many layers.

When I came in the front door, "Go, Bellefontaine" started. It followed me down the hall.

It was hard not to smile and wave to my fans. Before I got too carried away, I remembered the guy who would whisper to the

Roman generals during their triumphal processions, "You're only a mortal man."

I don't know if that ever really happened, but it was good advice.

I saw that Coach Stone had already had our trophies placed in the trophy case in the main entry lobby. I wondered if they were like my National Bull Riding Championship trophy. It was three times the size of any in the trophy case. Currently, it is in my bedroom, and I am using it as a clothes rack.

Mum was complaining about me hanging my clothes on it. I used to hang my clothes up in my closet out in the hall of North Detroit Street. Now I had a closet in my bedroom, and I wasn't using it.

In homeroom, the announcements included the strong finish of the golf team and that I had advanced to the finals in Columbus this weekend.

I liked Rodney Humphrey's comment, "You play a wimpy sport, but at least you're good at it. 'Go Bellefontaine.'"

I may be a wimp, but at least I was their wimp.

Chapter 50

Looking at Rodney, something clicked. There is a pecking order established among the boys around junior high. Rodney had been bigger than me, both in height and weight. I was now at least three inches taller and forty pounds heavier.

I filed that thought away for future consideration. I didn't want to be a bully like him, but at the same time, I didn't have to be bullied.

I also wondered if I could get fighting lessons somewhere. I knew they had golden glove boxing in Columbus, and in the movies, they showed mysterious techniques like judo.

In a small town, we had none of that. A fight would be a pushing, shoving match with a black eye and bloody nose thrown in for good measure. Fighting lessons were something else to think about, maybe when I was in California for the movie.

Classes were almost incidental to the day. I attended and handed in the work required, knowing I had finished the next day's assignments. I read or worked on problems ahead during class where I could. My teachers knew I was doing this and seemed okay with it.

On rare occasions when we were officially working on problems, I would raise my hand for help. I requested help on future lessons, but help was given with no comment.

Study halls were spent writing essays that would never be turned in. I had one interesting learning experience several weeks ago. My world history teacher Mr. MacMillan asked me to see him after class. I wondered what I had done. It was what I wasn't doing.

The essays I had been handing in were a common variety of high school plagiarism. You would go to the referenced text and copy the words, citing that text in your bibliography. Ninety-nine percent of all essays would only have one reference in the bibliography.

He asked me if I was ready to take it to the level demanded in college. I told him yes while having no idea what he was talking about. He was ready for me. He pulled out a paper he had done in college; he also had the reference texts. He had me read the text, then what he had written.

He had written in his own words what he thought the message was and cited specific statements in the text to support his assertions. I see where he used citations from several books to form an argument against what was being taught.

So besides having the title of the book, author, publisher, and dates, he would have the specific page and paragraph identification. This was a whole new level!

He told me, "Rick, you show great promise as a student and scholar. Would you please try this method? It will not hurt your grade in any way, I promise. If nothing else, it will give you a firmer understanding of the material."

I did try it and was blown away by what I was seeing. Now, thinking about what the author had written, I questioned the facts and conclusions. This led me to look at the author's bibliography.

Very quickly, I learned to have little faith in poorly researched work. If the book had no bibliography, I didn't bother but would hunt up other books.

This took so much time that I quit trying to do every essay question at the back of the text. I spent my time doing a quality job on one issue. This spread out to my other classwork wherever there was an essay-type question.

I was asked about this change by several teachers. I referred them back to Mr. MacMillan.

Miss Bales told me, "It's a shame we don't have a grade higher than A-plus; you would receive it."

She continued, "This is college-level work. I have read in my professional journal that there is a move underfoot to have advanced classes in high school for which you can receive college credit. Your work would qualify."

Yeah, I had a fat head for the rest of the afternoon that day. Mary took care of it when I walked in the door that evening when she came out with, "*Hola, gran hermano.*"

My four-year-old sister was speaking Spanish! I recognized the hello, but not the rest. I asked her. She giggled as she explained,

"Hello, big brother."

At least she didn't tell me I had a big nose, as I feared.

I asked her where she was learning Spanish.

"From Mrs. Hernandez next door, silly."

I immediately asked Mum who Mrs. Hernandez was.

"She just moved in with her husband's brother's family, the Wingers. Her husband is in jail in Cuba, and she had to flee the country.

"Why is her husband in jail?" I inquired.

"I don't know the ins and outs, but a dictator by the name of Batista runs Cuba, and several groups are trying to overthrow him. Her husband was arrested. She happened to be in Miami, so she didn't go back. I guess she was also involved. Now she is working on her teaching certificate to get a job teaching Spanish in high school.

"We don't have a Spanish course in Bellefontaine."

"You will next year."

That was interesting. Maybe I could hire her to tutor me after the golf season, then take Spanish with a head start. Learning Spanish was in the future. Now I had to get through the school day.

Things had changed at lunchtime because the golf team had previously joined Tom and me at our table. Today, a senior, Scott, was at another table with his classmates. Even the conversation at the table had changed. Gary, Tim, and Tom were sophomores, and their conversation was about tenth-grade classes. I was feeling a little left out but was content to listen.

I did look around at the other tables, particularly the ones with freshmen. There is no way that I would fit in with them. They all seemed so childish. Not that I was that more mature than them. Their interests were different.

Who cared what the latest Pez dispenser looked like? Who was Grayson who got Tom Dooley hung and that deep philosophical question, "Why did he stab her with his knife?"

What I thought was interesting and funny had changed without me even noticing.

I got together with Coach Stone after school. We went out to the country club; he had his Ohio State Scarlet Course map there. It was still raining, so there would be no outside work today. The Scarlet Course was interesting but had been laid out in favor of the long hitter, so I should be able to get by the sand traps on the course.

They had a lot of sand traps, but Coach, an OSU alumnus, told me that when they were originally put in during the 1940s, they were deep but had been allowed to deteriorate over the years and now were fairly flat with little in the way of lips. We came up with a strategy for each hole.

Coach told me there would be no sense in coming out here tomorrow if the rain didn't let up. It would only be to get in some driving range work. This was the latest in the year they had ever had the state championship, and he hoped the course would dry out by Saturday.

When I got home, there was wonderful news. It was in a certified letter from the Texas State Cattle Commission. Mum had saved it for me to open. It was the reward check for the capture and conviction of the rustlers. It was for eighty-five thousand dollars, as promised.

Dad got home from the railyard while I was still dancing around waving the check. He asked Mum to fix some coffee while he cleaned up. We had to talk about what was going to happen now. The kids were watching TV, so we had the kitchen to ourselves.

Dad started, "First of all, Rick, this is your money; you knew it was coming. Have you thought through what you would like to do with it?"

"I have thought about it, I would like to keep some for my personal use, some for my hairdryer project, and the bulk is for the family."

"How would you break that down?"

"Dad, I would like to keep five thousand for me, ten thousand for the hairdryer project, and the rest for the family housing business."

"You're willing to give us seventy thousand dollars?" inquired Mum.

"I consider it an investment in the future of our family. You and Dad won't be dependent on the railroad. My brothers and sister will have a chance to go to college. Remember, I will make another seventeen thousand five hundred dollars from the movie."

"Also, since you have set up a company that I will own if anything happens to you, it is an investment in my future in the long run. I know nothing about the stock market, but I know how hard my parents work.

"Money is not an issue right now. Unless you will let me buy a limo and hire a driver," I said the last with a smile.

"Well, no limo, so we might as well take the money," rejoined Mum.

Chapter 51

We proceeded to drink coffee and tea while talking about how to go forward. Dad would deposit the check, fifteen thousand in the savings account set up for me, the rest in the business checking account he had opened. He would buy the ten rental duplexes as planned.

Mum and Dad were developing a written business plan. They estimated that a duplex would cost twelve thousand dollars; to buy ten would be one hundred and twenty thousand. Putting twenty percent down would be twenty-four thousand dollars.

They figured it would take about two thousand a unit to bring them into condition. That would be another twenty thousand. So, they would have forty-four thousand dollars invested.

That would leave twenty-six thousand in the bank. A man with a particularly good job would earn eight thousand a year.

I thought, "Dad, you could hire two people to do the work for you if they had the right skills. You could save a lot of money and have the units ready to rent faster."

"Rick, I've thought seriously about that. I have been studying for the Ohio State Contractors Examination. If I am a licensed contractor, it will make everything go easier. I think it will take a year to get the first ten purchased, brought into shape, and rented out."

At the same time, we will watch how many other units we can work within Bellefontaine. We may have to buy some in Urbana or Kenton."

"The quicker, the better. In the *Examiner* the other day, I read that the recession is about over, and the economy will take off."

"Well, that's what your godfather wants us to think," Dad said with a scowl.

He didn't like Ike.

"Now, Jack," said Mum.

It was that tone of voice that said settle down or else. Dad settled down.

"Things seem to be better locally, so maybe he is onto something," Dad added.

About that time Mary came in, she asked, "*Madre ¿puedo ver el espectáculo que quiero?*"

Mum never blinked, "*Si*, Denny, and Eddie, it's Mary's turn to choose the program."

"You both speak Spanish?"

Mum laughed, "No, but it has been the same question every day for a week."

"I would like to speak to Mrs. Hernandez about tutoring me in Spanish if that is all right with you."

"That's fine, but why do you want to learn Spanish rather than German or French?"

"You know I do a lot of research on my essays for World History. History suggests that the birth rate drops as a population makes more income. If that is the case in my lifetime, we will have to import workers. Where is a source of plentiful cheap labor?"

I went on, "I know President Eisenhower deported many Mexican workers, but that is a problem that won't go away. It may be handy for me to speak Spanish. Besides, you never know when Elvis and I may want to go back for more wine, women, and song."

Mum shook her fist at me, "You will get it, boyo."

She is English. Where is she coming up with Irish terms? I asked her.

"Your great grandfather was Irish; I can remember him calling my dad boyo when I was young."

"Your Dad was a grown man by then."

"You're always children to your parents."

I had plenty to mull over that night, but I still did my nightly reading. It would be neat to have a lens giving you almost superpowers. The grey suit sounded sort of plain. I think Superman had the right idea. I would chase the Boskones all over the galaxies.

Tuesday morning, the rain had stopped, but there was standing water in our yard. I was still able to run. I hoped the Ohio State University Golf Course would dry out. Breakfast was quiet. I tried coffee again, and it didn't seem as bad as yesterday. I was drinking it without cream or sugar. I was going all the way.

Tom met me for the walk to school. Eleanor Price came out in front of us. She was wearing a short ski jacket; I noticed something about her dress.

"Hey, it's snowing down south."

She turned around and asked, "Is my slip showing?"

Both Tom and I assured her it was, not just a little but a lot. She went back home for an adjustment. Before we got to school, she caught up with us.

"Thanks, guys. I would've been teased all day."

There was something a little exciting about a girl's slip showing. It sort of made you think of everything else under it.

It seemed every teacher decided to have a pop quiz on Tuesday. I had one in every class but Latin. She waited till Wednesday. They weren't a problem; they helped my schedule. I flew through the exams, turned my papers in, and then got to work on my future assignments.

Since I would work on every problem in the back of my English and Math books, I was doing more work than most other students. I hadn't taken any work home in the last six weeks, using my class, study hall time, and bus rides for golf to study. I did take the time in study hall to write a letter to Judy.

I met Coach at the pickup spot for the ride to the country club. We rode out, and I worked the driving range. He watched my swing for any glitches. Since I was banging my driver out over 250 yards and some even close to 300, I didn't think I had anything to worry about.

This yardage was with no roll. The ground was still wet. I bet they would have to dig about half of the balls out of the ground if they could see them.

Coach and I talked about why my drives went so far.

"Rick, you are like a giant human lever with your height. Your timing is a natural wonder. You also have another advantage that most golfers don't seem to have. Your exercising has given you enormous core strength. This provides power to your swing.

"Your swing looks easy, but it whips through the ball. When you watch the next pro tournament, notice the physical condition of the golfers. They aren't in bad shape. They just aren't in great shape."

I hadn't given it any thought, but I could see what he meant. I wondered what other muscle groups I should develop to increase my strength. More importantly, I could learn what to do and what equipment I needed after knowing which ones needed work.

Coach continued, "With the way you play, there is no reason that you can't turn pro right out of high school."

Now, there was something out of the blue. I knew I was good, but I had never thought about earning my living playing golf. I liked the game, but I wasn't certain I liked it that much.

Coach also told me, "There will be a pep rally for you Thursday before we leave for Columbus."

"Oh, good, I love being the center of attention."

This got Coach laughing. He was well aware that I hated it.

When I got home, there was a phone call from Bush Electric that my electrical components had arrived. It was too late for me to pick them up.

Dinner was fun that night; we had pancakes with Dad cooking. It was always like a little party. Normal sit-at-the-table rules were suspended. While Dad was trying to get ahead of us, we could take our plates to him.

Between the four of us, he didn't get caught up till we were all full. I noticed Denny didn't try to out-eat me tonight.

I made several different sketches of how I wanted the insides of the hairdryer to fit together. I needed something to attach the basic parts as a framework. The framework would have screw holes to attach the motor, fan, and controls.

Once they were attached to the framework, I would attach the housing to the framework. The heating element would stick out of the framework, and the barrel snap-fit around it.

The result would look like a gun with a grip and a barrel. The body would have to be much fatter than any pistol, but it would still be only about four inches wide.

That night I started another book, this one about some Russian brothers. I gave up. I didn't like any of the characters in the book and thought that they should all die and then rot and stink up the place. So, take that!

Chapter 52

Wednesday came clear and cool. It was autumn. Summer was over. The ground was drying out, so I had hopes for good rounds on Saturday and Sunday. At breakfast, Dad was excited about several properties he had looked at. He wanted Mum and me to go back with him for a second look at them after school today.

I couldn't tell him anything useful about their condition, but I could see that he just wanted to show them off to us. Of course, we said yes.

School was a typical day with one exception. At lunch, a senior girl Rita Harrison sat with Tom and me. She fawned all over me. For a senior girl to even notice a freshman was alive was amazing. To flirt as openly as she was, ran up all sorts of red flags.

I met Coach at our usual spot, and he suggested we skip practice tonight. If I weren't ready now, I would never be. He did have a present for me. It was a white cardigan-type sweater with a sports letter.

I was now a letterman for golf! I had never given it a thought, but I was now officially a jock. Rodney Humphreys would tell me that it wouldn't equal a real sports letter like football or basketball. What a poor kid, having to put everyone down to build himself up.

Coach told me to be sure to wear it to school tomorrow. I told him I would. It would've taken an act of Congress to stop me from wearing it.

I got home early, and Dad was ready to go. I did talk him into stopping at Bush Electric to pick up my parts. After that, we toured the duplexes with John Tapp of Tapp Realty. They all just looked like houses to me.

Dad was pleased with the general condition and thought he could fix them up for less than he had budgeted.

He told Mr. Tapp, "I like what I see. Let's put in offers for all of them. I will talk to Tom Harrison down at the bank and start the ball rolling.

The Harrison name caught my attention.

"Dad, does Mr. Harrison have a daughter named Rita?"

"Yes, he does, Rita. I met her when I picked up her dad to attend an AA meeting."

"Rita started flirting with me at lunch today. She is a senior, and they never do that."

"Hmm, right after a large deposit. I would tread lightly there, son."

"I guess that is the danger of living in a small town."

"It is, but he had no right to spread our business around, even with his family."

"Jack, don't get too excited. After all, you are about to ask him for a lot of money," put in Mum.

"I won't, but it just bothers me."

In the car on the way home, Mum brought up, "You don't have to say anything. John Tapp heard it all. It will be all over the business community in hours."

"You're right, Peg; it couldn't have gone better if I planned it that way."

There was a letter from Judy waiting for me; the biggest news was that she had talked her parents into inviting Coach Stone and me to dinner at the OSU Clubhouse on Friday evening. I will see Judy!

Before dinner, I had my soldering iron heated up and made the control circuit as Mr. Robinson had sketched out. He had added a bimetallic switch that would turn the unit off if it reached one hundred and forty degrees. It would prevent people from getting burned. I wished I had thought of that.

There was also a fuse in the circuit that would trip if there was an electrical overload. I would also have a guard on the front of the barrel so that kids couldn't stick their fingers in and burn them on the heating element.

At dinner that night, I asked my parents if they knew any engineers who could help me with the unit's internal assembly layout and drawings. They didn't know anyone off the top of their heads, but Dad knew Jim Willis, the plant manager at Rockwell, who had plenty of engineers working for him. He would give him a call after dinner.

I had shown my letterman sweater to my family. I wore it to dinner, and it was noticed immediately. Everyone admired it, but my brothers kept looking at each other and giggling while Mary practically danced in her seat. Something was up, but I couldn't even begin to guess.

Dad called Mr. Willis as promised, but he had no engineers he would recommend. This said something about his engineering staff.

I was too wound up; I couldn't read later, so I just listened to records. When it was lights out, I lay there for a long time, thinking of everything I had going on.

Thursday, the weather was beautiful again. The weather forecast remained this way for the rest of the week. We had an Indian Summer.

I wore my letterman sweater to school. Even Eleanor Price made a positive comment, "Looking Good, Go, Bellefontaine."

I must have heard "Go, Bellefontaine" five thousand times that day. There were about six hundred students in our high school.

Even Mr. Gordon got in on it with his morning announcements over the intercom system. That was right after he announced the pep rally immediately after the lunch period.

Rita Harrison sat at our table and tried to grab my attention at lunch, but so many kids came up and wished me luck that she didn't have a chance.

I ignored her as much as I could. She would figure out I'm not interested. Since she is a girl, I'm interested, but not under these circumstances.

I always thought the gym was noisy up in the bleachers. Down on the floor, it was pandemonium. (I love learning big words when I read.) They presented the team trophy for second place in the district. This was the furthest any team from Bellefontaine had got in a state tournament.

It was like the Sweet Sixteen in basketball. After that, I was singled out for my trophy for the lowest score for the tournament.

The cheerleaders had been leading cheers and jumping around, waving their pom poms before the presentations started. Now Coach Stone announced we would have a cheer led by the golf team's own cheerleader.

Mary ran out in a BHS cheerleader's uniform and pom poms! I saw my family standing front and center, yelling with everyone else.

Mary did us proud. If she got one of the cheers wrong, there was so much noise that no one would know. Then something horrible happened. They handed me the microphone.

"Thank you very much for this show of support. I will do my best to bring home the State Championship for the Bellefontaine Chieftains. I want to thank Coach Stone for his training and support this year, my teachers for their support, my teammates for pushing me on, the Logan County Country Club for the use of its facility, my parent's support, and most of all, the littlest cheerleader, my sister Mary. Go, Bellefontaine!"

That worked. I think I got everyone. Maybe I should go into politics. Nah.

I carried Mary off the floor with me so that she wouldn't get crushed. Now I know what was up at dinner last night. They were all in on it.

Coach drove us in his car since it was only the two of us. He had packed our clubs yesterday. We quickly stopped at my house to get my airline garment bag. It was perfect for a short trip like this. Mum, Dad, and the kids beat us home, so I was able to get hugs and well wishes. Mum took pictures.

Mary, of course, had on her black sweater with BHS on the front and an Indian Chiefs Head on the back. I wondered how they got one in her size on short notice but didn't have a chance to ask.

During the ride over to Columbus, I told Coach about the dinner invitation. Judy wrote that information would be waiting for us at the information desk. I always got a kick out of going through New California on the way. They had a statue of a Union Soldier in the middle of the intersection on the main and only crossroads.

In Europe, it would've been used as a roundabout, but they had only widened the road a little, so it was more of a shift-lane deal. The poor soldier was in a circle with a low iron fence about ten feet long. Why some drunk hadn't taken it out, I didn't know.

A known speed trap was through Dublin, down Riverside Drive to Fishinger Road to Upper Arlington. There we got a glimpse of the OSU Golf Course on our left. From there, we went to the Visitors Center at the university.

No camping this week. They had a check-in desk, and there was a message from Mr. King; he would see us in the morning at the tournament sign-in.

I roomed with a kid from Akron; the only thing I remembered about him later was that he could fart louder than anyone I had ever met. His first name was John, which I thought was appropriate. Luckily, they didn't smell that strong. Of course, I stayed as far from the guy as I could when in the room, but the room wasn't that big.

Chapter 53

In the morning, I got out of the room of Rolling Thunder as I thought of it as soon as I could. It was a beautiful day, so I had a long run around campus. It is a nice campus, and I would consider going to school here. I wondered how their School of Engineering was rated. More research to do. I heard that the only engineering schools by reputation were MIT and Georgia Tech.

I met up with Coach in the Visitor's Center restaurant as arranged. The whole place was set up like a hotel. After a nice breakfast, we went over to the golf course. Our first stop was the valet to unload my clubs, then parking. We retrieved clubs and went to the, you guessed it, white pavilion to register. I bet someone was making a living off renting tents. It would have never occurred to me.

Mr. King was there helping, but when he saw us, he waved us over.

"I'm glad you made it; a certain young lady would make my life not worth living if I didn't get Rick to dinner this evening."

Coach just shook his head and murmured, "Young love."

Mr. King laughed and said, "Ain't it grand."

I wish they didn't make fun of me. I knew it wasn't love. We hardly knew each other. I would use words like infatuation or maybe even lust, but not love. I decided not to say anything about what I thought it was, especially lust. I may be slow and oblivious at times but not completely stupid.

Coach and I walked the course. I saw what he meant about the sand traps; they had been deep potholes at one time that would be a nightmare. They had been allowed to fill in over the years, and the lips guarding the green had crumbled so you could make a pitch and run to the green. Someday they may restore the course, but I wasn't complaining today. This course right now was made for my game.

I could see how The Golden Bear could tear this course up. My long game was longer than his, but not by much. He would kill me on the greens. It would still be fun to play with him one of these days. I put that on my mental list of things to do.

I no sooner thought this as we walked off 18 to return to the practice area than Jack Nicklaus walked by. Of course, he didn't know me from Adam, so he kept going. Even if he knew me, he probably would've kept going.

Though I had heard he was a nice guy. Maybe he would've said, "Hi," as he kept moving.

The practice round on the 7455-yard-long par 71 Scarlet Course went well. As usual, I didn't keep score. I was trying to understand how the course played. None of the sand traps guarding the normal landing zones for drives would cause a problem. I would just hit past them. I could roll through the traps surrounding the greens.

If my putting was on, I should do well. This course didn't give me the same fear that Inverness did. Now that was a course you had to respect. This one was like a down on its luck brother.

Thinking "down on its luck brother" made me think of my Uncle Wally. That made me pause for thought; even someone like Wally could cause problems. I better not get too big for my britches, as Mum would say.

We went back to our rooms and cleaned up for dinner. I had brought my cowboy suit with me this time. Mum had taken it to the tailor to have the pants let down. The coat was a little tight so I wouldn't be wearing it much longer, but it would do.

My shirt had cool-looking pearl buttons, and I wore a bolo tie with a turquoise slide. Of course, I wore my alligator skin boots, belt with the large rodeo championship buckle the size of a small dinner plate, and black hat.

I had several calls of "Hey, Tex" in the lobby. I had even put my Texas Ranger badge and I.D. in my pocket, more to show off if I could. I was dressed to impress. Coach just shook his head when he saw me.

We made a small stir when entering the restaurant. I removed my hat and followed the hostess to our table. There were comments from other diners as we passed through. None of them were bad, just like, who is that guy? The Kings were already seated, and Judy had saved me a seat next to her. She was dressed in a white blouse with a black pencil skirt and a nice set of pearls. I said, "It is my pleasure to sit next to you, ma'am," in my best Western drawl, which was atrocious, to say the best.

Then the most wonderful thing happened. Two small kids came up and asked for my autograph. They were a brother and sister, eight and ten years old. The younger sister told me that I had better be nice to Annette and not try to kiss her again!

This opened the conversation up at the table. I worked hard not to have it all about me as dinner proceeded. Judy didn't contribute much except for an occasional question. Most of the questions came from her parents. I started to think they didn't approve of me being allowed to roam last summer.

In an attempt to change the conversation, I told Mr. King I was his customer. Of course, he wanted to know what I was buying, which led to a description of my control unit and my hairdryer idea. He liked the electronics; the women liked the hairdryer.

I told him that I had breadboarded a control unit but would have to hire a professional electrical engineer to lay it out to work and be manufactured. He wanted to know where I had heard about manufacturability versus engineering.

I told him how Mr. Robertson, my merit badge instructor, talked about engineers designing things, then throwing them over the wall to manufacturing without knowing if they could be made to specification or cost-effectively.

Mr. King sighed, "I've over five hundred engineers on staff. I wish they could understand that concept. I fight that battle every day."

He continued, "We have some sharp junior engineers that do some moonlighting. Would you be interested in paying one of them to design what you need?"

"Sure, as soon as we get a nondisclosure agreement signed.

"I learned about NDAs with my movie contract. Mum, Dad, and I had to sign one not to disclose the movie plot or script."

That brought Mr. King up short.

He gave me a long look and said, "You aren't just a pretty face."

Now how does a guy respond to that? I just smiled. Coach, in the meantime, was following the conversation like a tennis match.

Coach now put in, "He hasn't been tested, but most of the teachers at school think Rick has a genius-level I.Q."

I just smiled; I wasn't about to dig my hole any deeper. In the meantime, Judy was beaming like her pet puppy had performed an amazing trick. Even her mother looked approving. Maybe I had dodged the parental kiss of death.

It was a good sign that Judy and I were allowed to walk alone after dinner for a short walk. When we were out of sight, she took my hand and talked as we walked. When we got to a more secluded area but still near the clubhouse, she said, "You aren't allowed to kiss Annette, but you can kiss me."

I was so quick into that kiss that we bumped teeth. I backed up, went slower, and got it right. It wasn't a fancy French kiss or anything like that, just a pressing of the lips. That was the correct level of kissing for a first kiss. She hugged me, and we started back.

We all said our goodnights, and I was wished good luck in the tournament. It wasn't until we were in the car that Coach told me. "You might want to wipe that lipstick off, Tex."

Even my roommate John didn't bother me when I got back to my room. Everything was bright in the world. Love, infatuation, lust, whatever I was enjoying, the feelings.

I was still feeling that way two days later. I had beaten the Scarlet course at Ohio State University into submission. I played a round of 67, followed by a 63. I destroyed the course with my 130 for the two rounds. Not a course record but close.

My nearest competitor was Tom Logan from Athens, who shot 139 for the tournament. The trophy was presented to me by a previous champion, Jack Nicklaus, almost as big as the rodeo trophy. He even said he would look forward to playing me someday.

I wondered if I could keep the trophy as another clothes rack or would it go to my school. I suspect Mum would make certain the school would have it.

I saw Judy in the gallery on Sunday, but her parents whisked her away immediately after the awards, so all I got was a small hug and congratulations from her. I had been hoping for another kiss. Life was still good, and the ride home was fun. I think Coach enjoyed my win more than I did.

He did enlighten me a little when he told me that while he wasn't looking for a job, it wouldn't hurt to have me on his resume. He asked me if I had given any thought to turning professional since he had mentioned it.

I told him probably not. There are too many things I want to do in life. Golf was fun, but it wasn't all-consuming to me. Getting up every day to play golf would be like work. I didn't think I wanted to turn my play into work.

Coach came back with, "Think of the money. You can win a year's salary from winning one tournament; they pay up to eight thousand dollars for first place."

That's when I enlightened Coach about my income.

"Coach, I made twenty-five thousand dollars last year catching two bank robbers, and eighty-five thousand dollars breaking up a gang of rustlers. I will make over seventeen thousand dollars next spring for seven weeks of work in the movies. Money is not an issue with me."

The only news I was giving him was the movie work, which would come out soon anyway. I tried not to think about the gold in the safe deposit box.

"You are only fifteen; I wonder where you will be when you are twenty or forty. I bet you will know the president, whoever it will be.

I thought about telling him who my godfather was, but I didn't know if he had a heart condition. The rest of the trip home was quiet.

He dropped me off at my house. It wasn't late, just after dinner, so everyone was up. Mary did her cheering.

The trophy said it all.

Finished for now.

To Be Continued in:
Book 2: School Days The Richard Jackson Saga[1]
https://www.enelsonauthor.com/

If you want information on hiring Janet E. Rupert to edit your fiction project, email:

janeteditorrupert@gmail.com

---

1.   *https://www.amazon.com/Richard-Jackson-Saga-Book-School-ebook/dp/B07W8B7Q69*

Other books by Ed Nelson

The Richard Jackson Saga

Book 1: The Beginning

Book 2: Schooldays

Book 3: Hollywood

Book 4: In the Movies

Book 5: Star to Deckhand

Book 6: Surfing Dude

Book 7: Third Time is a Charm

Book 8: Oxford University

Book 9: Cold War

Book 10: Taking Care of Business

Book 11: Interesting Times

Book 12: Escape from Siberia

Book 13: Regicide

Book 14: What's Under, Down Under?

Book 15: The Lunar Kingdom

Book 16: First Steps

In The Richard Jackson World

Mary, Mary

Stand Alone Stories

Ever and Always

The Cast in Time series

Book 1: Baron

Book 2: Baron of the Middle Counties

Book 3: Count

Book 4: Earl

Book 5: Earl of the Marches

Did you love *The Beginning*? Then you should read *School Days* by Ed Nelson!

The Richard Jackson Saga, Book 2: *School Days*. Coming-of-age stories don't have to be all teenage angst; they can be fun-filled adventures. With humor, we follow a young man's coming of age in the late 1950s. Starting in the summer before his freshman year, the saga follows him through high school and beyond. He finds wealth as an inventor and fame in Hollywood as he searches for a girlfriend. Wealth and fame prove far easier than girls. The second book, *School Days,* shows Rick in the first semester of the ninth grade. Using the lessons learned on the road, Rick makes a serious start on being an excellent student. He still has to navigate the pitfalls of the Homecoming Dance, Sadie Hawkin's day, and other dangers encountered with the fair sex. His thoughts of being a football star go, but he finds that chasing a little white ball around a field can be fun and that being a hero is not all it is cracked up to be. This tongue-in-cheek saga is all true, give or take a lie or two.